ADVANCE PRAISE FOR *SICK KIDS IN LOVE*

★ "The excellent character development lends depth and sweetness to the romance... A highly recommended work that's thoughtful, funny, wise, and tender."

—*Kirkus Reviews*, starred review

"*Sick Kids in Love* takes on serious issues in an original, thoughtful way. Isabel and Sasha are vivid, warm, complex characters, and I fell in love with them both."

—Jaclyn Moriarty, author of *Gravity Is the Thing*

"Romantic, refreshing, and brimming with empathy. Isabel and Sasha captured my heart."

—Rachel Lynn Solomon, author of *You'll Miss Me When I'm Gone* and *Our Year of Maybe*

"An empathetic, hilarious, and honest window into living with a chronic illness, *Sick Kids in Love* is an insightful and vital addition to disability representation. I love this book with my whole heart!"

—Laura Silverman, author of *Girl Out of Water* and *You Asked for Perfect*

SICK KIDS in LOVE

SICK KIDS in LOVE

HANNAH MOSKOWITZ

Entangled Publishing, LLC
2614 South Timberline Road
Suite 105
Fort Collins, CO 80525
rights@entangledpublishing.com

Entangled Teen is an imprint of Entangled Publishing, LLC.

Visit our website at www.entangledpublishing.com.

Edited by Lydia Sharp
Cover illustrated by Elizabeth Turner Stokes
Interior design by Heather Howland

Print ISBN 978-1-64063-732-0
Ebook ISBN 978-1-64063-736-8

Manufactured in the United States of America

First Edition November 2019

10 9 8 7 6 5 4 3 2 1

entangled teen
an imprint of Entangled Publishing LLC

ALSO BY HANNAH MOSKOWITZ

*For Garrett, Benni, and Jack, who wait
for my love story with me.*

WHAT'S YOUR FAVORITE PLACE
IN NEW YORK?

The High Line. Is that too cliché? If you go like midday on a weekday it's not super touristy. You can get brussels sprouts and doughnuts at the market and then go up there and feel like you're about to fall off the edge of the world. Plus if you're there midday it means you're not in class, and there's nothing wrong with *that*.

> —*Maura Cho, 16, basketball player*

Dumbo. The bars don't card and I like hanging out under a bridge and feeling like a mole person.

> —*Luke Stellwater, 15, currently starring as Pippin in "Pippin"*

My favorite place in New York isn't there anymore. It was called Kelly's Diner, and it was on 31st Street in Astoria. 31st and…I can't remember. 23rd. 23rd. I used to go there every Wednesday during my residency, and I'd have a tuna melt, coleslaw, and a chocolate shake. Every Wednesday. I was there when I found out I was getting my fellowship, and I was there when I found out I was going to be a father. Now it's a Wendy's.

> —*John Garfinkel, 49, Physician in Chief at Linefield and West Memorial Hospital*

The Octagon on Roosevelt Island. It's like someone built a church to honor a place and then keeps on forgetting it exists. It's beautiful, though. You can really think there.

— *Claire Lennon, 16, dead*

I don't know. What's wrong with right here? Are you gonna buy something?

— *Helen, ???, manager at my bodega*

CHAPTER ONE

"Hospital" should be a setting on white noise machines. The nurses laughing at the station and the sound of their squeaky sneakers on the floor. The rush of the pneumatic tubes sending blood back and forth from the lab. The rhythmic beeping of someone rolling over onto an IV. Every once in a while, that flurry of activity like an awkward dance break.

It always sounds the same here.

I get infusions at Linefield and West once a month, after school on the first Monday. I could do injections at home instead, but those are twice a month instead of once, so I'll trade the inconvenience for half the needle sticks. Plus I'm here all the time anyway. It's not that much trouble to go down to the drip room—that's what we call the Ambulatory Medical Unit, because come on—sit in one of the comfy chairs, eat Goldfish crackers, and study for two hours.

It's always kind of awkward because the other people there are usually cancer patients, and I know they probably assume I'm a cancer patient, too, and it feels like lying to let them assume that. Some of them are dying. I'm not dying. I'm just sick, and have been for eleven years now. And I don't look like I'm dying. People come down from their rooms to get chemo wearing their hospital gowns and scrub caps over their heads, and I'm looking like I just walked out of high school, because I did.

I think they hate me. The cancer people.

This is only my second month doing infusions. I was fine on pills for a long time, but lately my fingers have been swelling and making it hard to type, and my ankles have been keeping me out of gym class, which is sort of fine by me but also sort of not, in that complicated way like when you win an argument but by doing something really shady and gross. My doctor wanted to try something else, so here I am with a new treatment plan and a new set of people to look at me and think I don't look sick enough.

I should stop wearing makeup on infusion days. Blush makes anyone look healthy.

So I look away when people come in, and I study, and sometimes I drift off a little because of the hospital noises. Today, there's nobody else in the infusion room, just me and the florescent lights and a bird on the tree outside the window who looks like he's trying to pick a fight with another bird on the tree outside my window, and I close my eyes for what feels like a second, but must have been longer, because…now there's someone here, in the chair two over from mine.

The first thing I notice is he's the first person I've ever seen in here who looks about my age.

The second thing I notice is the way his hair curls behind his ears.

He's watching something on his phone, but I'm thinking *you're pretty you're pretty you're pretty* hard enough that I guess he hears it, which honestly is probably possible considering exactly *how* hard I am thinking it, and he looks up at me with an eyebrow quirked.

"Sorry," I say.

He keeps looking at me.

"Not a lot of young people here," I explain.

"There's that six-year-old with leukemia," he says. "He's always bringing those trucks that are the size of his arms and just"—he mimes it—"smashing them together. I think it's supposed to be violent, but there's something kind of…romantic about it? Like the trucks just can't stay away from each other. They don't want to drive around like the other trucks. They want to…I don't know. Dance. He's a little kid. I'm sure they're just dancing."

"What," I say.

"Oh, you don't know the kid?"

"I'm only here once a month."

He cranes his neck to look at my IV bag, like it's going to be some special color. They all look the same. "What are you in for?" he says.

A lot of the people here have central lines, but I just have an IV going into my hand, since it's not like they need easy access to my veins. He has the same setup.

"DMARD infusions," I say.

"I don't know what that is."

"Rheumatoid arthritis."

"Oh, no way," he says, in the same voice you'd use if someone told you their uncle had the same birthday as you.

"Mmhmm, since I was nine."

He nods at the notebook in my lap. "What are you working on?"

"What's on your phone?"

He grins. "I asked you first." I hope he doesn't have cancer. His eyelashes are so long. He can't lose those eyelashes. This is the worst thing I've ever thought.

I hold my notebook up to my chest and stare him down. He's pale, in both a white way and a sick way, but his eyes are this bright sparkly green.

He smiles and tilts his phone toward me. Oh God, he has dimples. Just slay me in the drip room. "It's this woman who makes robots, and then she posts videos of them not working correctly. Like this one's supposed to be tying her shoe, and instead it rips the shoe open. This is what I want to do with my life."

"Build robots that don't work?"

"Yeah."

I show him my notebook. "I have an advice column in my school newspaper. Or…I edit the advice column. Every week I come up with a few questions, and then I gather people's answers and pick the good ones and write up a summary of it, sort of. I think of a way to bring everything they say together and make some kind of point about it. So…there you have it."

"Oh, neat, that's what I want to do with my life now. Forget the robots."

"You can't, I'm doing it."

"You're gonna do this forever? You're gonna want to retire at some point."

"So you want to take over for me when I get old? I don't know, what do you have? How long are you living, here?" Well, now I have the worst thing I've ever said to go along with the worst thing I've ever thought. It sounded cute and edgy in my head, but now that it's out I just can't believe I said it in the room where the cancer people come. They might not be here right now, but if he could hear my thoughts earlier, then they probably can, too, wherever they are. Cancer people *know*.

Plus, he could, y'know. Actually be dying.

"That was beautifully distasteful," he says.

"I can't believe I said that."

"No, it's good. Now we've established we have the same sense of humor."

I don't know if I do have that sense of humor or if I was just trying to be the cool girl because of his eyelashes, but I'm willing to try.

"And," he says, "lucky for both of us, I have some hipster disease you've never heard of, and it's not fatal, so nice try. Though I wish it were, just for how awkward you'd feel in this moment now."

"I'd know if you were dying," I say.

"Oh yeah, how?"

"Wouldn't be wasting your time talking to me."

"You talked to me first. Maybe I'm just being polite."

"And I bet I have heard of it," I say. "My dad's a doctor. I know a lot of shit."

"Gow-Shay disease," he says, or something to that effect.

"Yeah, I don't even know how to spell that one. What is it?"

"Google it, you have a phone."

"I can't. I don't know how to spell it."

He grins. "Your dad's a doctor?"

"Yeah, sick girl with a doctor dad. Pretty lucky."

He does this low whistle then points through the window of the drip room at a guy signing paperwork at the counter.

"That's your dad?" I say.

"It is." He looks young, maybe late thirties, and like he does a lot of hiking. Probably not with this sick boy next to me. "He comes with me every week," he says. "I'm sixteen and three months, and I've been doing this my whole life, and he comes with me every time."

"That's sweet."

"It is, yeah."

"You're younger than me."

"That's why it's up to me to take over your advice column." He coughs a little. "How old are you? Thirty-five?"

"Thirty-five," I say. "Seriously?"

"Do you have a career? Are you retired?"

"I'm sixteen and nine months."

"So I was close. What's your name?"

"Isabel."

"That was my grandmother's name," he says.

I laugh accidentally.

He puts his hand on his chest like he's offended. "Hey, she was a lovely woman," he says. "She wasn't allergic to poison ivy. Used to pull it right out of the ground with her bare hands. I tried to copy it once."

"Didn't go well?"

"It did not."

"Is that how you got your disease?"

"It's genetic, *doctor*," he says. He pushes his hair back from his eyes and smiles at me. "Sasha."

"What?"

"That's my name. Sasha Sverdlov-Deckler."

"No shit," I say.

He tilts his head back and grins. "No shit."

"That's quite a name."

"Eh," he says. "It's no Isabel. So what's your answer?"

"What?"

"To your question. What's your favorite place in New York?"

"Oh," I say. "I don't answer the questions. I just ask them."

"Hmm," he says.

"It's actually for the best." I shift around in the chair some. "Sometimes I can sneak in, like, questions about me and my life and make people answer them."

"That's smart," he says. "That's some clever shit right there."

"Sometimes I get way too specific, and then I can't use them in the paper," I say. "But I still get the advice. And an excuse to talk to people. I like to talk to people."

"Sure, how else are you gonna ask them when they're going to die?"

"Please," I say. "We're gonna pretend that didn't happen. We have to."

"So ask me your question, then," he says. "Change the subject."

"Okay. What's your favorite place in New York?"

"My favorite place... I think it's right here."

"The drip room."

He laughs. "Not the drip room specifically. Just...here. Linefield and West Memorial Hospital."

"You like the hospital."

"I know," he says. "It's weird."

"No, I...I've never met another person who likes

hospitals."

"I don't always like them," he says. "But hey, you're not always gonna like anywhere, right? At least here you get to just relax and be sick and not have to be anything else. You should see me when I'm admitted. Just total sick caricature. Demanding Jell-O and shit. Plus they know me here. I live in Chelsea and I still trek out to Queens every ten days to visit this place."

"I grew up here," I say. "My dad's the chief physician."

"No shit," he says.

"No shit."

"Well," he says. "I like your house."

"I need a job title for you," I say, showing him my notebook. "See, it'll say Sasha, uh…"

"Sverdlov-Deckler."

"Right. And then sixteen. And then your job. You can pick something funny if you want. I let people put down whatever they want."

"Brother," he says. "Put brother." He looks at my IV. "Looks like your bag's done."

"Oh. Yeah."

"See you next time?" he says.

"I'm only here once a month," I say.

"Yeah, but you live here, right?" He closes his eyes, smiling. "I'm just kidding," he says. "I can be patient. Probably. Well, I can try it. I like trying new things."

Cathy, one of the nurses, comes and tapes up my IV. "Bye, Sasha," I say.

His eyes are still closed. "See ya, Grandma."

I take my phone out of my pocket on the way to the elevator and open up a text to Maura, but my fingers feel cold and stiff, like frozen tree branches. I stretch them toward my palm and back up to my wrist.

Me: **Met a cute boy.**

She always answers immediately, which is why she's always the first person I text for play-by-plays.

Maura: **NO BOYS!!! You know your job.**

I roll my eyes and press the button for the cafeteria. I love Maura, but she has no idea the real reason why I don't date.

Not that it matters. The point is that I don't. If that boy's waiting for me, he'll be waiting a long time.

WHAT WOULD YOUR LAST MEAL BE?

Pecan-encrusted salmon with mango coulis, a peanut butter and banana milkshake, flourless chocolate cake, and some really, really greasy fried chicken. Oh God, put me to death right now so I can have it. Is this like one of those TV shows where you're gonna bring it out now? Do me a solid, Ibby.

— *Ashley Baker, 17, just got an A on her Physics test*

I can't remember who it was, but I read about some movie guy—I think it's one of those actors who turned out to be a really shitty person, but that doesn't exactly narrow it down, I know—who needed to gain weight for a role, so he'd microwave buckets of ice cream and just drink them. That's what I want. I do it now with the low-fat shit, but I'm sure it's a whole new world with the real stuff.

— *Luna Williams, 16, professional lesbian*

My last meal was just some chicken broth because I wasn't really feeling up to anything else. My mom fed it to me while I lay in bed and watched birds fly outside my window. They were swooping in long, slow circles, like kites. That's the last thing I remember.

— *Claire Lennon, 16, dead*

French fries and whiskey. Most people here, though, when they think they're gonna die, they all want food from home. I always think, you must come from a different home than I did, that's for sure.

> — *Leon, 30-something, Linefield and West cafeteria worker*

Spaghetti with NO vegetables in the sauce. Mom thinks I don't know. I know.

> — *Mina Eisenhower, 7, visitor*

CHAPTER TWO

I don't know why hospital cafeterias get such a bad rap. I'm not saying it's five-star cuisine or anything, but it's as good as your standard mall food court. We have a whole soft-serve ice cream bar that's sold by weight, and pizza, and some sandwiches, and some seriously underrated lasagna. I think people just associate hospital food with being in the hospital, and most people don't associate hospitals with somewhere they'd like to sit and enjoy a nice meal. Unlike me.

I fill up two cups with soft serve and grab some apples and ask Mario, the hot food server—as in the food is hot, not Mario, who is very nice but about sixty and has grandkids—for two big slices of lasagna. He forces me to take two salads, even though I hate salad.

"Make your dad eat both of them, then," he says. "Your dad could use some more vitamin D. Locked up in that office all the time."

"Salads have vitamin D?"

"Haven't you seen *Popeye*?"

"I think that's iron," I say.

"You're a smart girl."

I pay for the food—I get to use my dad's discount, which I always feel kind of weird about, even though I'm paying with his money—and head back toward the elevator. The cafeteria has this atrium between the real seating area and the elevator, and often people will come out here to eat their food instead. Birds fly in from the patio and get stuck sometimes. When I was eight I watched two cafeteria workers and a patient's entire extended family rescue a blind pigeon that was accidentally terrorizing everybody trying to eat.

Even though I've seen the atrium a million times, I always used to really love it, but lately I'm more concerned with counting steps. The number of steps it takes to get around the cafeteria. The number of steps from the cafeteria to the elevator. And the atrium is just extra steps right now.

I balance the cardboard containers in the crook of my elbow and hit the button for the sixth floor. Dr. Garrison, who works in radiology and has been here since I was born, is in here and trying to read an X-ray by the elevator's frosted-glass light.

"Hey there, Ibby," he says. "How's the joints?"

"I'm fine. How's Marsha?" His wife.

"Due any day now," he says. "Petey can't wait. He's been wearing this *I'm a Big Brother* shirt every day, y'know, just in case."

The elevator dings on my floor. "Can't wait to see pictures," I say.

"Thanks, sweetheart. You take care now," he says. I'm careful not to limp as I go.

My dad's office is at the end of a long hallway with glass ceilings and abstract pastel paintings. The door's not fully closed, but I still knock a little as I go in.

He looks up from his desk and smiles at me. When I was a kid he was always running around, seeing patients in the ER, responding to codes, fetching test results, laughing with the other doctors. Now he spends most of his time at a desk. When he got the promotion, when I was thirteen, he said it would be less vigorous work and he'd be able to spend more time at home. So far only one of those has been true.

"How's my girl?" he says.

I hold up the boxes. "Lasagna."

"Perfect." He opens the mini-fridge by his desk and takes out two bottles of coconut water, then neatly stacks his paperwork to clear off a place for us to eat. I pull up one of the comfy chairs he keeps by his coffee table. It's not as good as the drip room chairs, but it's nice.

"How'd it go today?" he says.

"Just fine. What are you working on?"

"Oh, you know…figuring out new stuff with insurance policies. Trying to keep the doors on this place open. You know how it is this time of year."

I nod, though I don't really know what November has to do with hospital finances, especially considering he'll say stuff like that any time of year. But I like that he thinks that I know.

"Did you get that Chem homework done?" he says.

"I'm gonna finish it when I get home."

He looks at me over his glasses, points at me with his fork. "We've talked about saving things until the last minute."

"I didn't! It's not due until Thursday."

He lets the fork go limp a little, relenting. "All right."

We eat in comfortable silence for a bit while he leafs through some papers and I look out the window at the people rushing around on the floor below us. There's nothing to look at inside the office, nothing I haven't already seen a thousand times. There are always boxes of files that need to be put away, and his gold clock on the wall that's two minutes fast, and four framed pictures of me on his desk. He swapped out some of the pictures recently.

I clear my throat. "Hey, Dad?"

"Hey, Isabel?"

"Do you know about, um, Gow-Shay disease?"

"Sure do." He wipes his mouth.

"Uh, how do you spell that?"

"This for your Chemistry homework?"

"No, I met a boy today who has it."

"At the infusion? Y'know, we can get you a private room for this. I didn't run this hospital so my daughter had to talk to people while she gets needles in her."

"I like talking to people," I say.

His eyes twinkle at me. "I know you do. Jewish boy?"

"Uh-huh."

"It's the most common genetic disease in Ashkenazi Jews. It's one of the ones we got screened for before we had you. Tay-Sachs, cystic fibrosis, and Gow-Shay."

I don't really know what to say about that for a few reasons, mainly that it's hard to hear about all the ways he planned ahead to try to have a healthy kid and then I went and got sick anyway. He'll talk sometimes about the irony of a doctor having a sick kid, and I always feel so weird and guilty. He doesn't talk about it much, thankfully. We don't really discuss me being sick unless it's a problem, and it hasn't been a problem in a long time. I'm doing fine.

I take a bite of lasagna. "Tay-Sachs and cystic fibrosis,

those are really bad."

"This one's not as bad. It's a…ho boy, it's been a while since my genetics rotation, let's see. Enzyme deficiency, causes a certain lipid to build up in the body. Hard life, but the fatal type kills you before you're two, so sounds like your friend's out of the woods." He takes a swig from his coconut water. "I think that's right. Don't quote me, if this is for your homework."

"It's not for homework."

"What about your column?" he says. "What questions have you got?"

"You've already done most of them," I say. "What's your favorite part of the city, time management advice…"

"Right."

"How about this one," I say. "What would your last meal be?"

"Hmm," he says. "The best meal in the world, huh?"

"Uh-huh."

"Well. This is some pretty good lasagna."

"I was thinking the same thing," I say, holding up my fork.

"That, my dear," he says, "does not surprise me." He taps his fork against mine.

WHAT'S YOUR BEST TIP FOR TIME MANAGEMENT?

Create a schedule ahead of time and stick with it. Stop putting things off as if that way it's going to be another person who has to do it. It's still you, just later, and that later-you hates you.

> —*George Mattrapolis, 41, 11th grade History teacher at The Markwood Academy*

Delegate. Don't feel bad about hiring someone else to take care of a task you don't have time for. That's what runs this company. Money flowing down. It's important to have good work ethic, but it's also important not to waste your energy on tasks that don't require your expertise. Remember that and you'll have a big head start going into college.

> —*John Garfinkel, 49, Physician in Chief at Linefield and West Memorial Hospital*

Honestly, I don't really have a good system. I kind of just put everything off until I have no choice but to freak out and do it, but like…it gets done. Sorry. You should probably ask someone else.

> —*Lisa Hamilton, 18, early acceptance at Yale*

*S*omeone once told me—there is nothing so terrible you can't survive it for ten minutes. No matter what it is, you can do it.

—*Claire Lennon, 16, dead*

*C*reate a rewards system. See? Answer a question, eat an M&M. Answer a hard question, eat two M&Ms. Take a break, eat five hundred M&Ms. Foolproof. And you have got to think of some more interesting questions, Ibby.

—*Maura Cho, 16, lacrosse player*

CHAPTER THREE

I don't celebrate Christmas, but I still love Christmastime in New York, and every second after Thanksgiving is Christmas as far as New York is concerned. When I was a kid, we used to go to Macy's in Manhattan and drink hot chocolate and wait with all the tourists for the moment they unveiled the Christmas windows.

I hold my hands in front of the radiator and look out my window, down the street toward Queens Boulevard. The train tracks are above ground here, with stained glass on the sides like some kind of art piece. It's sunny today, white light gleaming off the glass and probably the retro metal SUNNYSIDE sign on the other side of Queens Boulevard, but I can't see that from here. It's a massive street, and instead of a median there's the elevated train tracks, and underneath them, little chairs and tables in case you want to eat a bagel in a very strange location. There are snowflake lights strung up all across my street, between the trees and the streetlamps and off the apartment buildings. They aren't lit during the day, so they just hang like ghostly spiderwebs, waiting.

I blow on my hands and put on another pair of socks.

Our house is quiet. It's small, just the two bedrooms and a bathroom upstairs and a living room and a kitchen downstairs, but it's ours, which is saying something in New York, even in Queens. Still, it means Dad and I are constantly aware of whether the other one is home, always stepping over each other, keeping the other one awake. Which would be more of a problem if he were home more often, but he's not. So instead I'm usually very aware of how much he *isn't* here. He didn't get in until ten last night, and he's long gone now. It's been like this my whole life. Dad says when he was growing up, they called children in New York who were left alone a lot *latchkey kids*. Now they just call us children.

I make instant oatmeal and cup my hands around the bowl to keep loosening them up, then put on a sweater, joggers, and sneakers. I gave up on jeans earlier this year. I put on pink lipstick and mascara and tie my hair up in a messy bun. Scarf. Hat. Backpack.

And I'm out the door and into the November air.

It's just one block to the 46th Street–Bliss Street subway station, then my school is two stops deeper into Queens, in Woodside. There's no elevator at either stop, though, so you have to take the stairs down from the elevated train, and then it's a two-block walk from the second subway station to my school. For most New Yorkers, that's nothing. We walk everywhere. You can't complain about that, is the thing. I'm about to go to my posh private school where my friends are, wearing the warm clothes my dad bought for me. You can't complain.

I get up to the platform and blow on my hands while I wait for the train. A text comes in, and I roll my fingers around before I answer it.

Luna: **Topic???**

We have our end-of-the-semester research project starting today for our History class, and the two of us have been waffling on topics since it was announced. We have to go in-depth on the life of literally any historical figure, and it's just far too much freedom. I don't know how anyone else made this decision. I ended up going to the hospital library and asking Nina, the librarian, who she recommended.

Me: **Frida Kahlo**

Luna: **FUCK**

She doesn't care who I picked, really, she just cares that she hasn't decided yet. She keeps thinking of new people she wants to do and abandoning her old choices.

Me: **You'll figure something out in the lab.**
Something will grab you.

My train pulls up, and I shove my way inside. In the mornings it's all work commuters and students, and it's always packed, even though most of the traffic is going the other way, from Queens into the city. I take my backpack off and set it on top of my feet and wrap my fingers around the pole, one by one. My knees creak as the train jerks into motion.

It's only about five or six minutes of standing. And then down the stairs, and then just two blocks.

Then up the steps in front of the school. Down the hall to my History class. Only five doors down from the computer lab.

I can't complain.

Luna, Maura, Ashley, and Siobhan are waiting for me on the steps. "Didn't Frida hate white people?" Ashley says.

I say, "Just because I'm white doesn't mean I'm going to do my report on someone who was ignorant enough to like white people."

"Did Jane Goodall like white people?" Luna says, taking Siobhan's hand as we head into the building. "I might do Jane Goodall, but not if she liked white people."

"I don't think Jane Goodall liked any kind of people," Maura says. "That's why she went to live with monkeys."

"Chimps," Ashley says.

Maura rolls her eyes. "Whatever."

Maura and I have been friends the longest, since fourth grade, when we both had a crush on Luke Schivo and he told us he liked both of us, but he liked two other girls more, Maura third and me fourth. Maura and I hated each other over that for about a day and a half before we decided that we were going to hate him instead, and we wrote a no-dating pact that she honored for three months, until Johnny Lupo transferred in, and I've honored for seven years. We started hanging out with Ashley—who, incidentally, was Luke Schivo's number-one girl, and they dated for two weeks and had a very emotional breakup on the playground after he kissed girl number two—in seventh grade, when the three of us chased a field hockey ball that rolled away during gym class, got poison ivy, and sat on the sidelines scratching ourselves and bonding for the next week. Like Jane Goodall and the monkeys. Chimps.

"Did you do the Bio assignment?" Laura asks Siobhan.

"I did not," Siobhan says.

"Me neither. We're screwed."

"I told you not to take that class," Luna says. "Too many APs."

"You're supposed to take APs junior year," Siobhan says. "It's how you get into college."

Luna fluffs up her hair and says, "I'm gonna be just fine."

"I know," Siobhan says, and they give each other sappy smiles.

Luna, we met in high school. She'd just moved here from Jamaica with her family, and she was really into tarot and was doing everyone's readings, and she told Ashley something good was going to happen to her the day she found out her mom was pregnant, so we became completely obsessed with Luna and her tarot powers and basically stalked her until she agreed to be our best friend. Siobhan is her girlfriend, who is cool and artsy and used to only hang out with other cool and artsy people but now splits her time with us.

We stop at our lockers to drop our stuff off before first period, and Maura, whose locker is two down from me because the fates are always on the sides of me and Maura, says, "Did you see the paper yet?"

"No," I say. "It's already out?"

"Yeah, Hattie's new boyfriend works at FedEx, so now she's getting it printed early or something." Hattie is our editor-in-chief, this kick-ass senior who looks and acts like she's twenty-five. She's amazing. Maura doesn't really understand my love for the school paper, but she still writes the sports column, so she at least gets it more than

the others do. She digs around in her tote bag. "Uhh...
here."

I flip through it and find my column. *Sick Girl Wants
to Know!* it says at the top in big pink letters.

"Y'know people were talking about it," she says.
"Laughing over the answers."

"Yeah?"

"It's been there for years and people still like it. You've
got crowd appeal, girl." She pulls out her compact and
eyeliner. Maura loves makeup but hates getting up early,
so she always sleeps as late as she can and puts her face
on one step at a time between classes.

I smile.

"Y'know, that's what's gonna get you into college,"
she says, tapping the paper without looking up from her
mirror.

"Crowd appeal?"

"Yeah. An interesting extracurricular. You really think
colleges want to hear about one more person taking AP
Bio? They want the girl with the weird advice column."

"It's not that weird," I say.

She lowers the mirror just to give me a look. "You
call yourself Sick Girl, ask people weirdo questions, and
then somehow turn them all into one little story. It's
brilliant, but it's weird. And that's why," she continues,
"you shouldn't go messing up your brand by dating some
boy you met in... Where did you meet him, anyway?"

"It doesn't matter," I say. "And I'm not dating him."
Like I could even think about dating someone without
wanting to run away. From myself. While screaming. Trust
me, it's for the betterment of society.

"Good. Because take it from me. Boys are terrible. And not worth messing up your reputation as…you know."

"As what?" I say.

"The even-keeled spinster."

"That is not my brand."

Luna appears over my shoulder. "It's sort of your brand," she says. "Can we go?"

"My brand is Sick Girl," I say. "Not single girl."

"Sick Girl *is* single," Luna says. "That's part of what makes her so wise. That's why she thinks to ask such lovely and insightful questions." She kisses my temple. "Come on. We're gonna be late."

Luna and I head to History, where Mr. Mattrapolis gathers us all up and then leads us to the computer lab to start our research for our project. Luna sits next to me, clicking through picture after picture of Jane Goodall.

"It's not working," she says. "The chimps just aren't speaking to me. Maybe I should do Bob Fosse. Do you think I should do Bob Fosse?"

"I don't know," I say. "Ask Mattrapolis."

"I'm asking you."

I'm scanning Frida's biography and writing down all the important early dates and some quick facts—I didn't know she wanted to be a doctor—when I get to the part about her bus accident. I think I knew about this, but I haven't heard about it in a long time. Mostly people just talk about her eyebrows. She had a pole go all the way through her, and she was in pain her whole life. One of her friends said she "lived dying."

I stretch my fingers.

"You're not even listening to me," Luna says.

I close the page. "Sorry."

"It's fine. I've decided. Bob Fosse."

I need a break, and Mr. Mattrapolis is all the way across the room, helping Katherine Lewis with her Ann Boleyn thing, so I open up Tumblr and scroll through for a while, and then I take a BuzzFeed quiz to find out what piece of furniture I am (I'm a bed) and then I Google my dad and see if he's been published anywhere new recently, and then I think *what the hell* and make sure no one's looking and type in "gow shay disease." A bunch of pages on Tay-Sachs come up, so I try one word, "gowshay," and Google asks me if I meant "gaucher" and like yeah, Google, probably.

Gaucher disease is a genetic disease in which a deficiency of the enzyme glucocerebrosidase (also called glucosylceramidase) leads to the overaccumulation of the sphingolipid glucocerebroside (also called glucosylceramide) and wow, okay, that's the least I've ever understood a sentence in my lifetime. I scroll down and look for some plain English.

There are three types of Gaucher disease. Cool, that's more my speed. It looks like one of the types almost always kills you before you're three, like my dad said, and then one of them, type three, you can live into "early teen and adulthood." There's only one type—type one—that doesn't say anything about a reduced lifespan.

I don't know why I'm sad about this. I barely know the guy, for one, and two, for all I know he has the type that doesn't kill you—he told me himself he wasn't dying—and three, you don't grow up in a hospital without developing some amount of comfort with death. I volunteer there once a week, just helping the nurses answer calls and bringing patients their water and things like that, but I've been very close to a lot of very dying people.

I guess when I met him I felt some kind of camaraderie. Here was someone who was just going to deal with the everyday slog of being sick for the rest of his normal-length life until he died of something completely unrelated, just like me. That's a weird and special and boring kind of existence that you don't get to share with a lot of people. If he has some illness he's dying of, he's not part of the Long Slog Club anymore. He's in the Shiny Dying People Club, and he's all important and significant and not just…this. Waiting.

And also, you know. I'd rather people weren't dying.

The main symptoms are severe anemia, bleeding problems, weak bones, and enlarged spleens and livers. The less common symptoms basically boil down to "and whatever the fuck else it wants," like lung problems, seizures, and severe bone pain.

I wonder what severe pain feels like. You have to know if you have it, right? There must not be any question about it. You don't doubt yourself. You just know, yep, this here qualifies as severe pain.

This is a fucking legit disease, I guess is what I'm saying.

"Learning anything good?" Luna says.

I close the page quickly. "About Frida?"

"Yeah, what else?"

"She had a pole go all the way through her," I say.

"Pretty punk rock."

"It hurt forever."

WHAT'S YOUR IDEA OF A GOOD TIME?

Honestly? I like to go to the casino. I only go a few times a year, and I have a budget and everything… which is good because I always lose. But I don't know. There's that hope that this time I won't. Why? I don't know. I think a "good time" is being someone different from who you usually are. I'm usually so responsible. Going to a casino and blowing money is like a vacation from myself. And it's not like I can afford to take a real vacation.

— Tyson Yugosoft, 24, Law Student

Oooh, hiking! Or rock climbing, but not in a gym, like out there with actual rocks. Honestly anything out of the city. I don't know what I'm doing here. If Billy Joel had written about a seventeen-year-old girl instead, I'd be the piano man. Does that make sense?

— Ashley Baker, 17, from Connecticut

A stiff drink, a good book, and a long ride on the Staten Island Ferry. And my daughter right there with me. What else do you need?

— John Garfinkel, 49, Physician in Chief at Linefield and West Memorial Hospital

I'd like to go on a picnic in Central Park, where you can see the sheep. I'd bring a big checkered blanket that I could lie out on and tea sandwiches and lemonade, and I'd have everyone I love there, and they could eat while I slept.

—*Claire Lennon, 16, dead*

Nothing you can print in the paper. What is it you call yourself, "Sick Girl"? Aw, I could make you feel better.

—*Brad Levington, 17, Student Council Treasurer*

CHAPTER FOUR

After school, we get boba and frozen yogurt at a place near the subway station. It's actually a little past the subway station, so you have to double back to get home.

Siobhan got a bad grade on a Calc exam, so we're all brainstorming ways to cheer her up. She's slumped over her frozen yogurt, giving us all these pitiful little smiles every time we suggest something new, to show she appreciates it. Even her freckles look sad.

"My parents are still in Korea," Maura offers. "We can go to my place and make a stew with their overpriced wine. And also drink it."

"I'm in for that," I say.

Ashley checks her phone. "I have to be at the animal shelter in…forty-five minutes. Don't you have the hospital thing today?"

She means my candy-striping work, not the infusions. "Tomorrow," I say.

"I should probably go home and study anyway," Siobhan says.

Luna rests her chin on top of Siobhan's head, giving herself this curly red beard. "You're not going home and studying," she says. "I won't allow it."

Ashley puts her phone down and claps her hands. "Got it." Ashley doesn't wear makeup and still looks like a Chapstick ad all the time, all blond and fresh-faced and healthy, and the cold air's stung her cheeks a little and put me and my layers of blush to shame.

Siobhan raises an eyebrow.

"My parents were going to use their ski house this weekend, so they didn't rent it, but now my mom has a sinus infection, so they're going to stay home, aaaaand since it's already not rented…"

"Seriously?" Luna says.

"They just texted me," Ashley says. "It's ours. I'll bring Justin, you and Siobhan bring each other, Maura can meet some cute ski instructor, and Isabel can interview them all."

I raise my cup in agreement, despite the feeling at the bottom of my stomach, because a lot of friends wouldn't be supportive of my choice not to date. They'd keep saying, *well, once you meet the right guy*, or *come on, it's just for the weekend.* Or they'd try to fit me into a box and tell me I'm asexual—which I'm not, not that there's anything wrong with that—or a closeted lesbian—which, again. It's just a choice that I've made, and the stupid excuse that it's for the column either satisfies them or they're willing to act like it does, and either way that makes them pretty awesome friends.

The problem with having awesome friends, though, is they want to do stuff like go skiing with you on the weekends.

"It's supposed to snow in the mountains this weekend, too," Ashley says. "It's gonna be gorgeous."

"Who's driving?" Maura says.

Ashley says, "I can, but we won't all fit… Maybe if we take Justin's dad's car? How many is that?"

They count people and arrange seats and talk about

snacks and double black diamonds and I chew balls of tapioca between my teeth and look out the window. A man walks by in a big overcoat, bowed down against the cold. He's holding a newspaper and wearing a structured hat and looks like something out of another century.

I hear them get quiet all of a sudden, and I know they've finally gotten to *oh wait, Isabel*, so I put on a smile, turn back to the table, and play dumb.

They're all looking at me. "I'm sorry," Luna says. "I got excited—I wasn't thinking…"

"We can do something else," Maura says. "I'll hide all the wine before my parents get back, and we'll bring it to Luna's and watch Netflix. Or to your house, do you want to do it at your house?"

"Guys," I say. "It's fine."

"There are tons of other things we can do," Luna says.

"Yeah, and there's tons of other things I can do at the ski house," I say. "I'll like…go to the lounge and hang out and do puzzles and drink hot chocolate, and you guys will break your ankles and get all sunburned and be suuuuper jealous that I had an excuse to sit around in the hot tub all day."

They look really unsure.

"Come on," I say. "What are you supposed to do, not go skiing because *one* of us has arthritis?"

Honestly, it's not a rhetorical question, though I know none of them has the answer, either. I know they're not supposed to sit around planning a whole ski trip with me, even though it's fine and I'm not mad. But they're also not supposed to just secretly go without me, and I honestly can't expect them to plan everything around me and what I'm supposed to do. So like…what is the actual answer here? I think it's that I go and I hang out in the ski lounge, and that's fine. A weekend at a ski resort, for free? I'm going to complain just because I can't actually ski? Of course not.

Ashley says, "Okay, well, I have to run, so we'll work out all the details of this later?"

Everyone else has places to be, too, basketball practice or study group or couple-y stuff. I think about going to the hospital and having dinner with my dad, but I just had all that frozen yogurt, so I'll probably be eating late, and anyway I'm tired. I just want to go home.

They say goodbye to me and head back to school or toward the subway platform. I don't want to have to walk fast enough to keep up with them, so I make an excuse about how I left something inside the boba place and they should go on ahead. I go inside the store for a minute and just wait, soaking up a little bit more warmth before I go back out.

I think about Claire, like I usually do when I'm feeling like this. She would never have gone outside in weather this cold. Nobody would have let her. Claire's mom sat inside with her, bundled her up in blankets and made her tea, and they distracted themselves watching Christmas specials on a tiny TV and talking about candy.

I step back out onto the sidewalk and take a deep breath against the wind. I'm on the west side of Queens Boulevard, so the traffic is headed out toward Manhattan, the right direction for me to get home. I just need to walk a block back, then cross to the middle of Queens Boulevard. Climb up the stairs. Get on the train. Take it two stops toward Manhattan. Go down the stairs. Walk back to the west side of the boulevard. Walk one block to my house. Up the front steps. Up the stairs inside. Into my room.

It's not far.

But the thing is that there's a cab waiting at the light, with its numbers on top lit up. I could stick my arm up and in three minutes I'd be right at my door. No waiting outside for the train. No holding on to that frozen pole. No stairs, except the ones in my house.

It's not like we're hurting for money, but my credit card is my dad's, and he checks the charges, and he'd ask me why I took a cab to go fifteen blocks. Plenty of people wouldn't even pay to take the subway that far. They'd just walk. Old people and pregnant people. And people with arthritis who are just better than me.

The cab driver would judge me. I'd tell him the address, and he'd say, "In Sunnyside?" and he'd think I was some tourist who didn't know how close she already was to where she needed to be. Or he'd just roll his eyes at how lazy I am, how in his day…

The light turns green and the cab blows past me.

I walk to the end of the block to get to the subway.

It takes me about twenty minutes to get home. I shake my hands out and fumble with my key and take my shoes and coat off in the kitchen.

It is so, so quiet, and my dad won't be home for hours.

I look at the stupid third chair around our breakfast table that we haven't moved because this is a tiny house and we don't have a place to store a chair that nobody's using, and we're not just going to throw it out because probably there will be three people in this house again at some point, so there's no reason to just put a chair out on the sidewalk like some sort of sculpture about how lonely we are.

It could be worse. I could be Claire, wrapped up with her mom and waiting to die.

I go up to my room and get into bed.

WHAT'S THE STRANGEST COINCIDENCE YOU'VE EVER EXPERIENCED?

My cat died when I was eleven, and I was just completely devastated. Her name was Moulin Rouge because that was my favorite movie. Not that I understood anything about it, because I named her when I was eight, I just thought it was really sophisticated and I wanted everyone to hear my cat's name and think about how sophisticated I was, I guess. Anyway, after a while my parents wanted to get a new cat, and I felt like I wasn't ready, and then my mom found a kitten on Petfinder that was named—you guessed it. And like, what are the odds of that? Maybe if her name had been Mittens or something, sure, but Moulin Rouge? You're going to find two cats named Moulin Rouge in the same borough? I guess they weren't alive at the same time, but…still. Pretty wild.

—Siobhan O'Brian, 17, sculptor

The only time I've ever driven a car, I wrecked it. Is that a coincidence?

—Justin Trainer, 17, boyfriend

Well, I've told you about that diner in Astoria? And how every time I went in I'd get coleslaw, a tuna melt, and a chocolate shake. Well, I had a favorite waiter there, named Sal. They always put me in Sal's section. Anyway, one day I was in Manhattan, and I walked into a diner, and who should be sitting there at the counter having lunch but Sal himself. And what was he eating? Coleslaw, a tuna melt, and a chocolate shake. I just turned around and went home. Too much for me.

—John Garfinkel, 49, Physician in Chief at Linefield and West Memorial Hospital

I died on my birthday.

—Claire Lennon, 16, dead

Biggest coincidence? I don't know, one time I walked into a store and they were playing the same song I was playing in my car. My mom used to say all coincidences were signs from God. Not sure what that one was a sign of. Sign that we need more radio stations, maybe. Now you get back to work.

—Sheila Bellequest, 58, orthopedics charge nurse

CHAPTER FIVE

'm sitting at the nurses' station, in front of the monitor that tracks the patients pressing their call buttons. They press it, their room number pops up, I pick up the handset and ask them what they need, and then the same thing happens. Every time.

The monitor dings and I pick up the phone. "Hi, room seven ninety-one, can I help you?"

"I need my nurse," a woman says.

"Can I ask what it's about? I might be able to help you."

"I just want my nurse."

"Right, but there are some things I can do, and some things an orderly—"

"Hello? I need my nurse, please!"

So I hang up the phone, and I flag down Brenda, and she's pissed at me for not finding out what the patient wants before I send her in, and then she's going to come back here and complain that I sent her in to do something an orderly could have handled. Every time.

I like the patients, and I like nurses when I am a patient, but good lord can both of them be hard when you're a volunteer.

"Sorry," I say to Brenda as she groans her way to seven ninety-one.

Two of the older nurses are in the station behind me, and Sonia says, in what I must assume she thinks is a low voice, "Brenda really should go easier on her, with what she's going through."

"I know," Angie says. "Her poor father, *such* a nice man, really doesn't deserve—"

Saved by the buzzer. Thank God. I pick the handset back up.

"Room seven forty-two, can I help you?"

"Hi, my nurse was supposed to be here with meds a while ago, but I think she might have been abducted by aliens. Or maybe she was taken, like in the Hollywood hit *Taken.*"

So…that voice sounds awfully familiar.

I clear my throat. "Who's your nurse?"

"Katherine," he says. "She's been great, which is why I'm concerned about the whole 'taken' scenario. I don't have a special set of skills."

"I'll track her down."

"Great, thank you."

I hang up and scroll down through the patient logs, and…there it is. A. Sverdlov-Deckler, room 742. What the hell is he doing on orthopedics?

I grab Katherine when she breezes past and say, "Hey, Sasha needs his meds."

"Ah, shit. Thanks."

I decide not to bother him—after all, he barely knows me, and he probably looks like shit and doesn't want unsolicited visitors—but about half an hour later, Sonia asks me to check the water refills. That's my other major job besides answering call buttons. There's a whole procedure to prevent contamination, where they keep big bulky cups in their rooms and I bring them thin plastic cups full of water and put them inside. Hospitals are so full of small, strict little rules. You always have to wonder what went wrong for someone to come up with them.

I get the water cart from the back of the nurses' station and push it down the hall to the water fountain to fill up the cups. I wonder who's going to answer the call buttons while I'm gone. Whenever it's a nurse on that job instead of a volunteer, they'll let their room sit there blinking on the screen for ages. I guess they have bigger things to do. And it's a small floor; if something's really wrong in one of the rooms, you wouldn't need a call button to hear it.

Still, it bothers me. But it's not my place. And anyway, I'm the one who abandoned the job because I didn't want to sit there and listen to them gossip anymore.

I'll do the rooms on the left side, then the ones on the right. I drop water off with two sleeping patients before I hear a muffled call from someone on the other side of the hallway.

"Isabel! Iiiiisabel!"

I turn and look, and, sure enough, that's Sasha, lying in bed with a cast on his left arm and an oxygen cannula in his nose. He raises his eyebrows at me through the window.

I grab a water cup and push his door open.

"I knew that was your voice," he says.

"Yeah, well, you were supposed to be patient. It's been two days."

"I told you I wasn't good at being patient." His eyes light up. "Is that water?"

"Yeah, here." I set it up on his tray and watch him work

on sitting up. "You want a hand?"

"Mmhmm, c'mere," he says. I come around to his side, and he holds onto my arm and pulls himself up. It makes my shoulder ache a little, but it's a productive ache, a doing-something ache.

"So what'd you do?" I say while he drinks.

"Fell off my bike. It's no big deal. Only a flesh wound! My bones break really easy."

"Yeah, I read that."

He grins. "You googled me!"

"I googled you."

"So I did that yesterday and I'm really anemic, so it just…" He gestures vaguely. "I don't know. I'm lying here for a few days. What about you? You working here now? I thought you were an advice columnist."

"Volunteer work."

"You're sick *and* you help the sick?"

"I know. I'm amazing. The ill Clara Barton. How are you doing, do you need anything?"

"Besides a shower? Nah, I'm okay." I start to go, and he says, "No, hey hey hey!"

"I have work to do!"

"Doing what, helping patients? I'm a patient, help me." He takes his pillow and throws it on the floor. "See, look at that, I need your assistance."

I roll my eyes and brace myself with a hand on the wall.

"What are you doing?" he says.

I kick the pillow up in the air and catch it. "Getting your pillow. Ta-da."

He wrinkles his nose a little. "It hurts to bend down,

huh? I'm sorry. I'm an idiot."

"Shut up. I'm fine. Lean forward," I say, and I situate the pillow behind his back. He's thin and cold, but he smiles at me.

"Y'know I googled you, too," he says.

"You did?"

"Yeah, well first I had to look you up because you said your dad was the…y'know, the head guy, and I was curious. And then I found out your last name was Garfinkel and realized you must be Jewish, and so now I'm in love with you."

"I know, after you told me your last name I realized I should have just told you I was Jewish, too. People don't guess, with the blond hair."

"And then," he says, "I looked up RA because I realized I didn't actually know very much about it."

"Oh yeah? Learn anything?"

He coughs. "Totally. I thought it was just like, y'know, arthritis, but no! It's a whole thing!"

I laugh. "It is, yeah. It's a whole thing."

"Do you want to sit?"

I pull up the armchair in the corner and unload the stuff from it. There's a little duffel bag and a ton of board games.

"Sorry," he says. "My brothers were here earlier. They bring board games whenever I'm in the hospital."

"That's okay."

"Anyway, yeah, I learned a lot. And I'm impressed! I'm a wimp about pain. I'm drugged to my gills right now or I'd be whining about my arm." He coughs a little more and sips some water. "So that's me. I stalked you."

I lean forward onto the bed. "Want to know what I did?"

"Of course."

"Calculated when the next time was that we'd be at infusions on the same day. The next, like, intersection of once a month and every ten days." I can't believe I'm admitting to this. I can't believe I did it in the first place.

But he doesn't seem scared off. "All right, when is it?"

"Five months from now."

"Five months! Well, holy shit, I'm glad I broke my arm, then."

I don't know what to say to that, so I just blush and look down and play with my bracelet.

"Do you have to be on your feet all day for this job?" he asks. His voice is gentle.

"No, no. Most of it I'm sitting at the nurses' station. I just wanted to take a break from that…" I clap my hands together. "Don't worry about it. Reasons."

He's looking at me the same way he did in the drip room. Like I'm interesting. Like he'd be fine saying nothing forever and just waiting until I have something else to say.

"I really do have to get back to work, though," I say.

"Orrrr you could stay and play Monopoly with me."

"What if I get back to work now, and then I come back tomorrow and I play Monopoly with you? You still gonna be here tomorrow?"

"Yes, ma'am."

"Don't call me that, or I'm not coming back."

He raises one eyebrow, and I deliver the rest of the water with a flutter in my chest.

He's sleeping when I get there the next day. I wake him up by tossing a copy of the school paper onto his chest.

He drags his hand over his eyes. The IV catches on his eyebrow.

"Is this your column?" he says.

"Uh-huh. Your answer's in there."

He rips into it like it's a birthday present. "Ha! Look at that! I'm famous. *Sick Girl Wants to Know?* Are you Sick Girl?"

"I am."

"So it's like a secret thing?"

"Nah, everyone knows it's me." I think about pulling the chair up, but it's covered in games again, and it just seems like a long walk for a short drink of water, so I sit down on the edge of the bed instead. "It's kind of like a pen name, I guess. I joined this forum online right after I got diagnosed, and it kind of…stuck, I don't know."

"I like it."

"My dad's always been horrified by it," I say. "He doesn't want me to define myself by my illness or whatever."

Sasha widens his eyes. "Healthy people are *so weird* about that."

"Right?"

"I don't know how they've developed this fear of it," he says. "Was there an after-school special that they all saw? Like, at some point every healthy person saw some TV show about how you shouldn't let sick people define themselves by their illness, whatever the fuck that even *means*, and they were all sitting there taking notes like uh-huh, oh yes, very smart, thank you, I *will not let them.*"

"Well, okay," I say. "To be fair to healthy people—"

"Ugh."

"—you *can* define yourself by your illness…as long as you're an Olympic athlete who's overcoming it."

"Yes! You either have to be overcoming it or you have to be *completely* disconnected from it. God forbid it be an important part of your identity that you're just living with. Why *is* that?"

"It's because they can't imagine it," I say. "They think it's completely ridiculous that a person can just…have a sick life and be fine with it. So they have to build this story around you kicking the illness's ass. You can't coexist with it. You can't incorporate it into yourself. Because they don't. So you can't."

He points at me. "That's it," he says. "That's exactly right."

That makes me feel very good.

Except it also makes me feel like some kind of fraud. Because I'm sitting here talking to him like we have the same experience, but I know we don't. He has a tube in his nose to help him get oxygen. He's in the hospital often enough that he knows his brothers will always bring board games. And me? I haven't stayed overnight at a hospital since I was born, unless you count the times I've fallen asleep on the couch in my dad's office. Arthritis is supposed to be a footnote, not an identity. I mean, my friends forget it exists for long enough stretches to plan a ski trip. Are people around him forgetting that he's sick? I'm going to guess not.

And I'm letting him think we're the same.

"Ugh," he says again. "I can't stand healthy people. Besides my family, I just avoid them."

"What about your friends?"

"I only have sick friends." He adjusts the cannula in his nose. "Fuck healthy friends."

I stare at him. "I'm so jealous right now. I only have healthy friends."

"Well, you might be jealous, but I'm offended as hell. What about me? Do I look healthy to you?"

"I'm sorry."

"Healthy friends. Sounds exhausting."

"Really, all yours are sick? Where do you find them?"

"Online, mostly. My only good friend in real life goes to school with me. He has cerebral palsy. I've known him since I was, like, six. I like you more, though, don't worry."

"You like me more than the friend you've had since you were six."

"I said what I said."

I laugh. "Are we playing Monopoly?"

"Yes please." While I'm setting it up, he says, "Is this okay with your hands?"

"What?"

"Holding all the pieces and stuff. Your hands are swollen."

"I'm fine."

"Okay," he says. He helps me sort out the money. "Y'know, my disease can come with arthritis. And 'bone crises,' which I hear are just as horrifying as they sound."

"Yeah, I read about that."

"But not me," he says. "And it's pretty common, too.

And then lung problems are pretty rare, but I got those, so I guess it all evens out."

"Yeah, what type do you have, by the way?" I say. "Because I read that there's three, and one of them kills you when you're a baby, and I'm really just not interested in being friends with a dead baby." I thought of that line a while ago. I thought he'd like it.

"Type one," he says, and I smile a little to myself. That's the normal-lifespan kind.

I kick his ass at Monopoly. He challenges me to a rematch tomorrow.

We exchange numbers, since he's not a dead baby.

On Friday, I wake him up with frozen yogurt. "I got you gummy bears because I like you."

He licks the spoon, then says, "Y'know, I'm going home tomorrow."

"So you've mentioned." He's been texting me all day. "Is your family gonna be here for that? If your family's so great, how come I never see them?"

"Because you come by at the same time every day, and so do they," he says.

"Last night I was here for four hours."

"Yes, and my brothers are very small and were asleep by then. My dad comes and spends the night every other night. My sister drops by before school, and the little guys come when the babysitter can bring them. They're more enthusiastic about it when I'm really sick. No one's gonna skip school and come weep at my bedside for a broken arm."

"You still like this place?" I set the game up.

"Yeah. I mean, I get the un-appeal of it, but I don't get why more people don't appreciate the freedom to just... be sick. There's nothing else you're supposed to be here. You can just lie around and do it. Get taken care of. Isn't that what everyone wants?"

That's a question I can't really answer comfortably for very complicated reasons, so I just choose the thimble before he can and roll to see who goes first.

"I lied to you," he says a few minutes in. "The first time we met."

"Did you?"

"Yeah." He collects the deed for St. Charles Place. "My dad doesn't come every time I get enzyme replacement."

"That's too bad."

"I understand if that's a deal breaker in our friendship," he says. "If that's something you look for in a guy."

"Shut up," I say.

"He used to," he says. "Fourteen dollars."

"Yeah, yeah."

"But this past year he started dating, and now he's... Look, I don't want to talk bad about him. He's a great guy. Works really hard. He's just got more on his plate now."

I look up. "Your parents are divorced?"

He says, "Yeah, since I was four. They're still best friends, though, so it's fine."

"Where's your mom now?"

"She travels, her wife's a photographer. Right now they're in central Africa. Taking pictures of bonobos. She calls every week." He pauses, dice in his hand. "How about your mom?"

I shake my head.

"Nothing? No mom? You spawned from the sea like Aphrodite?"

"She's not in the picture," I say. "She's a nonentity."

"And you don't want to talk about it."

"No."

"It's recent, huh?"

"It's recent," I say. "And that's all I'm gonna say about it."

"Okay," he says. "I'm sorry. Fifty-six dollars."

"Fifty-six?"

"I have all three."

"Goddamn it." I count out my money. "I do feel like I owe you something personal, though, since you told me about your family, and all you know about me is I'm Jewish and have RA."

"That's all I need to know to be in love with you," he says.

"Y'know, if I actually took you seriously when you said that, you'd probably have a panic attack, and you already can't breathe."

"I can breathe! You're very dramatic. I just take free oxygen when it's offered."

"Okay, something personal..." I take a Community Chest card. Second prize in a beauty contest, and it reminds me of how I met Maura. "So you know my healthy friends?"

"Yes, all of your friends."

"Let me talk."

He zips his lips.

"They're going skiing this weekend. Or, we're going

skiing this weekend. Or, I'm sitting in the lodge, drinking hot chocolate while they go skiing this weekend. We're leaving at the crack of dawn tomorrow morning."

He looks at me.

"Okay, you can talk," I say.

"Why?"

"Why what?"

"Why skiing."

"I can't expect them to just plan their whole lives around me."

He waves his hand. "Yeah, sure, they're going skiing. That's kind of mean, but it's not outside the realm of... whatever. Fine. But why are you going skiing?"

"Because my friends are going. They invited me, I don't want to like…"

"All right," he says. "I'm presuming you can't ski. Can you ski?"

"I cannot. Or, I mean… See, that's the thing, right? No one's ever told me, *Isabel, you cannot ski.* My doctor didn't give me a list of things I can't do. And exercise is supposed to be good for me. And I'm sure there are plenty of people with RA who ski."

He wrinkles his eyebrows. "But we're not talking about them."

"No, but I'm not, like, I don't have some special severe form of RA. I'm the same as everybody else. And there are people out there doing all sorts of shit."

"But it would hurt. If you went skiing. And you wouldn't have a good time."

"I don't want to be, like…like stealing the experience of people who actually can't do anything because maybe

I just don't understand how much pain is normal," I say. "Like, most people get sore when they go skiing. They deal with it. What if it's just that? And I'm acting like I'm some sort of…like I need accommodations that I actually don't."

"All right," he says. "Let's say, theoretically, that that's true. So what? The amount of pain you'd be in would not be fun for you."

"Yeah, but…"

"And also—sorry, but you told me I didn't have to shut up anymore, so I'm not—it's, y'know, not true, and you have an illness, and it might not have caused your leg to fall off or your spine to break in half, but your hands are all swollen, and your leg is next to me here, and I can *feel* how hot your knee is, and that's not some kind of euphemism. And that's not even to mention that I'm kind of the poster child for the fact that, even if you looked completely normal, even if your hands were perfect and your knee was…knee-temperature, that doesn't mean you're healthy, necessarily, because invisible illnesses are a thing. I look fine most of the time. Stunning, in fact. C'mon, you're a doctor's kid! You volunteer at the hospital! You know this."

"Yeah, but…"

"You just said it yourself," he says gently. "You're not an exception."

I sigh. He flops back on his pillows, looking annoyingly triumphant and also casual and also hot, with his broken arm lazily over his head and that sleepy smile on his face.

"So don't go skiing," he says.

"I'm just gonna drink hot chocolate."

"Hang out with me instead. I'll be out of here. We can

go out somewhere. We'll get hot chocolate."

I roll the dice around in my hand. I think it's my turn. "I don't date."

"Good," he says. "You don't want to be the kind of person who blows your friends off for a date."

I'm smiling. I can't help it. "Okay. It's not a date."

WHAT ARE YOU LOOKING
FORWARD TO?

Skiing. Are you seriously not coming? Come on, I'll do the bunny slope with you. You can do the bunny slope! And then we can just hang out in the lodge, and there's a hot tub, and come onnnn, it's gonna be so fun! You can't miss it. We'll be so sad without you.

> — *Luna Williams, 16, professional lesbian and Bob Fosse enthusiast*

Looking forward to today being over, honestly. I'm here for an ultrasound because they thought they saw something—this happened with my last kid, too, and she's fine. I just want them to do that high-tech ultrasound, see that nothing's wrong, and let me keep going to my regular OB with her, apparently, very blurry ultrasound machine. I don't want to be in a hospital again until a baby's coming out of me. A healthy baby.

> — *Jennifer James, 33, pharmaceutical rep*

When you were younger, I'd look forward all year to Take Your Daughter to Work Day— What? It's Take Your *Child* now? We're supposed to not celebrate having daughters? I swear...

> — *John Garfinkel, 49, Physician in Chief at Linefield and West Memorial Hospital*

Haunting some very choice people.

—Claire Lennon, 16, dead

In the 1970–71 season, the Fordham Rams had the best season they've ever had. Twenty-six wins, three losses, thanks to the spectacular coaching of Rodger Frederick Phelps, better known as Digger, nicknamed such by his father, who was a mortician. He was only with the Rams for one year, and we've never been able to reach that glory again. Digger Phelps retired in 1991. But I look forward to the day that he wakes up, realizes his destiny lies back with the Fordham Rams, and comes back to the Bronx to elevate New York basketball back to the number nine team we once were. I look forward to the day the Fordham Rams celebrate twenty-seven wins. It's gonna happen.

—Sasha Sverdlov-Deckler, 16, brother

CHAPTER SIX

I wake up at noon on Saturday feeling like I've been run over. My whole self is throbbing. A full-body sprained ankle.

My friends are skiing right now. I wonder if sitting in a car for three hours feeling like this would have been worth the hot tub I could be soaking in. Probably not.

"Dad?" I call, even though I know he's at work—and even if for some reason he's here and he answers, what am I going to say? I can't sit up, but actually I can, it just hurts, but I don't actually want you to do anything, because I'm fine, except I'm sort of not, but I will be, and I don't want to comfort you about it, so let's just say I'm fine?

I don't even know what to do with me, and I'm expecting someone else to?

I sit up slowly and force my feet and knees into a butterfly pose and bring my forehead down to my ankles. It hurts, but it feels so much better than not stretching. My ankles are hot and swollen against my face.

I need a shower. I need to eat something.

I'm supposed to go out with Sasha tonight.

That's not going to happen. I know it's not going to happen, but I refuse to acknowledge that right now. I don't want to cancel on him the first time we're supposed to hang out. I cancel on my friends all the time—hell, I canceled on them *today*—and every time I cancel, I feel like I'm taking a step backward on some kind of friendship-plank, and at some point soon I'm just going to run out of chances and plunge into the water and off the ship.

The friend-ship. Ha.

Anyway. I'm not going to get into a pattern of that with him. Except that I am, but I'm refusing to acknowledge that right now.

I can go out. It's just a series of steps, just like going to school. Shower—the hot water will feel nice. Find something to wear—I have plenty of options that don't require messing with buttons or zippers. Makeup—I can put some of my pencil grips on my brushes to make them easier to hold. I do that sometimes. Shoes—I have flats with some support in them. And then it's just to the train, into Manhattan, and then…and then the actual date. The not-date. And then getting home.

So, see. Totally possible.

I make it halfway down the stairs to make a cup of tea before it becomes screamingly obvious that it is not totally possible. It doesn't matter that the date's six hours away. At this rate, it would take me six hours to get ready for it, and then I would have absolutely nothing left in me.

I want to feel bad about it, but I don't. I don't feel anything but tired. I could go to sleep right here on this skinny wooden stair.

I take out my phone and will my fingers to work.

> Me: Hey, I'm really sorry, but I need to postpone tonight. I'm really not feeling great, and I just don't think I'll be any fun. Can we reschedule? Really sorry :(

He'll be understanding. He's got a disease way worse than mine. He probably cancels on people all the time.

He responds quickly.

Sasha: **ok**

Ok? That's it? Not even the four-letter version? All it needs is a period at the end and that's a text-speak *fuck you.*

Me: **I'm really sorry**

I don't hear from him again for the rest of the weekend.

"So wait," Maura says at our lockers on Monday. Her cheeks are burned red from the snow and the bridge of her nose is already starting to peel. "You blew us off to hang out with some guy?"

"No, I blew you off because…you know, I had homework to do, and my dad's been so busy, and he had the day off on Sunday, so he wanted to actually spend time with me, and it's not like I could have done much on the trip anyway, y'know?" None of this is technically a lie. "And then he wanted to hang out. They were, like, separate events."

"And you said yes?"

"It wasn't a date," I say.

"A guy asking you to hang out is a date until proven otherwise."

"Well, it was proven otherwise, because I said I don't

date and he said it wasn't a date."

She wiggles on her mascara. "That's what boys always say when they ask you out, so that if they decide halfway through that they don't like you enough to pay for shit, they can go, *well, this isn't really a date, so...*" Maura hasn't trusted a boy since Luke Schivo.

"Okay, well, it doesn't even matter because, like I said, I didn't go. And now he isn't talking to me."

"He sent you that one text and then nothing else?"

"Nothing. All weekend. And I texted him on Sunday, too."

"Sounds like a jerk."

"I guess. He seemed nice."

She slings her arm around my shoulders. "C'mon. I'll walk you to History." The others went ahead without us because they were sick of watching Maura pick at her sunburn, and honestly, that's fine with me. I'm good with just one person knowing about how I totally bombed my chance at the non-date I bailed on them for.

"How was skiing?" I ask.

"Oh, it was really fun. Would have been better if you were there. So this is the boy you met during your medicine thing?"

"Yeah."

"Does he have the same thing you do? That'd be cute."

"No," I say, "And we're not dating, so it wouldn't be cute. It wouldn't be anything."

She looks at me. "Is he like for real sick, then?"

"Yeah."

"Eesh, that must be rough," she says. "You're a good person. But you're not...ugh, this sounds awful. You're not gonna start, like, habitually ditching us for hospital friends, are you?"

"No," I say. "C'mon. I just didn't want to go skiing."

"Okay. We'll do something that's more, like, inclusive next time."

"It's not a big deal," I say. "C'mon, I've spent ages at the hospital for as long as you've known me, and I've never picked hospital friends over you before, right?" I've never really had any hospital friends, even. There was a girl who used to volunteer with me who I liked, and that's about it. Mostly I just hang out in my dad's office.

"That's true," she says.

"So see, why would I start now?"

She squeezes my shoulders and I try not to yelp. "Okay," she says.

We're back in the computer lab for History class. Luna sits down next to me and says, "Maura texted me."

Of course she did. "So what do you think?" I say.

"I'm confused. Sick Girl's dating now?"

"No, he's a friend." I open up some of the Frida Kahlo websites I have saved to check out today. "Sick Girl makes friends now."

"Sick Girl has always made friends," Luna says sweetly.

"So what do you think?" I say. "Do I text him again?"

"No, don't go crawling. Make him come to you."

"It's kind of too late for that. I sent him a bunch of texts he didn't answer."

"All the more reason not to go crawling," she says.

Siobhan appears on my other side and logs on to the computer. "Hi."

"What are you doing here?" I ask.

"Free period. Bored. Thought I'd come and pretend I have a History project."

"Or you could study," Luna says.

She waves her away. "What's going on?" she asks me.

Maura hasn't texted her anything, turns out, so I fill her in on the whole situation, again trying to minimize the part where I didn't go skiing with them.

"Did you know that skiing sucks?" Siobhan says. "It's paying money to fall. I wish I'd had a good excuse to skip it."

"We did it for you!" Luna says.

"Yes, and the thought that counted was very…thought," she says.

I say, "What do you think I should do about this boy?"

"You should make that your question of the week," Luna says. "Ask everybody."

"Should Sick Girl date Sick Boy?" Siobhan says.

"That's not the question," I say. "It's if I should text him or not."

"So make that the question," Siobhan says.

"Maybe I will."

"Girls?" It's Mr. Mattrapolis. Oh, right, we're supposed to be working. We all smile at him.

He comes up behind our computers. "What do you have for me?"

Luna rambles on about Bob Fosse for a while, with hand gestures and a couple of tap dance moves and a little bit of vibrato, and Mattrapolis smiles in a way that's probably supposed to look indulgent, but you can tell he's actually entertained and just trying to act disconnected.

He turns to me. "What's the plan, Isabel?"

"Frida," I say.

"She's a big topic. What are you thinking of focusing on?"

"The bus accident," I say. "How that changed what she was planning to do. Shaped the rest of her life. And the love affair with Diego."

"Connecting the two?"

I nod. "Trying to do something with the way chronic pain affected her. How it made her...not suited for relationships."

"Good," Mattrapolis says. "Keep it up."

He walks away to check on someone else, and Siobhan and Luna stare at me from either side, like curious lesbian bookends.

Luna says, "Is that why you—"

"No," I say. "That is not why I don't date."

I don't get a consensus on whether or not to text Sasha, so I don't do it. And he doesn't text me, either. And honestly, maybe that's fine. If he's so insensitive that he can't even respond well to an apology, he's not someone I need in my life. I'm always just going to be worried about disappointing him, and I have enough people I worry about disappointing without throwing a whole new one into the mix. I'll run into him in five months when our infusions overlap, and I'll pretend to be asleep, and then I won't have to think about him for another five months. And that's fine.

Except on Wednesday I'm at the nurses' station, today on the pediatric surgery wing, and I look up, and there he is.

"You know how hard it was to find you?" he says. "There are a lot of nurses' stations in this hospital. Do we really need that many nurses?"

He has more color in his cheeks than he has the other times I've seen him. It's also amazing how healthy *not* having an oxygen cannula in your nose can make a person look. He looks just like anybody else. Just a normal jerk.

A normal jerk who came here looking for me.

"I wouldn't say that so loudly if I were you." I act like I'm really busy with some paperwork.

"Hmm. Fair point." He leans down on the counter. "Working hard?"

"Mmhmm."

"What's wrong?"

I stop shuffling papers for no reason and look up at him. "What's wrong? *Ok*, that's what's wrong."

He looks confused.

"I had to cancel on you, and I sent you a really nice apology, and all you said back was *ok*, and then you didn't talk to me for four days. Can you not stand there like you don't know why I'm upset?"

"I'm not—"

"And you know what, I really thought you would be more understanding. You talk a lot of shit about healthy people for someone who goes and acts exactly like one of them."

"Isabel," he says.

"What?"

"I was not acting like a healthy person. Can you let me explain?"

"Not...not here." I can feel all the nurses leaning in

and listening. This is going to give them gossip fodder for weeks. I guess I should be grateful they have something else to talk about besides me and my poor little dad. Now they can speculate about my pathetic non–love life.

We find a little nook close to the elevators. He says, "I was an idiot to make those plans in the first place. I got home from the hospital, and I was a fucking zombie. I'm gonna say that I would have canceled on you if you hadn't canceled on me, except I'm honestly not sure I was awake enough to remember that we had plans. I've barely been awake for four days. That's why I haven't texted you."

"Oh," is all I can think of to say.

He's not a jerk. He's sick.

"I'm not pissed at you for canceling," he says. "I understand, c'mon. How could I not understand? Canceling on people is my middle name."

"Sasha Canceling on People Sverdlov-Deckler."

"Aleksandr," he says. "Spelled the Russian way. See, it's even worse. Aleksandr Canceling on People Sverdlov-Deckler. You can see why I didn't tell you ahead of time. It's just too many syllables."

His dimples are a goddamn nightmare.

"I understand," he says. "And you understand me being too tired to function."

"Of course," I say. "I just didn't… My brain didn't go there, I guess."

"Of course it didn't, you don't have sick friends."

"Yeah."

"Okay, so, we're good? This actually isn't something we need to be off in a corner fighting about? Because I would really rather hang out with you than fight."

I smile a little bit.

He takes my hands. "I am awake now. And I came here to make new plans. And you seem okay. Are you feeling better?"

"Yeah, I am."

"All right then. How about this Saturday. Do you have plans?"

"I don't have plans."

His eyes are so sparkly. "Good," he says. "This Saturday. Unless it turns out you need to cancel."

"I'm not going to cancel."

"Good."

"Unless I do."

He smiles. "Exactly."

WHAT'S YOUR FAVORITE
SUBWAY LINE?

I like the 4 a lot because you get right up close to Yankee Stadium, but honestly I'm never up there, so it's gotta be the N/Q. Reliable, as long as it's not late night and you're not trying to take it actually *into* Queens, which honestly I think is kind of ridiculous. You're gonna name something Q and then shortchange Queens? Pick a different letter. Queens gets shortchanged enough as it is. I mean, it could be worse. We could be Staten Island.

—Ashley Baker, 17, future Snow Ball Queen
through the power of positive thinking

The G. *HA.* Just kidding. Can you imagine? I've taken the G once. Once. Do you know what happened? It flooded. A subway train flooded in the middle of the summer. I bet the G floods every day.

—Mitchell Yarsburg, 14, math genius

I've always been partial to the 1. The 7th Avenue express? In my younger days, I used to just get off at every stop and have a drink, get back on, new stop, new drink. Of course, that was when the subway was a dollar fifty a ride. And we used tokens! Kids these days, you'd never last with tokens. You don't even have pockets.

—Lucas Ursick, 48, Oncologist

To be honest, I think I'm forgetting some of the specific lines and where they go. Do any of them take you out of the city?

— *Claire Lennon, 16, dead*

You're going to think I'm just trying to suck up here, but I swear: it's the 7. And I probably shouldn't say that, as Manhattan-trash, and any self-respecting Manhattan-trash will claim they never go to Queens, but since I've been going to Queens every ten days since I was four…here we are. And honestly, Manhattanites should love the 7, because it's the best view of Manhattan you can possibly get. When you're at Court Square and the train finally breaks above ground, and BAM, there's the skyline. There's really no place like it. Tourists haul themselves to the top of the Empire State Building for that kind of view. You want to actually *see* the Empire State Building, you get on the 7. There's no better view in the city that you don't have to pay for. Well, except for one.

— *Sasha Sverdlov-Deckler, lopsided*

CHAPTER SEVEN

Neither of us cancels. Sasha tells me to dress warm, and since it isn't a date, I don't have to worry about looking cute, so I go all out. Two pairs of socks, boots, fleece leggings, a huge sweater, my warmest gloves, a big hat. My joints are going to be so warm they'll think they're being toasted. They are going to behave.

"Now, tell me again who this boy is?" my dad says as I circle the kitchen in search of a necklace I swear I saw in here. He's on his minigrill, making something that smells so good it almost makes me want to stay home.

"I told you," I say. "He's the boy I met at the hospital."

"With Gaucher."

"Mmhmm."

"What's he like?"

He jokes about everything, and his hair is like ink, and he sleeps a lot, and his wrists are skinny, and his eyes disappear when he smiles.

"He's nice."

"Is he sick?"

I find the necklace and work on the clasp. "I don't know how to answer that."

"I'm just looking out for you, Ibby. You know that."

"He's not going to drop dead in the middle of our... whatever."

"Date."

"It's not a date."

He sighs. "I knew this day would come. I knew having a daughter who didn't date was too good to be true."

"We're just hanging out," I say. "It would be nice to have a friend who's…"

"A boy," he says.

"No. Who's like me."

He looks at me. "What do you mean, like you?"

And we just stare at each other, and I can't tell if he's honestly confused or if he's playing dumb. I can't read him.

I know my dad doesn't think of me as a sick person. Why should he? I'm out living life. I'm not coughing up blood or fainting. He'd acknowledge that I have pain, sure, but sick? Sick is a whole different thing. When he reads my column, he skips any mention of Sick Girl. He doesn't get it, so he pretends it doesn't exist, and we don't talk about it anymore.

And the thing is, it's good. That he doesn't think that of me. He's a doctor, so there's always the risk that he'd look at me and see me as a diagnosis instead of a person, and he doesn't. He sees his daughter. He thinks I'm strong and don't need to be insulated because I have a condition. And he spends his whole day around sick people, so he knows what sick looks like, so it's not as if his opinion isn't valid here. It's just as valid as mine, and he doesn't think I'm sick.

It's a good thing.

But it puts me in a very awkward position if I ever accidentally say I'm sick in front of him.

So I deflect.

"Jewish," I say. "None of my friends are Jewish."

"Well, far be it from me to argue with that. Come here,

let me help you with that necklace."

"Thanks, Daddy."

Sasha is waiting on the platform at my subway stop. He's wearing a huge plaid scarf, a brown leather jacket, and thick gloves. He smiles when he sees me.

"You look nice," he says.

I do a little twirl. "I look like an arctic explorer."

"The two aren't mutually exclusive." He looks to the right, toward Manhattan. "I love the view from this stop."

You can see the Empire State Building from here. It's lit up blue tonight.

"Where are we going?" I ask as the train comes in.

"Huh?"

I raise my voice. "Where are we going?"

"Oh," he says. We get on board. There are enough seats for both of us. Thank God for small favors. "I thought we'd go to LIC Landing."

I look at him.

"In Long Island City?" he says. That's a few subway stops from here—still in Queens, but closer to Manhattan.

"I figured that's what LIC stood for," I say. "But I don't know the place."

"Haven't you lived in Queens your whole life?"

"I don't really...go anywhere," I say.

"Hey, that's cool. I get to show you for the first time. Are you cold?"

"I'm okay."

"Good. It's about a five-minute walk from Jackson Avenue, is that gonna be okay?"

"That's fine."

"Cool."

We're quiet on the train. He stretches his legs out and crosses his feet at the ankles. The underside of the tongue of his boot says *NADIA* in scratchy pen.

"Who's Nadia?" I say.

"My sister. A couple years ago she got mad at me and wrote her name on all my stuff."

"Are you the oldest?"

"Mmhmm." He holds out four fingers. "So there's me, then Nadia, she's thirteen. Then my parents got divorced and my dad got remarried, and they had Josh and Nick. They're little. Seven and five."

"None of them are sick?"

"Nope, just me." The train slows to a stop at Court Square, and he pulls his legs in to make room as people enter. "My sister was already born before they figured out what was going on with me, but they tested her and she's fine. And the boys' mom didn't have the gene. Both parents have to be carriers."

"And then he got divorced again?"

"Yeah, and now he's dating for, like, the first time. I don't think he really dated when he met his second wife. He just kind of found a woman who seemed nice and married her."

"I guess that didn't work out so well," I say.

"I dunno. The boys are cute."

We get off at Jackson Avenue and head west. It's almost eight, so this time of year it'd be pitch black outside if not for the city lights and the twinkling Christmas garlands strung up between the lampposts.

"It's not even Thanksgiving yet," he says.

"You don't like Christmas lights?"

"I'm Jewish," he says. "You're Jewish!"

"Lights are nondenominational."

"I bet you like Christmas music, too."

"I do. I really do."

He laughs. "So do I. Doing okay?"

"I'm fine. How's your arm?"

"Looks totally normal under the jacket and glove, right? You'd never know."

"Eh. You hold it kind of funny."

"Yeah, well, you walk kind of funny."

"Hey."

"I'm just saying," he says. "We make a good pair."

"We are not a pair."

"So are you going to explain that to me?" he says. "Why you don't date?"

I carefully step over a crack in the sidewalk. "Well, it was part of what really got my column off the ground. My school newspaper is, like, weirdly selective, and colleges pay attention to it for journalism programs. It's a good school."

"Where do you go?"

"Markwood Academy? In Woodside."

"Sounds fancy."

"It's small," I say, which is what we always say to that, the same way people who go to Harvard say they go to school *outside Boston*. "So when I was pitching the column, I said, y'know, I'll ask questions, I'll get people's answers, I'll write up a summary of what those answers mean and how they all come together. And they said, okay, but why you, what makes your perspective interesting? And I had the Sick Girl thing, but they thought that sounded... I can't remember the word they used. Like it would only be applicable in certain situations."

"I mean, I certainly find that being sick only affects me in really specific situations," he says, and the relief of hearing someone call that out, of someone just grabbing that and pouncing on it and identifying it as the bullshit that it is... God, it's like coming up for air.

I clear my throat. "Yeah. But then I told them, well, I don't date, so I have more of an objective perspective on dating-type questions. They thought that was kind of cool. Like I became kind of a sexless Dear Abby kind of person. It made me seem more adult, I guess. I'm the closest we get to a grownup giving advice, but I'm still a kid that people will listen to."

"And you don't actually give advice."

"Oh, God no, I'm not going to be responsible for people's decisions. I don't even want to be responsible for my own decisions."

"So, what, if you started dating, they'd stop running your column?"

"No, probably not," I admit. "But it just... It's just easier."

"Fair enough," he says. "Here, check it out."

LIC Landing is, it turns out, a little waterfront park with café tables out on a dock. It's right on the East River, and it feels like I can see all of Manhattan glowing and moving like something alive.

"Wow," I say.

"This is my favorite view in New York," he says. "Go

sit down, I'll get us some food. Do you like burgers?"

"Uh-huh."

"Perfect. Sit tight."

I take a seat in one of the little metal chairs and watch him walk back toward the counter. He doesn't walk like someone who's worried about his bones breaking at a moment's notice, I'll tell you that. He has this long, loping walk on those skinny legs. It's happy.

I smile a little and look out at the water. I can just barely see the cars speeding around Manhattan, scurrying around like little animals.

"Okay," Sasha says, "here we go." He plunks down a tray with two hamburgers, two milkshakes, and a ton of fries. "Truffle fries," he says. "They're amazing."

"You eat like a skinny person," I say, grabbing some fries. "You are a skinny person."

"My limbs are skinny," he says. "But I have an awesome distended stomach like a starving orphan because my spleen and liver are enormous. It's super sexy."

"I bet," I say.

"I hate ordering food," he says.

I laugh. "What?"

"You don't?"

"No, what?"

"Ugh, I don't know. Ordering food, making phone calls, anything that feels like I'm making demands of people, I get so anxious."

"I get like that with, like, complaining to doctors," I say. "I have it in my mind what I'm going to say to my doctor, but as soon as I get there, I'm like *nope I'm great everything's fine don't worry about me.*"

"Oh, I'm good at that," he says. "If it's illness-related, I will squeaky wheel like it's my job. When I was little, before I was diagnosed, they thought I must have had leukemia because my white count was high and I told them all I was dying."

"Mmm, before I was diagnosed they told me there was nothing wrong with me."

He sips his milkshake. "Not really the same, huh."

"Nope. Must be nice to be a boy."

"It is," he says. "I recommend it."

"Maybe next time."

"But you can do other stuff?" he says. "Order food?"

"I mean, you *can* do it," I say. "You just did it."

He holds out his gloved hand for me to see. It's shaking.

"You should have had me do it!" I say.

"I was trying to be impressive! By doing something it turns out was totally unimpressive to you!"

I laugh. "I don't know. I'm not scared of talking to people. When I was little, I was basically raised by a committee at the hospital, so I was bothering doctors to play with me before I knew how completely inappropriate that was, and I guess I never fully learned, because I still go up to random people and ask them questions for my column all the time."

"Okay," he says. "So like…" He points to a couple eating a few tables away from us. "You would walk up to those people right now and ask them your question of the week. The subway-line one."

"Sure."

He stares at me with wide eyes.

"What?"

"I am *so scared* of you," he says.

"Oh my God."

"Do it. Do it right now."

"You talked to me the first day in the drip room," I say. "Explain that."

"Uh, you talked to me first. I was prepared to sit there the whole time pretending I didn't notice the pretty girl sitting next to me. And what did I even say? I babbled to you about some kid and his trucks."

"I thought it was charming," I say.

"And that's very lucky for me. Go ask them."

"This is how you learn things, y'know? By gathering opinions. I don't know how you learn anything."

"Books," he says. "Go ask them. I want to see."

"I don't want to be too spooky for you."

"It's too late. I'm terrified. Do it."

I roll my eyes, stuff a few more fries in my mouth, and go over to interrogate some people on their favorite subway lines (the 3 and, inexplicably, the 6). I come back to Sasha triumphantly.

"You didn't type anything," he says.

"I recorded them; I'll write it down later. It's actually easier for me to write by hand than type on my phone. Oh God, your nose is bleeding."

"Oh." He grabs some napkins and leans forward. "Don't worry, this happens all the time."

"Promise?"

"Like a few times a week," he says. "Seriously. It's gonna take a while, though, so get comfortable."

"Can I, like, eat?"

"Totally, yeah."

I take a bite of my burger. "Feels kind of rude when you're just sitting there with your nose open."

He laughs, then groans. "Don't make me laugh. It makes it worse."

"That's gonna be hard. It's pretty easy to make you laugh."

"Yeah, yeah."

"Maybe that's why you have so many nosebleeds," I say. "Laugh too damn much."

"Isabel."

"All right, all right, should I shut up?"

He shifts around, still bent over. It's easier for me to talk when I don't have to look at that face. He could go on thinking I'm witty and fun forever if he has nosebleeds this often. That could work.

"No, don't shut up," he says. "Just tell me something definitively not-funny."

"Um…okay, I'm thinking." I fiddle with my phone while I think, putting my interviews with the couple in the folder where I keep my column stuff, and that gives me an idea. "I have a dead imaginary friend," I say. "And I ask her all the questions I do for my column."

"What," he says, and it reminds me of how I answered him the very first time he talked to me, when he told me about the boy with leukemia and his renegade trucks. When he was scared. That feels like a long time ago. I try not to laugh so he won't.

"Her name's Claire, and she died when she was sixteen, and she's imaginary. She always died when she was the same age I am, so when I first thought of her, she was dying when she was thirteen, then fourteen…and every time I think of a question for my column, I ask her, too. I don't turn her answer in to my editor or anything, it's just for me."

"How did she die?"

"Some autoimmune disease. She would have lived, but she didn't have health insurance."

"Wow. That sucks."

"Yep." A pigeon lands on our table, so I give it a french fry. "Her parents were really great, though. Held her while she died and all that crap."

"You're right. This is extremely not-funny."

"She's not real," I say. "Just remember that part."

"Someone named Claire has probably died because they didn't have health insurance," he says.

"Oh, sure, but this isn't just some stand-in person. She's fully formed. I know her middle name and her birthday and, y'know, her answers to all sorts of random questions."

"So what's her favorite subway line?"

"New Jersey Transit."

He shakes his head sadly. "Claire."

"I know, but we can't blame her. She's a ghost. She doesn't care about crowds."

His nose keeps bleeding for a while, so I leave him alone and drink my milkshake and watch the water taxis glide across the East River. Finally he straightens up, dabbing at his nose and looking more than a little pale. He doesn't apologize.

"All done?" I say.

"I think so."

"Here." I hold his milkshake out to him. "Sugar."

"You look cold," he says. "We can go soon."

"Take your time."

He starts to take his scarf off.

"Stop," I say.

"I'm not cold. Here." He wraps it around my neck. It's big and soft like a blanket, and he winds it all the way around my shoulders. I burrow into it despite myself. It smells like cinnamon.

He looks out at the water, and I try not to stare at the way the light coming off Manhattan outlines his profile like someone painted him here.

"This is really beautiful," I say. "I can't believe I didn't know about it."

"My dad used to bring me here when I was a kid," he says. "He's really into boats, so anywhere you can see them, we were there. Did you ever do that thing off Battery Park where you can ride on a ship, like one of those old-time ships? You can even help them haul in the rope if you want to."

"Uh-uh."

"We should do it sometime," he says. "We don't have to haul in the rope."

I smile. "Okay."

"Boats and the castle in Central Park."

"There's a castle in Central Park?"

He claps his hands together. "Oh my God, there is so much we have to do. I am so excited."

I shiver a little. I don't mean to.

He smiles at me. "Not tonight, though. Let's get you home."

"No," I say, a little because I feel like I'm supposed to, but mostly because I don't want to.

He laughs. "You're freezing."

"We just got here, though."

"So? We can hang out a million more times. We don't have to fit everything in tonight."

"Okaaaay."

He gives me a hand to help me up.

"How are you?" I say. "I think you lost a couple pounds of blood."

"I'm all right. I'll go home and sleep it off."

"I thought you said it happens all the time!"

"It does," he says. "I sleep a *lot*. You'll see."

We start back to the subway, but my body is not behaving. It's never easy for me to go from still to moving, and refrigerating my joints and then expecting them to immediately work correctly was clearly too much to ask.

He tilts his head at me.

"Don't look at me." I feel like a marionette.

"But you're cute."

"Watch it."

"Okay, I honestly wasn't actually thinking you were cute, I'm just trying to be nice. Not that you're not, but...I was actually wondering if you'd like a hand."

"I'm okay."

"You can grab onto the cast. I won't even know."

"I'm fine," I say.

"Okay," he says.

I clear my throat. "Are we getting on different trains?"

"Nah, I'll bring you home and then switch directions."

"You don't have to do that."

"I want to," he says, and my frozen heart thumps and grows.

By the time we get to the train, though, all I'm thinking about is my ankles and my neck. All I want to do is collapse into a heap, and of course the train is packed. Of course. We crowd around a pole, and I try to stay upright when the train lurches forward. He's standing facing me, and I stumble a little bit into him.

He makes himself shorter so he can look me in the eye.

"I'm fine," I say.

"I didn't say anything. God, I'm tired. You know what will be fun?"

"What?"

"When we can stop pretending that we're interesting people who go out and do things and instead we can hang out and just do nothing."

It's incredible to hear those words out of someone's mouth besides mine. Not that I've ever said them, actually. Who would I say them to? "That sounds amazing," I say.

"You want to come over after school on Monday and... Do you play video games? Bash the shit out of some monsters?"

"Not really, sorry."

"Do you watch TV?"

"Yes, I watch TV."

"Perfect. Come over on Monday and watch TV."

"Okay."

We get to Court Square, even more people pile on, and when the train starts again, I put my hand on his chest to steady myself and accidentally make a noise in my throat.

"Yeah, okay," he says softly. "Hang on."

"What?"

"I'm just picking someone. Mmkay. Him. Excuse me?" he says to a man sitting near us. "I'm sorry to bother you, but my friend here—I know she looks fine, in fact she's very beautiful, wouldn't you say?—but she actually has, well, we call it an invisible illness. It's a joint condition, and she's having a hard time standing for this long. Do you think she could sit down?"

I can't even look at him, but the man stands up, and Sasha guides me into his spot. He leans against the pole in front of me and smiles down at me, his ankles crossed. He's proud. He still has a little bit of blood under his nose.

I say, "Y'know, you're standing there all smug, and you should probably literally be at home on oxygen right now."

"I only need oxygen when I'm sick," he says.

"Oh yeah, and what are you right now?"

The train goes above ground, and I slowly twist my head enough to see the skyline rise up over the tracks. I turn back at Sasha, expecting him to be watching it, too, but he's looking at me.

"Right now, I'm good," he says.

I still feel awful, but I don't really mind at this moment.

WHAT'S YOUR IDEA OF
A PERFECT DATE?

I love doing something weird, like paintball or geocaching or just, like, something that he's really passionate about, y'know? I can be interested in anything if the person telling me about it is interested in it enough. It's, like, infectious, y'know? People's excitement for things. So I want to know what it is about him that makes him special. When you see someone really light up like that...that's how you get to know them. Now whyyyyy are you asking?

—Maura Cho, 16, romance expert

Wherever she wants to go and whatever she wants to do. Trust me, three years into a relationship, you learn these things. Some things you can compromise on. Some things you can have great, invigorating discussions about. Not where you're going on dates. Men out there, listen to me: just let her pick.

—Sheldon Bartlett, 17, feminist

Well, if you ask my father, it's... I'm not sure. If you see my father, can you ask him?

—Sasha Sverdlov-Deckler, 16, Snarkmaster 5000

*O*h, wow. Something with candlelight. Dinner somewhere romantic, with a view, and maybe fireworks. And then afterwards we'd go for a walk in the park. Or a carriage ride! And, of course, a kiss. That sounds like the perfect date, don't you think?

—Claire Lennon, 16, dead

*S*eriously, you're gonna ask me this right now?

—Ashley Baker, 17, single

CHAPTER EIGHT

Ashley and Justin broke up this weekend. They'd been together since the very beginning of sophomore year, so something like fourteen months. She texted us about it on Sunday, and he's not at school today.

"He's taking it really hard," she tells us at lunch.

The walls are covered in paper snowflakes that are already starting to peel off. Our cafeteria's made up of tiny circular tables which seem like a bad design choice, because people are always dragging them around to put two together and teachers are always yelling at us not to. When Justin would eat with us, we'd have to squish an extra chair around our table for him. Now, we all fit.

"What happened?" Maura asks.

"He just… I mean, you know he was pissing me off the whole ski weekend. He's always trying to show off, and half the time he has no idea what the hell he's talking about, so he looks like an idiot, and everyone around him *knows* he looks like an idiot. I mean, his friends are always, like, exchanging looks about him when he says something stupid, and he doesn't even notice. And I feel bad for the guy, but like, at some point you're just wondering… Why isn't he noticing?"

We nod and sip our sodas.

"But, I mean, it's sad," she says. "But once I made up my mind, I just, I, like, couldn't even stand to be around him anymore until I did it. I just knew it was the right call. I wanted to wait until after the Snow Ball, but I just, like…once you know, you just *know*."

"Totally," Maura says.

"I remember when I broke up with my first girlfriend," Siobhan says. "It was like, I wrestled with the decision for ages, but then once I made up my mind, that was *it*. Like I didn't waver for a second."

"That's exactly it," Ashley says.

"There's just this relief about deciding," Siobhan says. "And once you get there, all you want is to not have to deal with the relationship anymore, and as quickly as possible." She kisses Luna's cheek. "Not you."

"But now he was too sad to even come to school?" Ashley says. "And just…ugh, I was so *happy* once it was over, and he can't even come to school. I feel terrible."

"Well hey," Maura says. "At least we're free of boys now."

Ashley takes a bite of her sandwich. "That's true."

"Except for Ibby's boy," Luna says.

I roll my eyes.

"Hang on," Ashley says. "What? What did I miss? How long have I been breaking up with Justin?"

"Did it take a long time?" Maura says.

"It felt like years."

"Ibby's going to some guy's house today," Luna says.

"You say *some guy* like he's some random guy I met on the way here and agreed to go home with," I say.

Maura says, "I mean, he's kind of a random guy you met at the hospital and agreed to go home with."

"You met him at the hospital?" Ashley says. "Does he volunteer with you?"

"Not exactly," I say.

Ashley raises her eyebrows.

"He's coming to get me after school," I say. "You all can meet him and form your own opinions."

"Do I get to have an opinion about Sick Girl dating in general?" Siobhan says. "Because I'm pro."

"Sick Girl is not dating," I say.

"Sick Girl should date Sick Boy," Luna says. "I think it's romantic."

"I don't know," Ashley says. "Seems to me like one of you needs to be able to shovel snow in the nuclear winter."

"That's what my dad's for," I say.

"Mmm. He could shovel my snow."

"Gross, Ashley."

Luna adds, "And what does that even mean? Is that some straight thing?"

"It's nothing," Maura says.

Ashley licks yogurt off her spoon. "This single life is not for me."

Sasha's waiting outside school when it lets out. His school day ends at 2:15, and ours keeps going until 3:20. Ridiculous. He looks a little pale, leaning against the railing at the bottom of the stairs, but he smiles when he sees me.

"You're wearing my scarf," he says.

"I didn't want to forget to give it back again." I start to unwind it.

"No, I like it on you." He looks around at my friends. "Hi."

"This is the welcoming committee," I say. "Ashley, Maura, Siobhan, Luna. They, uh, let's see. Siobhan makes sculptures, Luna does theater, Maura's on, like, every sports team, and Ashley...also a lot of sports teams."

"And newly single," Ashley says.

I give Sasha a look, and he sticks his tongue into his cheek and grins. "And newly single," I say.

"It's very nice to meet you," he says. I look at his fingers gripping the railing.

"We should go," I say. "Lots to do."

He nods.

"See you guys later," I say to the girls, and I slip my arm into his. He looks a little surprised—though not half as surprised as the girls—until he gets what I'm doing, and then I feel him relax into me a bit. It's just this small shift, but it feels like the best compliment I've ever gotten. He's telling me I'm helping. That my impulse was right.

I give him a little tug on the arm and walk away with him.

"Bye!" they screech after me. "Have fun! Wear a condom!"

"Sorry about them," I say.

He takes my hand.

"I gotcha," I say. "You okay?"

"I am. I just...long day. School was one thing after another, and...I don't know. Sapped all my energy." He's breathing kind of hard.

"We don't have to do this," I say. "I can just go home."

"We're going to my house and lying around, right?"

"Yeah."

"Then no, come," he says. "It'll be a lot more fun doing

that not-alone. Do you mind if we take a cab?"

"Of course not, whatever you want."

"Cool. Am I hurting you?"

"You're totally fine."

"How are you? How was your day?" He puts his arm up for a cab.

"It was good. Ashley broke up with her boyfriend, so that kind of dominated the conversation."

"She's the other blond one?"

"I'm the other blond one," I say.

"Never."

"No, Ashley's, like… She's a thing. She's captain of the basketball team, does great in school, up until yesterday was half of a power couple. She's killing high school."

"You don't want to be one of those people who peaks in high school," he says.

"Why not?"

"I have no idea," he says. "That's just what I tell myself."

"I feel like everyone's gotta peak somewhere. I think saying it can't happen in high school is just people who sucked at high school being bitter."

"Do I strike you as bitter?"

"You really don't, actually."

"So," he says. "It must be good advice."

"I'm not doing so bad," I say. "I get good grades. I've got my column. I'm thinking about college."

"That doesn't mean you're peaking here," he says. "We're juniors, we're all thinking about college."

"Where do you want to go?" I ask.

He laughs. "I don't know."

"Do you...think you'll stay in the city?"

"Oh yeah, definitely."

I try not to smile. "Me too."

We get into a cab and Sasha tells the driver 28th and 7th in Manhattan and asks him to take the bridge. He slumps down in his seat and rests his head against my shoulder, just a little, just carefully.

"Is your family gonna be home?" I say.

"My sister will be home from school. The boys are at their mom's house."

"Will your sister like me?"

"She'll probably stay in her room, honestly. I warned her there was gonna be someone over. It's nothing against you, she's just not super social."

"That's okay."

"It's kinda sad," he says. "She's really sweet, and she doesn't give people the chance to know her."

"Oh, so like the opposite of us."

"Exactly. Not sweet, and forcing people to know us."

I stretch my legs out as far as I can without moving him off my shoulder, point my toes.

"What are you doing for Thanksgiving?" he asks me.

"What are you doing?"

"Upstate to see my dad's parents and my cousins and everything, like every year. Aaaand you?"

"Just me and my dad," I say.

"Is this the first year just you and your dad?"

"It is, yeah."

"Eesh." He turns his head to look up at me. "Want to come upstate?"

I laugh. "Can I bring my dad?"

"Does he speak Russian?"

"Do *you* speak Russian?"

"Nope. He'll fit right in."

Sasha has the cab drop us off right in front of his building. I always just tell them "Oh, this is fine" and end up walking a block.

"I thought you couldn't ask people for things," I say after we're out.

"That's for non-illness stuff. This is accessibility. Trust me, in my family, they train you early to ask about accessibility."

That sounds incredible. I wonder what I was trained for early.

I remember my mom saying I was a natural at posing for pictures.

"Fourth floor," he says. "Don't worry, there's an elevator. You good?"

"I'm good."

"You get stiff when you first stand up, huh?"

"Don't…take notes on me."

"Yes, God forbid I keep track of what you need," he says.

"I don't need anything."

"Mmmhmm."

"I'm invincible."

"Yep."

"I'm a stereo that just plays the high notes."

"Oh, so you're broken?"

"Yeah."

"That adds up," he says.

Sasha says hi to the doorman so I say hi to the doorman, and I resist the urge to ask him what his idea of a perfect date is, and then halfway into the lobby I give up resisting the urge and go back and ask him. Sasha waits, leaning against the wall by the elevator, watching me the same way he did the other night on the train.

"What's the verdict?" he asks me after.

"Breaking into a public pool after midnight."

"Well, that sounds like a good way to murder someone."

"This is why you gotta talk to people," I say. "Everyone is actually so weird."

"Plus, now we have an idea for what to do the next time we hang out."

"Sure, active, athletic activity. Sounds like us."

He swipes his key in the elevator and we take it up to the fourth floor. The elevator's creaky and crimson carpeted. He leads me down a skinny hallway and unlocks his front door.

"It's a mess," he says. "Just to warn you."

"That's okay."

It's not really a mess, though, it's more…disheveled. There are little kids' soccer cleats stacked unevenly at the front door, and coats thrown over a chair in the living room instead of put away, and books flopped open on the kitchen table. The rooms are small, but it's a four-bedroom apartment in New York, so it's a palace.

"So, living room, which is kind of uninhabitable right now, thanks to Nadia's science project." He gestures at a bunch of poster board and half-full plastic bottles. "It's an acids and bases thing. Don't drink them. And then I'm down the hall." He knocks on the closed door across the hall and says, "Nadi, I'm back," and shrugs at me when he doesn't get an answer.

"This is me," he says, opening the next door. He has a plaid bedspread and a small TV and blinds instead of curtains. It's very generic teenage boy, if you ignore the oxygen tank tucked into a corner and the collection of pill bottles on his nightstand. I keep mine hidden away in the medicine cabinet.

Which reminds me. "Where's your bathroom?"

"Oh, it's…" He leads me back out of the room and past the living room. "Sorry, it's kind of a walk. Here."

"Oh my God," I say.

"What?"

"You have a bath tub." And it's not just any bath tub. It's a claw-foot and huge and deep enough to cover my knees. Or their knees. It's not mine. It would cover a person's knees.

"Yeah?"

"I don't have one," I say. "We just…my bathroom's small, so we just have a shower. Whenever I'm at a hotel or something I get really excited about the bathtub."

"Do you want to take a bath?" he asks me.

"Ha."

"I'm serious," he says. "You can take a bath."

"What, like right now?"

"Yeah."

I look at him.

"It's not a trick," he says. "There's a second bathroom. It's not like you'd be inconveniencing anyone."

"Well, what would you do?"

He pushes his hair back from his face. "Take a nap, probably."

"Are we being serious right now?"

"Yeah. There are towels under the sink. And also—hang on." He roots around under the sink, says "Aha" quietly to himself, which is for some reason so goddamn charming, and hands me a bottle of bubble bath. "Here."

"I can't believe I'm about to take a bath the first time I'm at a guy's house."

"There's a lock on the door," he says.

"No, I'm sorry—it's not that I don't—"

"You don't have to explain," he says. "There's a lock on the door."

"Okay."

"Just wake me up when you're done. Don't be too quick. I'm tired."

I laugh a little. "Okay."

He leaves. I lock the door and take off my clothes, feeling really naked in that special way you feel naked when you're changing at the doctor's office. I run the bath as hot as it will go. This is going to take forever to fill up. I should have kept my clothes on.

The bathroom actually is pretty small and dominated by the tub, not that I'm complaining. It's tiled in white to make it look bigger, but the grout is gray at this point, and some of the tiles are chipped. There's a big gouge in one of the tiles by the sink where someone must have hit it with something. The sink itself is covered in stuff—toothbrushes, deodorant sticks, contact lens solution, more pill bottles—all crammed together and leaning against the wall to stay balanced like some kind of art installation.

It looks like people live here.

I use just a little of the bubble bath—I'm guessing this

is his sister's, since it's vanilla scented and Sasha didn't seem to share my bath enthusiasm—and get in once I'm too cold to wait anymore. I sink below the water and try not to moan.

You stop noticing pain, is the thing.

You notice it when it's really bad, or when it's different, but...on the rare occasion someone asks me what it's like to live with RA, I don't ever know what to say. They ask me if it's painful, and I say yes because I know intellectually it must be, because the idea of doing some of the things that other people do without thinking fills me with dread and panic, but I always think about it mechanically. *I can't do x. I don't want to do y.* I don't continue the thought into *I can't do that because it would hurt. I don't want to do that because then I would be in pain.*

You can't live like that. There's only so much you can carry quietly by yourself, so you turn an illness into a list of rules instead of a list of symptoms, and you take pills that don't help, and you do the stretches, and you think instead of feeling. You think.

And you don't soak in hot water and feel the tension bleed out of your joints because it's just going to remind you that it will come right back.

I wipe my face off with wet hands.

But just for right now...I close my eyes. Just for right now, I'm good.

It stops feeling awkward as soon as the heat fully takes me over, but I still drag myself out after twenty minutes and dry off and put my clothes back on. I come out of the bathroom, and a girl sitting in the living room turns her head to look at me. She's found a sliver of the couch that isn't taken up by science project supplies and is curled up with a book.

"Hi," I say. "You must be Nadia."

"Hi," she says.

"I'm Isabel. I was…taking a bath at your house. I guess that's pretty weird."

She shrugs. "Sasha told me."

"What are you reading?"

She holds up her book. I go over and look.

"You smell like my bubble bath," she says.

"I do. In my defense, your brother told me it was okay."

She rolls her eyes. "It's fine."

"Sorry."

"No, it's okay."

She's reading *The Fellowship of the Ring*. "I never actually read that one," I say. "I love the movies, though."

"Yeah, I wanted to read them because I like the movies so much. They're…a lot different."

"Aren't all the characters, like, sixty?"

"Yeah! And if I wanted to read about a sixty-year-old, I'd just read…"

"Literally anything they assign for school, yeah."

"I'm trying to not think about that," she says. "I mean, they live to be, like, a million, so I guess proportionately their sixty is our…whatever."

"Sure," I say. "It's like the Torah. Jacob lived to be like a hundred and fifty, and we're supposed to treat him like he's not some kind of cyborg."

"That would make the Torah a *lot* more interesting."

"You're not wrong there," I say. "All right, I'm supposed

to wake your brother up."

She laughs. "Good luck with that."

"Oh yeah?"

"I know anemia makes you tired, but I don't think it makes it harder to be woken up," she says. "I think that's just him trying to make me late for shit."

I can't imagine my dad ever mentioning something about my illness casually like that. Wild. "All right, I'll get creative," I say. "I'll see you later."

"Bye."

I head to Sasha's room. His door's slightly open, but I knock anyway, then push it open slowly when he doesn't answer. He's asleep on the bed, on top of the covers, his body sprawled out like a starfish. I smile a little.

Once I get closer to him, I can see what he was talking about the other night with his stomach. It's swollen and sticking out through his shirt. I wonder if it hurts. Probably not—he said he was a wimp about pain. Good.

I squeeze my hair out onto his face.

He jerks awake, reaches behind him for his pillow, and smacks me with it. "I hate you," he says.

"I know."

He rubs his eyes and sits up. "Good bath?"

"Amazing. Thank you."

"Sure, any time."

I sit on the foot of the bed. "I met your sister."

"Oh yeah?"

"Yeah, she's sweet."

"She is, right?"

"Mmmhmm. And I love your house."

"This place?"

"Do you have another house?"

He laughs. "It's a mess."

"No, it's…alive."

"Like a monster? Okay, maybe I like it more, then."

I scoot myself up the bed and lie down next to him. "Everything is monsters with you."

"Yeah," he says.

There's a knock on the door and I sit up quickly. It's Sasha's dad, with a suit jacket slung over his arm and his tie loose around his neck. "Oh, hey," Sasha says. "I didn't hear you come in."

"Hi," I say.

"Hi there."

"I'm Isabel," I say.

"Oh, right! Sasha's mentioned you."

"Don't listen to him," Sasha says. "He's a pathological liar. He's not even really my father. Who is this man? Call the police."

"Sorry about my son," he says. "I'm Dmitri."

I laugh a little. "That's all right. Hi."

"Is it cool if she stays for dinner?" Sasha says.

"Of course, but I actually just left Nadi money for pizza."

"You're going out," Sasha says.

"I am. How are you feeling?"

He does a so-so hand. "Tired."

"You look a little bit like shit."

"Thanks, Dad."

I can't believe this conversation is happening. It's like I've stepped into some alternate dimension where people talk about things. Or some culture outside teenagers on Tumblr and me and Sasha where being sick isn't something to bury and talk around.

He has no idea how lucky he is, which is a strange thing to think about a boy born with a genetic illness, but there you go.

So when his dad asks, "Where did you two meet, again?" and Sasha says, "At the hospital," I chime in with "I have RA," like it's a completely natural thing to add.

And Dmitri just acts like it is. "Oh, my friend has that," he says. "How are you doing?"

"I'm…" *I'm great. I'm fine. Don't worry about me.* "I'm doing okay," I say.

"Glad to hear it. Well, thanks for coming by and sorry I'm such an awful host. Come over another night, and I'll make dinner. I'll make brick chicken!"

I have no idea what that is, but how do you say no to brick chicken? "Sounds great," I say.

"Take it easy tonight," he says to Sasha. "Don't go throwing any wild parties."

"Damn, there go our plans."

"I'll have my phone," he says. "It was nice meeting you, Isabel."

"You too."

"Door open or closed?"

"Closed," Sasha says. "Thanks." Once it's closed, he says, "So, that's my dad."

"He seems really nice."

"He is. He also used to be around more, instead of, y'know. Going-out-after-work Dad."

"Staying home, making brick chicken."

"Brick chicken is incredible," he says. "Just wait."

"I will."

He rummages around on his nightstand and finds the remote. "Ready for a movie?"

"Yes." I lie back down.

"Want a blanket?" he asks.

"Yeah."

He fishes one up from the bottom of the bed and spreads it over me. "Are you comfortable?" he asks. "You need another pillow, hang on—" He goes to the closet. "All right. Here. Pick your head up."

"You don't have to do this," I say while he fusses with the pillow.

"Actually, this is part of what people do when they like someone," he says. "So in a way I do have to. Part of the package." His hand brushes my temple as he adjusts the pillow a little more. "There. Good?"

"I'm good."

He climbs over me carefully and lies down next to me. "What are we watching?"

"Something scary."

"Goooood call."

He scrolls through Netflix. I just watch him. He's so focused on the screen, eyes narrowed, pale chapped lips just barely open.

That hair curling around his ears.

"How about this?" he says.

I keep looking at him. "Perfect."

WHAT ARE YOU THANKFUL FOR?

*Y*ou know what? A lot. I have a very good life, Isabel. I have a girlfriend who loves me. I have a family who… They're giving me time. They're not upset that I'm not doing better than I am. They just want to help. I have a very good therapist. And I have a whole, whole lot of time to sort myself out, if everything goes as planned, so…so I have a lot to be thankful for. Thanks for this question. I need to think about this stuff more often.

> —*Siobhan O'Brian, 17, artist*

I'm thankful for you, munchkin. What else?

> —*John Garfinkel, 49, Physician in Chief at Linefield and West Memorial Hospital*

*S*o. The year is 1867. It's December…somethingth. I don't remember. A young man is trying to catch a train from Cleveland to New York. He's running late, and back then if you were late you got seated in the back of the train because…punishment, I don't know. But! He misses it. No seat, back of the train or otherwise. He only misses it by a minute or two, but, train's gone. And then, that very train goes on to derail on its way into New York. Only the last two cars—one of the ones he would have been sitting in. 49 people died, but not the man who missed the train, who, by the way, was none other than John Rockefeller, who went on to make a zillion dollars, donate half of it to New York, and start the first public health center in the country. So I'm very thankful that John Rockefeller missed his train so we're all not dead of yellow fever right now. Or, honestly, he ended up giving all that money to Nazi racial studies, so maybe we should have sucked it up and died of yellow fever. It's a good story, though!

—*Sasha Sverdlov-Deckler, 16, historian*

I suppose I'm thankful for sixteen years on this earth. Not everyone gets that. Hell, before you turned sixteen, even I didn't get that.

—*Claire Lennon, 16, dead*

You know what they say! As long as you have your health.

—*Lynette Davis, 59, Principal at The Markwood Academy*

CHAPTER NINE

My dad blows through the door at eight thirty. I turn the volume down on the TV but stay where I am, facing away from him.

He comes over and kisses the top of my head. "I know, I know, I'm sorry."

"What happened?"

"I got held up in this insurance meeting. You'd think some of them would have families... And then this patient came in who needed surgery—"

"You're not a surgeon."

"The procedure had never been performed at this hospital before. I needed to make sure it went according to plan."

"Sounds like Dr. Robinson's job."

"It is, but... You're right. You're right. I'm sorry."

"It doesn't matter. It's just pizza, anyway."

"Where is it?"

"In the fridge. The oven's preheated. Just stick it in."

He goes back to the kitchen, I uncharitably turn the TV up again, and we settle in for New York's most depressing Thanksgiving ever.

Not to get all cliché about it, but it was my mom's favorite holiday. It's not like she was homey, either—I was sitting in empty houses way before she left—but she'd undergo some kind of personality shift for Thanksgiving, and Dad and I would power through 364 days of cold takeout and boxed macaroni and cheese, dreaming about turkey and stuffing and pies. I guess I figured with her gone he'd step up and take the reins. Now I realize he probably thought the same thing about me.

So here we are, sitting across the kitchen table from each other, eating reheated pizza while that stupid third chair sits there staring at us. I didn't even make a salad. I've been sitting here for three hours, pouting that he didn't come home. I couldn't have gone to the bodega and gotten shit for a salad?

He's got to be thinking the same thing.

I hate salad.

"So, what are all your friends doing today?" he asks.

"Luna's with her aunt's family in Brooklyn. Siobhan went to Denver to see her grandparents. Maura and Ashley stayed home." Ashley's family comes from all across the country to cram into their three-bedroom apartment for Thanksgiving every year. I don't know why they do it, but Ashley loves it. She invited me, but I knew there wouldn't be anywhere to sit down. Plus, I couldn't leave Dad by himself. Maura invited both of us, but she has dogs and my dad's allergic.

He chews. "We could try getting it catered next year. I know people do that."

"Yeah, when they have big groups and everything."

"Maybe we should go down to Florida next year, see Grandma and Grandpa."

"Ugh."

He chuckles. "Yeah."

"At least Hanukkah doesn't have a big food requirement," I say. "We'll be set there as long as you can make it home by sundown."

"Sundown's pretty early this time of year, munchkin."

"Yeah."

"I'll do my best," he says, but we both know what that means. I guess it's better to let me down a month in advance than to walk in at half past eight on Thanksgiving. "You could come to the hospital and we could do it in my office, like we used to." Mom and I would go over every night to light candles, if we weren't waiting around there already, and then come home. She hated it. I loved it, or I would have if she hadn't sat on the subway with that sour look on her face and then exchanged angry, whispered words with my dad all through the blessing.

I mean, what exactly are these happy holiday memories we're trying to re-create? The one day my mom stepped up? Eight nights of them doing exactly what they did every other night? Whose lives are we pretending my mom left, because they aren't ours. We're not holiday people. We're barely everyday people.

"I'm gonna go get some homework done," I say.

He gathers up our plates like he'd been waiting to do it. "I know this was a disappointment, baby," he says. "I'm sorry. Next year we'll be better. We just need to get into a groove."

I put a smile on. "Yeah. Totally. Don't worry about it."

I go up to my room, answer a few **happy thanksgiving!!!** texts from the girls with equally enthusiastic texts of my own, and then put my phone down and stare out my window. I don't want to do homework, but my usual ways of wasting time are out because everything on the internet right now is Thanksgiving stuff that I don't feel like dealing with. I'm looking through my bookshelf, trying to find some book that won't make me feel worse, when my phone rings on my desk.

I almost don't even check it, because I can't remember the last time someone called me who wasn't my dad or some cruise line trying to sell me a vacation package, but I do, mostly because I'd like to scold a telemarketer for bothering me on Thanksgiving right about now, and… it's Sasha.

He's supposed to be upstate.

Is something wrong? Why is he calling *me*? What does he think I can do?

"Hello?"

"Hi, Isabel." Okay, he doesn't sound like anything's wrong.

"Um…what's up?"

"Just calling to say hi. Are you busy?"

"No…"

"Something wrong?"

"I mean, do you know what decade we're in? It's nice to hear from you and all, but people don't really talk on the phone anymore. And didn't you say you hate talking on the phone?"

"You said texting hurts your hands," he says.

I can't believe he remembered that.

"Wow," I say. "I'm a jerk."

"I forgive you. How's your Thanksgiving?"

"Oh, it's…" I don't want to talk about it. I don't want to lie to him. It feels like there's a big difference between sending my friends a lot of exclamation points and telling him I'm okay, and I don't know if the difference is that it's out loud or that it's him.

So I just trail off.

"Well, mine has been an adventure," he says. "All my cousins are here, and… Okay, first of all, you should know that I don't come from a very, uh, politically diverse family. We're, y'know, Jewish, and as a group pretty gay, and they all have a chronically ill family member they love very much. But then my cousin David, he comes in and announces that he's been watching Fox News, and…"

"Wow."

"There were tears. Honestly, it's pretty fun watching my family just shut it right down. We are not having it."

"He can go hang out with my dad's parents. He'd fit right in."

"I'll let him know, if I get any urge to say words to him. Right now he's in the living room, trying to convert my dad. My dad. Imagine." I don't really know enough about Sasha's dad to get all the nuances of this, but I like Sasha acting like I do. Plus, I like that his dad is firmly against Fox News. "And I am outside in the freezing cold because if they knew I'd chosen a phone call over hanging out with the family for five minutes I'd probably be exiled worse than David." Somehow that's enough for me to form a whole picture. I have no idea what his grandparents' house looks like, obviously, but I create one in my mind, make a little yard out front for him to stand in. Give him clothes to wear. Make him bounce a little on his feet to keep warm, blow on his hands. Glow a little under the porch light.

I clear my throat. "Your family sounds intense."

"They are."

"So who's gay, besides your moms?" I say.

"Four of my cousins. Out of seven. We did pretty good. And then there's just me being like, possibly bi, but they don't know that, so I'm mostly just a disappointment."

"At least you don't watch Fox News."

"Yeah, and I'm sick, so I'm still, y'know. Interesting." His voice is so warm. "Are you okay?"

"What? I'm fine. I'm just in my room."

"Where's your dad?"

"Downstairs, cleaning up from our lukewarm pizza feast."

"Eesh."

"Not the best Thanksgiving."

"I mean, it's just Passover without the singing, anyway."

"That's true."

"I don't even know why we celebrate it. Just to make the gentiles feel better about themselves, I guess."

I flop down on my bed. "Well, you'll have to carry that torch alone this year."

"We can make up for it on New Year's."

"New Year's?"

"Yeah, next closest nonreligious holiday. What do you do on New Year's?"

"Nothing." That's not true; Luna always throws a party, but for some reason I don't say that.

"Well, this year we'll do something," he says.

Maybe that was why. "I'd like that."

"Me too," he says. "So, see? No problems."

"No problems now, huh? You've fixed everything?"

"Yeah, sure. Why think too hard?"

"Do you know what I like about you?" I say. I can't help it.

"I mean, hopefully a lot."

"You're not old."

He laughs a little. "And you are?"

"Yeah, I'm like a million. You said it yourself."

"I was flirting with you."

"Well, you were right."

"I was right to flirt with you? I knew that already. Listen, I should get inside before I freeze to death. It's very cold and I don't have my scarf."

"You told me to keep it!"

"I know. And I do have a scarf. Just not my favorite scarf."

"You told me—"

"Yes. Now it's with my favorite person." He pauses. "Is it okay that I called?"

"I liked it."

"So I'll call again?"

I snuggle into my pillow. "Right now?"

"Yeah, right now."

"Okay," I say. "Sounds good."

"See you," he says.

"Bye."

I hang up and let my phone rest on my chest and just lie there for a little with my eyes closed. I can hear my heart pounding like I've done something other than lie still and listen to that boy's voice.

Or like I've done just that, I guess.

His voice. It's always a little scratchy. Crackly and deep. Like a campfire.

Fuck.

I am so incredibly screwed and I do not care right now.

I just want to think about the smile in his voice, and how he called instead of texting, and how he asked if it was okay, and how he said I was his favorite person.

And of course it all happens on a day that seemed like it was otherwise created to remind me why Sick Girl does not date. Like, this would be the hardest day in existence for someone to convince me it's overkill for me to put absolutely any safety measure in place to make sure that thirty years from now I'm not leaving Sasha and a teenager alone to eat cold pizza on a national holiday.

I don't know what to do, which seems like a ridiculous thing to think, because it's not as if Sasha's asking me to do anything. He's not making demands. He's not rushing me. We're not even talking about it. We're just…

Somewhere in the background I can hear a ticking clock.

It's so slow. It's so inevitable. It's like I'm watching a movie I've already seen before. Or watching a car crash in slow motion.

Or sitting on the train, waiting for that moment between Court Square and Queensboro Plaza when the train comes up for air and you see the skyline and everything is all right in the world.

Maybe it could be like that.

I am so incredibly screwed and I don't know how to not care.

There's a knock on our front door. I sit up and listen to my dad go and answer it. I entertain this idea for a minute that maybe it was all some setup, that Sasha isn't actually upstate. The whole time I was picturing him outside his grandparents' made-up house, he was actually on my block, waiting to rescue me from my shitty Thanksgiving. Hopefully with pie.

But I recognize the voice immediately. It's Maura.

Come to rescue me from my shitty Thanksgiving.

She comes up to my room with Tupperware containers full of pie and kisses my cheeks and primps in my mirror, and I sit there and smile at her.

"This is really sweet of you," I say.

Maura says, "I figured…you know. It might not be the easiest Thanksgiving." She sits down on the bed next to me and gives me a hug. "I made lemon meringue pie *just* for you. Everyone was like, why is there lemon meringue pie on Thanksgiving, and I was like *don't you dare even touch it*."

"Thank you," I say. "This is exactly what I wanted."

WHO'S THE LAST PERSON YOU TALKED TO ON THE PHONE?

I literally have no idea. Oh! I do. It was the Seamless guy. He couldn't find my apartment. Do you remember when Seamless had all those ads on the subway that were like, *order food like a New Yorker. Use Seamless.* And we were like, are they trying to get tourists to use Seamless while they're here, or are they trying to shame us into feeling like we're not *real New Yorkers* unless we use Seamless? Anyway. This Seamless guy couldn't find my apartment. I feel like this happens *so* often. And like, are they real New Yorkers if they can't find anything? Maybe they should try ordering from Seamless instead of just delivering for them, and that would turn them into real New Yorkers who can...you know. Find shit. I am so sick of having them call me and ask for directions. If I wanted to talk to someone, I'd just go to the restaurant! It's two blocks away!

— *Maura Cho, 16, New Yorker*

I had to do that dreaded phone call home to a parent a few nights ago. And no, I can't tell you what it was about. I can tell that teachers hate them probably more than the kids do. All right, probably not that much. But a lot. Can you guys stop being jerks so I don't have to do them? I'd consider it a personal favor.

— *George Mattrapolis, 42, 11th grade History teacher at The Markwood Academy*

*Y*ou're expecting me to say you! Ha! But you're wrong. It was actually my mom's wife. She called last night to wish us a happy Hanukkah. It is, as I'm sure you're aware, not Hanukkah. My mom said she told her that as some kind of a prank, but knowing my mom, she legitimately forgot what day it is. My mother is a lovely woman, but she only has focus for bonobos. They're doing lovely, if you were wondering. My moms, but also the bonobos.

— *Sasha Sverdlov-Deckler, 16, enthusiast*

*M*y mother. She has to work really hard, but she says I can always call her if I need her and she'll drop everything to be with me. I try not to bother her because I know her work is important and we need the money. She's been fired because of me before. But she'd still never turn her back on me. She's my everything.

— *Claire Lennon, 16, dead*

*A*nyone who knows me well enough to have any business calling me knows not to call me.

— *Betty Ronan, 19, babysitter*

CHAPTER TEN

Sasha calls again on Saturday, the day he gets home from upstate. "I am so tired," he says. "I think my bones aged thirty years while I was gone."

"You're just trying to catch up to me."

"Doing my best. How are you?"

"I'm okay," I say. "I'm at the hospital." I'm sitting on the edge of the big fountain in the atrium with my books spread out around me, but I'm mostly just people watching. My dad said he'd have a lunch break in an hour.

"Appointment?"

"No, I just come here to study sometimes." A woman walks by with four kids she's trying to wrangle all at once. She looks like she's been crying.

"On a Saturday?" Sasha says. "That's bleak."

"It's not bleak! It's proactive."

"Isn't that the name of that yogurt for middle-aged women? See? Bleak. Why do women need their own yogurt, anyway? Judging by commercials, *all* yogurt is for women."

"Are you high?" I say.

"No, I just really like yogurt." There are kids chattering in the background.

I pull my legs up under me. "Are those your brothers?"

"Yep. Want to come meet them?"

"I'm studying!"

"Yeah, and I'm worn out as shit. Want to come babysit

them so I can take a nap?"

"Ah, there it is."

"Plus we have to watch more of…whatever it was. That scary show."

I watch a man rush by me. He looks happy, so maybe he's here for a baby, or maybe he's one of those people who looks like he's about to laugh when his world's falling apart. I've seen a lot of those. "I'll come over on Friday," I say. "How about that?"

"*Friday*. Damn. You really are trying to have a guy grow old. Okay. Friday."

"Are you mad?"

He laughs. "What? No, I'm not mad. I don't get mad."

That can't be true, but at the same time, I can't possibly imagine him mad. Sometimes he gets a little pissy when he talks about his dad, but even that is nicer than me at my mildest.

I used to be like that, but it was a long time ago.

"See you, Isabel," he says. Like always.

"Bye."

There's a text from my dad waiting for me. Something came up. Lunch is going to be delayed.

Screw it. Delayed for him, maybe. I dig my sandwich out of my bag, take a bite, and watch the people.

He calls me on Monday, during my lunch break at school.

"Do you have your infusion today?" he says.

"I do." I'm standing in the corner of the cafeteria by the trash cans after I hastily made some excuse about my dad calling to get away from my friends. They're looking at me and whispering, and I realize they probably think this has something to do with my mom.

"Mine's tomorrow," he says. "I'll keep you company today if you keep me company tomorrow."

"Deal."

My friends look at me with questions in their eyes when I get back, so I make up some excuse about my appointment being rescheduled. They say "Oh, okay" and change the subject immediately. I knew it would work.

I call him on Thursday. "What are we doing tomorrow?" I ask. I'm painting my toenails with my feet up on my desk. It's a good day.

"Ew, we have to do something?" He coughs.

"Well, we have to eat something. I'm gonna want to eat. And your apartment doesn't have a lot of food."

"We have tons of food!"

"Yeah, but it's all, like…ingredients. You have lots of parts of food."

"That's how you make the food."

I fold up and blow on my toes. "Seamless is how I make the food."

"Okay, well, I'll make something."

"Brick chicken?"

"No way. You only want my dad's brick chicken. Trust me. I'll make brisket."

"That sounds hard."

"It's not. I'll teach you."

I dig through my cabinets for a different color polish

for my fingers. "What do I need to know how to make brisket for? Can't I just sit there while you make it for me?"

"I don't know, maybe you'll want to make it for your dad sometime."

"He'll think I've been body snatched."

"Okay, well you can make it, and I'll make it, and my dad can make it, and we'll have my brothers and my sister do a taste test, and then we'll eliminate one of us, and then the other two go on to make dessert, and then the winner of that gets a million dollars."

I put the nail polish down. "Can we do that tomorrow?"

"Yes."

"You have to teach me how to make dessert first."

"On it."

He calls me at 3 a.m. between Monday and Tuesday.

"Did I wake you up?" he says.

I keep my voice low. "No, I'm still up studying."

"Your school works you too hard." His voice doesn't sound right. Pinched and heavy at the same time.

"They don't, really. I just couldn't sleep, so I thought I'd get some work done. You okay?"

"My stomach's all fucked up. I took my meds without enough food, and sometimes that... It's...gross. I don't know why I'm telling you this."

I staple some papers together. "If it makes you feel any better, one time at Six Flags I... Is there a delicate way to say *shat my pants*?"

"I mean, I feel like not at this point."

"All right, well, I once shat my pants at Six Flags."

"Is that like an RA thing?"

"Nope, that's just a me thing."

He laughs and groans. "Ouuuuch."

"Sorry. You okay? You sound kind of messed up."

"Everything just…goes haywire when one thing goes wrong. I get a nosebleed, my stomach decides it needs to hurt, my stomach decides it needs to hurt, my lungs get in on the party…"

"Okay, well, take it slow. Deep breaths. I'm not going anywhere."

We're quiet for a bit while I just listen to him breathe, and every once in a while I try something encouraging. He gives this little keel of pain that makes my own stomach clench up.

"You're doing so great," I tell him.

"What are you working on? Distract me."

"Yeah, sure. I'm finishing up my Frida Kahlo project."

"Frida Kahlo."

"Yeah, you know about her?" I move some images around on my PowerPoint presentation. I fucking hate PowerPoint presentations.

"I know she was a painter. Flowers in her hair. Eyebrows."

"She was this big revolutionary," I say. "One of the last things she did before she died was go to this protest against Eisenhower intervening in Guatemala. Like, days before she died. And she was really into, like, traditional Mexican culture and matriarchal societies and stuff like that."

"Badass."

"Yeah, but she was also just, like—she was really unhappy. When she was eighteen she was in this bus accident and a pole went through her, and she had problems from it her whole life. She had to get toes amputated later, and then when she got older—and she didn't live to be very old—she could barely leave her house."

He coughs. "That sucks."

"And she and her husband were always cheating on each other and fighting all the time and then they got divorced and then remarried. They wrote each other all these letters about how obsessed they were with each other, how they couldn't live without each other, and then they'd just turn around and be awful. It's like the messiest, most depressing love story. Are you wheezing?"

"A little. Why do you think it was like that?"

"What?" I can't remember what I was talking about.

He coughs. "Frida."

"I think it's probably hard to be happy when you're in the kind of pain she was. And I think if you're not happy, you're not good in relationships." He's still coughing. "Sasha, hey." I close my laptop.

"I'm okay."

"Honey." I didn't mean to say that. It just comes out. I don't know if he even hears me.

"I think…" He clears his throat. "I think I should wake my dad up."

"Good. Okay. Stay on the line, okay?"

"Okay."

He calls me the next afternoon on my way home from school.

"Happy Hanukkah," he says.

"You, too. How are you feeling?"

"Better. Just slept all day."

"Good." I turn right at the end of the block and almost walk straight into a woman who's got to be a hundred and five. Such a struggle not to hang up on Sasha and run and go back and ask her who the last person is she talked to on the phone. But. "You kind of freaked me out last night."

"Yeah, I'll do that. Is it too much?"

"Of course not. C'mon."

"Good," he says. "What are you doing tonight?"

I stop in at the bodega for a candy bar and an energy drink. The traditional Hanukkah foods of our forefathers. "Nothing really," I say.

"Nothing? It's the first night!"

"I know, but my dad has to work, so…maybe once he gets home we'll light candles late or something."

"Come over," he says.

"You're sick."

"Which is why I didn't offer to come to you."

I dig around in my purse for some pennies. "I can't just barge in on your family's Hanukkah."

"Do you want me to ask my dad? Would that make you feel better?"

"Yeah."

"Okay. Hang on." I hear him shuffle around in the background, hear his dad's voice. It's early for him to be home. I wonder if he stayed home with Sasha.

"Do you need a bag?" the bodega lady asks me. I shake my head no and stuff everything in my purse. I always feel like a thief when I do that, even though she just saw me pay.

Sasha's back. "My dad is *very* excited to find out you're Jewish," he says.

I laugh. "Is that a yes?" I push through the door of the bodega and out into the cold. My house is right at the end of the block, and the subway is twenty steps in the other direction, halfway across the boulevard.

"Yes," he says. "Please come."

"Will there be brick chicken?"

"*Yes.*"

"Well, finally." I turn away from my house. "I'm coming."

He calls me that night, right after I get home. "That was fun, right?" he says.

I'm going to smell like oil and onions from the latkes for days. "I love your family."

"They love you, too. Nick says he's gonna marry you."

I kick my boots off my feet. "Dad?" I yell.

"Still not home?"

"Doesn't look like it."

"Sooooo listen, I called because I had an amazing idea and I couldn't wait until tomorrow to ask you."

"Tomorrow?"

"Hanukkah's eight nights long. I assume you're coming back tomorrow."

I laugh. "Okay."

"So it's my sister's birthday next week, and we're throwing her this roller-skating party."

"That sounds fun. It's her fourteenth?"

"Yeah. It's a surprise, because she doesn't really... Stuff like that stresses her out because she feels like she doesn't have a lot of people to invite, so it's better just to leave her out of the planning stuff."

I hang my coat up. At Sasha's, we just throw them on the chair when we come in. "Uh-huh."

"Well, the thing is, she really doesn't have that many people to invite. And I know she likes you, so..."

"I'd love to come," I say. "I can't really roller skate, but I can definitely eat cake and bring presents."

"Well, I was thinking you could come, and you could bring all those healthy friends of yours, and they could roller skate, and you and I can, y'know... Bring presents and eat cake."

I head upstairs. "Sure, sounds fun."

"You're amazing. Do you need ideas for a present?"

"No, I know what to get her."

"Amazing," he says. "You're amazing." After we hang up, I curl up with those words and sleep beside them. *Amazing.*

I call him on Friday from the girls' bathroom on the third floor of my school. "I feel like shit," I say. "Why aren't you at school?"

"I am. I ducked out of class when I saw your number."

"Oh." I kick the metal trash can next to the toilet. "Sorry."

"What's wrong?"

"My wrists are killing me, and my neck hurts, and I'm so fucking tired, and I just… It's not a good day. I'm supposed to be in class right now, taking notes on this presentation, and I feel like my fingers are about to snap off."

"You should go home and get some rest," he says.

I shred some toilet paper in my lap because, arthritis or no arthritis, I need something to do with my hands, and I hate myself for that right at this moment. "I can't."

"Why not? Is this presentation life-altering? Is it about, like, falling in love or how to do your taxes or something else we'll actually need to know, or is it school bullshit."

"It's school bullshit! It's shitty, stupid school bullshit."

"Isabel," he says.

"What."

"Go home."

"I can't just go home in the middle of the day."

"I do it all the time!" he says.

"But that's different," I say.

He doesn't say anything for a minute, and when he says, "Why's that different?" his voice sounds funny.

"I didn't mean it, I just… It's different. With me." I sink my head down into my toilet-paper-covered hands. I shouldn't have called him.

He says, "You know there's nothing wrong with being like me, right?"

"Of course. Sasha, come on. Of course I know that."

"Whatever. It's fine. I don't care."

"Sasha."

"Seriously, it's fine. Listen, are you all right? I've got

to get back to class."

"Yeah, I'm…"

"Seriously," he says again. "Are you okay?"

"I'm fine."

"Are you still coming over tonight?"

I rub my forehead. "Yeah."

"Okay. I'll see you then."

"Yeah."

I call my dad after my rheumatologist appointment in Astoria, a couple hours before the last night of Hanukkah. "How did it go?" Dad says.

"Fine." I hunker down in my coat on my way to the train. "They took some more blood, and they had my results from last time."

"How'd it look?" He's walking, too; I can hear it in his voice. Rushing around the hospital, white coat swishing behind him. On his way to see some patient who's probably in critical condition, but making time for me and my blood tests.

"Good," I say. "Sed rate was normal. CRP was fine."

"Munchkin, that's great!"

"He told me if my knees keep hurting I should try losing weight."

"Want me to come over there and beat him up?"

I laugh a little. "It's fine."

"Listen, baby, I am going to try so hard to be there tonight."

I feel myself smile. "Yeah?"

"Yes. I'm getting the last of this paperwork done, and

then I'm going to be home. So at least we can have one night together, right? I'll call you as soon as I'm on my way out of here."

"Okay."

"That's my girl. So glad the tests were good! I knew they would be. I love you."

"Love you, too."

I get to the Ditmars subway station, or, at least, to the stairs in front of it, and look up at the people rushing up and down the metal steps. My phone is still in my hand. I duck underneath the elevated tracks and call Sasha.

"My tests results were really good," I say. "Everything came back normal."

He sighs. "Well. That's really frustrating."

And just like that, I'm crying. "Y-yeah. It is."

"Deep breaths, honey. I'm here."

I look up at the train and stick my arm in the air for a cab.

My dad calls three hours later.

"I'm so sorry," he says. "Something just came up, and…"

"I get it," I say. "It's okay."

"No, I told you I'd be home, and…"

"It's okay, Dad. There's always next year."

"I'll be home when I can," he says. "As soon as I can. Maybe you and I can do some kind of midnight candle lighting, how's that sound? That could be fun."

"Yeah," I say. "Yeah, sounds good."

I hang up the phone. Sasha's dad gives me a quick

squeeze around the shoulder and gets back to showing me how to make brick chicken while Nick and Josh wrestle on the floor.

Sasha reaches over to get the garlic and brushes his finger, so lightly, against the inside of my wrist.

All in all, a damn good Hanukkah.

WHAT SECRET ARE YOU KEEPING?

Ashley likes someone, and I've been threatened not to tell on pain of death, and like… What is this, fifth grade? We're practically adults. I think she's taking the single thing a little too seriously. Has to guard her new single-dom with her life, I guess. 'Cause she knows as soon as a guy found out she liked him, he'd be all over her. What is it about Ashley? She's magnetically charged. Amazing.

> *— Luna Williams, 16, proud owner of an A on her*
> *Bob Fosse project*

All right, I've got a good one. My husband and I have a place in Cape Cod, and we go to stay there sometimes. My husband, he likes to save money. So what he wants to do is turn off the heat—or the air-conditioning, y'know, depending on the time of year—at our place here the whole time we're gone, and then he wants our neighbor to come in and turn the heat back on for us a few hours before we come home. And also, neighbor's got to come every day and turn the heat on for twenty minutes and run the water so the pipes don't freeze, then come back, turn it back off. Can you imagine asking a neighbor to do this? It's so… I don't know what's going through his head. So what I do is, we turn the heat off right before we leave, and just as we're getting in the cab to go to the train, I go, "oh, hang on, I forgot something," and I run back to the apartment, and I turn the heat on, and then I tell him before we're leaving to go home, "oh yeah, I called the neighbor, she turned the heat back on for us." And he has no idea that it's always on the whole time. Look, I like saving money, too, but I'm first of all sure as hell not coming home to a frozen apartment, and I'm also not going to be the woman who asks her neighbor to come in and make sure the apartment's nice and toasty when we come back from our vacation. If I wanted someone to boss around, I would have had kids.

— *Doris Lancaster, 63, married for 42 years*

The same one you are. I'm you, remember? You think he'd still like you if he knew?

— *Claire Lennon, 16, dead*

All right, remember our hero John D. Rockefeller—I mean, he's not a hero, there's the whole Nazi-connection thing, but he's an established *protagonist*—who didn't die in a train derailment? Before he helped eradicate yellow fever in the U.S., it was going around killing people left and right. If you left your house, the world was like, hey, how about some yellow fever, like the people at Trader Joe's giving out free samples. But of yellow fever. And in New York, I mean, you can imagine, it was a yellow bloodbath. So they needed places to put the bodies of people who couldn't afford funerals—and also, y'know, people didn't want to have the bodies of people who died from it just lying around because they didn't know if you could get it from the dead bodies or whatever. So they developed these things called potter's fields where they'd dump the bodies. Eventually those became vaults, and the city built over them, and people forgot. But in 2015, when they were doing plumbing repairs or something in Washington Square Park, they were digging and they found this vault of yellow fever bodies. Now. My brothers *love* Washington Square Park. Favorite place. And every time I take them there, they're running around, and I'm like, *don't tell them about the bodies, don't tell them about the bodies.* It's a struggle. Honestly, they'd probably be into it. My family's so twisted.

—*Sasha Sverdlov-Deckler, 16, overeducated*

'm the Zodiac Killer.

—*Nadia Sverdlov-Deckler, 14, Zodiac Killer*

CHAPTER ELEVEN

Nadia's birthday party is at a roller rink in Jackson Heights. My friends show up decked out in eighties clothes they stole from their moms that they're probably pretending are ironic. Most of the crowd here is still just regular roller-skating people, if such a thing exists, but there are enough people here for Nadia that I think she's happy. She's smiling more than I usually see, anyway.

While EDM and synth-pop blast over the speakers and everyone else roller-skates around in endless circles, Sasha and I man the gift table. "What did you get her?" I ask him.

"This nail polish set that's themed after Disney villains."

"Badass."

"How about you?"

"Just some books I liked when I was her age. I figured then she'd have a built-in someone to talk about them with."

"I love that," he says.

I smile.

We sit on one of the tables in the eating area and scarf down cheese fries and watch everyone skate and dance a little to the music. Josh and Nick are bored of the kids' play area and run over every so often to climb all over us.

My friends come over for a break. "Well hey there," Luna says to Nick. "Who's this little guy?"

"That's Nick," Sasha says. "And Josh, here." Josh is currently hanging off his neck like a zoo animal.

"So cute," Maura says.

"They look like you!" Ashley says to Sasha. He raises his eyebrows at me, quickly, and I try not to laugh at the image of Ashley and Sasha together. She'd run him into the ground in the first ten minutes.

"Can I have some fries?" Nick asks me.

"Yep, right here…"

"She's great with kids, huh?" Maura says to Sasha.

I say, "Cut it out, Maura."

"She has all these little cousins," Maura says. "That's why."

Sasha looks at me. "I didn't know that."

"Yeah, well, they're my mom's family, so it's…" I wave a hand. "Complicated."

Siobhan says, "Oh, whoa, she told you about her mom?"

"Not really," Sasha says, but they talk right over him.

"That's amazing," Maura says. "She doesn't talk about her mom to anyone."

"You know I'm sitting right here," I say.

"She must really like you," Maura says.

Why do people have friends, whose idea were friends.

Ashley moves Josh onto her lap so she can sit down next to Sasha. He immediately squirms away and joins Nick to eat my fries, but she doesn't seem to mind.

"Are you two gonna go to the Snow Ball?" she says.

Sasha turns to me. "The what?"

"It's kind of like winter prom," I say.

"Isn't that homecoming?"

"What? No, that's fall prom. Who raised you?"

Maura says, "You haven't invited him?"

"I don't even know if I'm going," I say.

Ashley leans into Sasha like she's going to tell him a secret, but she talks loud enough for all of us. "Ibby has these *rules* about dating. Or *not* dating."

"That I know," he says.

"Well, if you don't go with her, I still need a date," Ashley says.

He's trying not to laugh. "I'll keep that in mind."

A new song starts playing, and Luna squeals and says this is *her song*, and they all hurry, or as much as you can in skates, over to the rink. Sasha watches them go. "Y'know, that's kind of how you look when you walk," he says.

I laugh. "Shut up."

"So. Snow Ball?"

I shrug and take the fries away from the boys. "All right, you two, you're gonna turn into fries at this rate."

"I want to turn into a fry," Josh says.

Sasha says, "Why don't you guys go back to the play place?" Nick hauls himself up on the table to squeeze Sasha's head and kiss him on the cheek. I bite my lips to keep from smiling.

I watch them run over to the play place, mostly for the excuse not to look at Sasha.

He talks to me anyway. "You don't know if you're going?"

"I'm not much fun at dances," I say.

"Nobody dances at dances anyway."

"Not at my school." I lean against him a little, just

enough to tap my shoulder against his.

He rolls a french fry between his fingers and watches it like it's fascinating. "There isn't anyone you'd want to go with?"

"C'mon, don't do the whole…thing. If I was going with someone, it would obviously be you."

He smiles a little. "Sometimes I need to check to make sure this isn't all in my head."

"It's not all in your head, it's just…"

Maura stops in the middle of a loop and leans over the little half wall closest to us. "Ibby!" she calls.

"Yeah?"

"You should totally come and do one round."

"I can't," I say.

"Just like one! We all want to do one together. You can do one, right?"

I hesitate because yeah, of course I could do one. I could do a hundred. I wouldn't die. So I'd be sore tomorrow. People do things that make them sore. That's something that people do.

But nobody in Sasha's family is trying to guilt *him* into skating, and it's *his* sister's party, and he wouldn't die, either, and I'm frustrated and pressured, and I don't know if I'm about to yell at Maura or go put on some damn skates when Sasha takes my hand.

He says, "She can't, we actually need to go talk about something."

Maura raises her eyebrows.

"Sorry," I say.

Sasha leads me back to the play area to quickly check his brothers, then down a few hallways until we find a spot with fewer people. He leans against a water fountain. "You okay?"

"Do you ever just…" I pick up my hands and then drop them. "I don't know. Do you ever just get really fucking mad at healthy people for doing nothing but… living their lives, and it's not their fault, and you love them, but you just fucking hate them?"

"I don't really hang out much with healthy people," he says.

"Yeah." I push my hair off my face. "I'm beginning to think you're onto something there."

"Plus I don't really get mad," he says.

"Come on. Everyone gets mad."

He shrugs.

"You know, that's not really healthy," I say. "Not getting mad."

He grins. "Good thing you don't like healthy people."

I point at him. "You got pissed at me the other day. When I called you from the bathroom at school."

"Okay, I'm not saying I was pissed, but…can we talk about what that was?"

I sigh. "I guess I walked into that."

"Mmmhmm."

"I wasn't saying what you thought I was saying. I just don't think that it… That it's fooling anyone if we act like you and I are on the same…"

He watches me.

"I mean, look! You have doctors telling you to be on oxygen; I have doctors telling me that my blood tests look great and I can do whatever I want. Before I got diagnosed, they told me it was nothing, that I was making it up or it was growing pains or something. Before you got diagnosed, they thought you had *leukemia*. I mean, nothing versus cancer, here, what does that tell you?"

"Well, it tells me I'm better at complaining than you are, which we knew already," he says. "And also that doctors are sexist and ignore girls, as you rightfully pointed out last time we talked about this, so we knew that already, too."

"It doesn't just mean that."

"You know I looked it up," he says. "And RA is the tenth most debilitating illness there is. Mine wasn't even on there."

"Yeah, because it was probably a list of common illnesses, right?"

"I mean…"

"I'm sure fatal familial insomnia wasn't on there, either, and nobody's acting like they don't have it harder than we do."

"What's that?"

"It's how it sounds—you can't sleep and then you die."

"Damn," he says. "Well, at least that's one we don't have to worry about. We sleep all the time."

"Ha, ha."

"I don't know why it's important for us to establish some hierarchy of who's sicker than who," he says. "Can't we both just be the same?"

"I know you don't," I say quietly.

He waits for me to say more, and when I don't, he says, "Well…okay, regardless, I wasn't pissed at you."

"Okay, well, hey, you're always pissed at your dad. How about that?"

"That's different," he says. "I just… The kids deserve to have him around the way that I did."

"Okay, but I've been at your house basically every day for the past week and a half, and he's been gone like, what, four of those nights? And he was always there for Hanukkah first."

"He used to be there every night."

"He just threw a huge party for your sister!"

"I'm not saying he's a bad father," Sasha says. "But he could be doing more, and he's not. I love the kids, but I can't be all that they need. They need him around."

"He is around," I say.

"All right, well…I don't see it that way."

"I don't know how you don't get mad," I say. I'm walking around in tiny circles like some kind of caged animal. "You know people talk about how being sick gives them some good perspective and makes them better people or whatever?"

"That's bullshit," he says.

"I know it's bullshit, but I thought it was bullshit because I was going to stay the same person I always was. But I'm not. I think it's changed me. I think it's made me just a mean, angry, worse person. And like…what is the upside there?"

"I don't know," he says.

I force myself to stand still. "I think I'm just going to spend my whole life being mad at people who aren't doing anything wrong. And that's… I'm just going to fuck people up. I can't be in a relationship or have friends. I'm just going to resent them. Maybe this is what happened with Frida Kahlo."

"Okay, but honey," he says. His voice is so gentle. "You're not Frida Kahlo. You're some white girl from Queens."

I laugh a little, mostly in frustration, partly at his voice. "I'm trying to be serious."

"Yeah, you picked the wrong guy for being serious." His phone buzzes, and he checks it. "All right, Dad says we're leaving soon. We're just taking a few of them back to the house to open presents. I guess my dad's sticking around tonight."

For some reason that's the last straw. "Can we make a detour?" I say.

"What?"

"You and me. I want to show you something."

"Now?"

"Yeah, let's just grab our coats and go."

"What about your friends?"

"Fuck my friends," I say. "Come on."

"We're going to your house?" Sasha says when we get off at the 46th Street subway station.

"Yeah."

"Am I meeting your dad? I want to fix my hair if I'm meeting your dad."

"My dad's not going to be there," I say. "That's the point."

I lead him up the front steps of my house and unlock the door. I leave the kitchen lights off, but there's enough light coming from the neighbor's house and the streetlamps and the snowflake lights on the street that we can still see pretty well. Sasha wipes his boots on the mat.

"Dad?" I call, just to make sure. He's not here. "All right," I say. "You see this?"

"It's nice," Sasha says. "What I can see of it, anyway."

"It's perfect," I say. "It's neat, and dark, and empty, and perfect—because nobody lives here! This is what a house without a dad looks like. Not your place. Not home-cooked meals and science projects in the living room and sports equipment from games that he probably goes to, right? Not birthday parties. You think my parents had time to throw me a birthday party?"

"I'm sorry," he says.

"No, I'm not... I'm not trying to get you to feel sorry for me. This is what it's like for most people. This is how most people live."

"So...I'm not feeling blessed enough?" he says. I can hear the smile in his voice. "In my charmed childhood?"

"Honestly, when it comes to this? Yeah."

"Not a lot of people would tell me that. I like that."

I sit down at the kitchen table. "We can go in a minute."

"Take your time."

I just sit there in the dark, listening to the clock ticking above the microwave. It's so loud. We've had it since I was a little kid. When my parents used to fight over dinner, I would close my eyes and try to hear every click of the clock instead.

Sasha sits down. In Mom's chair, but how would he know. He has this knit cap pulled down low over his head and a couple of curls escaping underneath. His lips have a little color from the cold, for once. I can see it even in the dark.

I take a deep breath.

"I don't want to… He's a great guy," I say. "My dad. He saves people. And he loves me. He never… I've never felt like he doesn't love me."

"Of course," Sasha says. "I mean, he's a doctor, he's gonna be busy. And at least, y'know. At least you had a doctor in the house, so that must have been good."

"Yeah."

"Although they still didn't believe you when something was wrong, so I guess maybe not."

I scratch the surface of the table with one nail. "I… fuck. Okay. I need to tell you something. And it's not like it's some huge secret, I just like… I've never talked to anyone about it before, and I don't know how you're going to take it."

He taps his fingernail against mine. "Okay."

"So I was… You were diagnosed when you were four, right?"

"Four, yeah."

"But you were sick."

"Since I was born, yeah. They just didn't know what it was."

"Okay." I need to do something. "Do you want some tea?"

"Sure."

I take the box out of the cabinet and put the kettle on the stove. "So I wasn't…it took me like a year to get diagnosed, but until I was eight I was fine."

"Uh-huh."

"But I always…" I stay facing away from him. "I always felt this…connection. With sick people. Mostly with, like, fictional characters, not actual people, but I mean, I didn't have Claire yet, but I always had some sick imaginary friend. And I was always reading books about kids with cancer and shit. And I used to…" I sort the tea bags in the box. "I would hide them, like, I'd read the books behind other books, because deep down I felt like I was doing something bad. After my parents went to sleep, I would sometimes…I would sit down here, and I would make Shirley Temples and drink them and pretend they were medicine. I was always… I was reaching for something."

He says, "So then when you got sick you felt like you'd made it happen?"

"No, it was…"

"You thought you were faking."

I shrug a little.

"You still think you're faking," he says quietly.

I'm losing him. I can feel him slipping away from me like it's something physical, and it hurts so much more than I ever would have guessed.

"It's not that I think I am," I say. "I just… I'm worried that I am. I'm sick, and I used to pretend to myself that I was sick. That's a weird coincidence, isn't it? And the doctors, you know, they spent ages telling me everything looks fine before they figured it out, and now they tell me my test results look good, so I should be feeling okay… And it's not like this is something I've stopped doing, this reaching thing. A couple of months ago, I had this dream that I was in the hospital and people were just taking care of me and no one thought I didn't deserve to be there, and now that's what I think about before I go to sleep.

That's like my happy place. Being in a hospital. That's not what I'm supposed to want, but I do. There's something wrong with me. So when I say that I'm not like you, it's not because I think there's something wrong with being like you. It's because I am so afraid that someone's going to accuse me of exaggerating to be like you. Because I don't think… If someone thought that, I couldn't handle it. If you thought that…"

"Ibby," he says.

I force myself to turn around. "Yeah."

"Is this… I know this isn't the point, but is this why you're like, you know. Why you're hesitating?"

"Hesitating on what?" I say, just automatically.

"Don't," he says softly. "Don't do the thing."

"No," I say. "I don't date. It's a policy."

"Right, and…I would like to know why, please."

I'm actually not sure anyone's ever gone right out and asked me before.

I don't know if I've been waiting to tell someone or if I've been waiting to tell him.

I swallow. "It's because of my mom."

His eyebrows come together under the hat. "I thought your mom only left a few months ago."

"She did only leave a few months ago, and before that she was already horrible. They had a great marriage, for a while, my parents, and then all of a sudden she just… She was biting his head off about everything. She couldn't stand his job, she wouldn't accept his choices, and she was just *mean* about it. And I figured, okay, my parents are just going to have a shitty marriage where they hate each other, or maybe they'll get divorced, and those things suck, but people live with it. But instead they kept on doing that for years. And then one day I get home from school and there's a two-line letter, to my *dad*, saying she's gone, and nothing for me and no way for me to get in touch with her. I have no idea where she is. I'm her *daughter.*"

"Fuck," Sasha whispers.

"And you know what? It shouldn't have been a surprise, because she was a horrible person. And it's not just her. You want to know why I don't date?" He doesn't say anything. I keep talking anyway. "Because the women in my family are horrible people. Every single one of them. My mom left us. My grandmother cheated on my grandfather and stole all his money. My mom's sister had her kids taken away because she got two DUIs with them in the car. My half sister, Alyssa, my mom's daughter, she's in prison for credit card fraud."

"I didn't know you had a sister," he says.

"Yes, I don't talk to her, because she's *terrible.* They're all terrible. So I'm the girl who's got a lot of odds stacked against her here that she's not going to be a good person, and then we've got my history of feeling like a sick person, and now I'm sick, and it *really* doesn't look like I'm going to be the one to break the pattern and head down the path of righteousness or whatever. I am a public health hazard. Your buddy John Rockefeller would shoot me in the street before I go around and 'black widow' a bunch of guys, so…okay? That's what it is. That's all my shit, and if you and I are gonna keep doing whatever this thing is that we're doing, you have to know these things about me, okay?"

His lips part as he watches me. "You're not saying no," he says.

"No, I'm not saying no, I'm just saying…"

"Okay." He stands up as the kettle starts to whistle. "Okay."

He comes over and takes the kettle off the stove and pours us two cups of tea. I stand there, leaning against the counter, feeling like the whole world's sitting at some angle and I'm just trying not to fall off. Or throw up.

"Do you like honey in yours?" he says softly.

"Yeah."

"Me too. Okay. Can I ask you something?"

"Yeah."

"Do you know that you're Jewish?"

I look at him. "What?"

He's not looking at me. He's concentrating on the tea like it's so important, but his voice is casual. "Do you know that you're Jewish," he says again. "Like…deep down. In your soul or whatever. Do you just feel it?"

"Yeah," I say.

"And when you try to explain that to non-Jews, they look at you like you're crazy, right?"

"Uh-huh."

"Okay then." He gives me my cup of tea and keeps his hands around mine when I take it. His cast is cold against my skin. "Why is it so ridiculous that you'd feel being sick deep down in you, then? It's a part of who we are."

"But I wasn't sick yet," I say. "I was just a normal girl pretending."

"It's not like RA is some contagious thing you happened to pick up when you were nine. Eight," he corrects quickly. "It was always in you somewhere, right? Just hadn't, y'know. Come out to play. Maybe it's like... like converts. They were always Jewish, they just didn't always know."

"Y'know, it's probably blasphemous to talk about being sick like it's a religion."

"Why?" he says.

"Because..."

"Because healthy people would think so."

I laugh a little. "Yeah."

He tilts his head to the side and looks at me. I just sip from the teacup.

"And I don't care about the other women in your family," he says. "I mean, I care about them because they've been shitty to you and I want to yell at them, but what I mean is...I care about you and whether or not *you're* horrible, and I think I know you pretty well at this point. And you're way too self-deprecating to ever trick me, so I don't think we need to worry about that. You'd sell yourself out instantly."

"That's what my dad thought about my mom," I say. "She had him tricked, too."

"Yeah, and I'm guessing she didn't give him a whole speech about how she was scared she was going to hurt him."

"She might have. I don't know."

I look down, and he touches his hand to my cheek until I look up at him.

"This isn't working," he whispers. "You're not scaring me away."

Just like that, everything straightens out.

Fuck, Sasha.

He says, "You think I'm going to think it's weird that you dreamed about being sick? Honey, nobody took care of you. Why would you have dreamed about anything else?"

I need a moment to collect myself. He lets me have it and pretends like it's nothing. He drinks his tea, looks around the kitchen, has no idea how goddamn incredible he is.

"Are you ready?" he says after a few minutes.

I nod.

"C'mon. Let's go home."

"Okay."

He takes my hand on the way back to the subway.

"So," he says once we're up on the platform, his voice light. "About that dance."

SHOULD SICK GIRL DATE SICK BOY?

Are you two seriously not already dating? Because I think you're basically already dating. You've already betrayed us by giving up the single life, Sick Girl! I'm just kidding. Yes, obviously, you should date him. You two are adorable together.

— *Luna Williams, 16, fangirl*

Listen to me, Isabel. Being in a great, supportive relationship is like... Okay. So before Luna, I dated some girls who were great on paper. And I felt totally amazing about myself because they wanted to date me. But then, now that I'm with her, I realize this is the only time I've felt amazing. Well, then, and when I was away from them. I'd always thought of relationships as this thing that you needed to, like, steel yourself against, y'know? You had to gather up all your power while you were alone to be able to stand the, like, *chip chip chipping* away of yourself that the other person was going to do to your self-esteem and your personality and your...you-ness, because that was all I'd ever been in. And now I'm with Luna, and I just... If you have any chance of feeling what I'm feeling, you have to feel it. You have to.

— *Siobhan O'Brian, 17, taken*

Nooooo! Who is Sick Boy?? All I know is Sick *Girl*, who is supposed to be, like, smarter than the rest of us and not messing around with relationships. If you're dating, what's gonna make you, like, special? You're just like everybody else.

— *Alicia Nichols, 15, some girl*

I don't know. I'm still a little worried about that nuclear-winter thing. He is cute, though.

—*Ashley Baker, 17, still going to be Snow Ball queen, even if she doesn't find a date*

Look at me. Girl. Look at me. Do not screw this up. No, I don't know what not screwing it up means! But I know that you screw things up and you *better* not. We need a win, Isabel.

—*Claire Lennon, 16, dead*

Okay, so here's what I'm thinking, and don't kill me here, but isn't it sort of... I mean, look, he seems really sweet, and if you like him then that's all that matters. But a part of me wonders if like maybe it isn't a little... convenient? Like, oh, you've got a thing, he's got a thing, so you have to pair up. I just don't want you to feel like you have to date him because, y'know, you've got that in common. Because you're good enough for anyone that you want. And if that's him, then fine! This isn't coming out right. Don't print this. Oh, I guess you're probably not printing this question at all, are you? That'd be weird.

—*Maura Cho, 16, best friend*

Sick Boy? This is so demeaning. Can't I be Sick Man?

—*Sasha Sverdlov-Deckler, 16, fully grown*

CHAPTER TWELVE

"**W**hat if it messes up our friendship?" I say.

"It won't," Sasha says. He's doing some really ineffectual job of cleaning his room while I lie on his bed with my existential panic. He rustles around in a box by his computer.

"Oh, that's your answer? *It won't?*"

"Yeah."

"You know, you could be a little more reassuring."

"Well, you could help me clean my room, so there's stuff we both could be doing."

"I'm not gonna clean your room! *My* room is clean."

"Yep, because you've gotta be perrrrrfect." He spills a box everywhere and coughs.

"I don't have to be perfect," I say.

He gets the coughing under control. "You're gonna feel really bad about not helping when I get, like, a mouthful of dust and my lungs stop working."

"Maybe you should clean more than once every ten years."

"See? How could we possibly mess up our friendship? We're already jerks to each other. And you do, by the way, have to be perfect."

"No I don't. My dad just likes a neat house."

"That's not what I'm talking about. Do you want this?"

I sit up. He's holding some kind of cord. "What is it?" I ask.

"It's an HDMI cable."

"What does it do?"

"It's for like…hooking your computer up to a different monitor. So if yours isn't working or if you want to play a game on your TV screen or something."

I stare at him. "Why…why would I want that?"

"I don't know!" He holds up one in his other hand. "I have two! I thought I'd offer you one! Tikkun olam!" He coughs into his elbow.

"Could you cut that out and come give your lungs a break, please."

He grumbles and clambers onto the bed next to me. "C'mere," he says, and he slings one arm up over my head. I scoot closer to him and rest my cheek against his chest.

"You could try taking me seriously," I say. "I'm wrestling with a major decision here."

"I've used up all the *seriously* I have for this issue over the past month and a half. I'm at capacity."

"I *don't* have to be perfect," I say.

I listen to him laugh, feel his scratchy breathing under my ear. "You asked people if you should date me," he says. "And you do it for everything! You don't do anything without asking twenty billion people first to make sure the way you feel is normal. You are so afraid of making the wrong choice. Why don't you just trust yourself? What do *you* want?"

"What I want isn't the point," I say.

"Do you even hear yourself?"

"No, because like…" I sit up. "What if I'm wrong? What if I do what I want and…"

"Lungs rested," he announces. He gets up and goes

over to his closet and starts rearranging boxes on top. "And you know, not that I support the practice, but most of the people you asked *did* say you should date me, so if you're going to make it your method…"

"Going with what I want could be a bad idea," I say. "What I want could mess everything up."

He turns around and faces me, his hands braced on the top frame of the closet. He says, "If I'm reading between the lines correctly, what you want is to go to the dance together."

"Okay, yes, but—"

He holds out a hand. "Just, just stop, right there. Think about how great it would to just stop at yes. I know I would enjoy it, personally."

"It could be a mistake," I say.

"So what!" he says. "Is the world going to end if we go to the dance together and have a terrible time? Or if we date for a while and then break up? We would still be friends."

"Everyone says they'll still be friends," I say.

He shrugs. "Everyone isn't us."

I sigh.

He pulls a box down and sorts through it, pulling out a bunch of what look like…Happy Meal toys, why does he save this shit? "Let me ask you something," he says. "When's the last time you made a mistake? Did something you knew might not end up well. Something reckless."

"I…I don't know."

"You don't *know*! Isabel, come on. That is no way to live and you know it."

"Garfinkels don't make mistakes," I say. "We make

decisions."

He barks out a laugh. "What is that, a motto? Is that on your family crest?"

I flop back on the bed. "Shut up."

"Fine," he says. "Maybe Garfinkels don't make mistakes. But you know what Sverdlov-Decklers do? Mistakes. Lots of 'em. Accidental babies, runaway trips to Africa, dating girls they meet at bars when they could be home with their lovely children, having the aforementioned lovely children without any kind of genetic testing, not cleaning their room for ten years... Just mistake after mistake. And since you've been basically living here for the past month, some of that *must* have rubbed off on you."

I groan as loudly as I can. I hear him put the box down and walk over, and the next thing I know he's gently pulling me up by both hands, his fingers carefully supporting my wrists.

"It would probably be a pretty major mistake to date the emotionally stunted goofball with the debilitating chronic illness," he says. "I mean, I think that'd be a decent way to make up for lost time."

I say, "You know that's not why I'm... The Sick Boy thing was just an alias to, like, go with mine, it doesn't mean—"

He cuts me off. "You think I think you don't want to date me because I'm sick? C'mon, we don't have to do the thing."

"Okay. Thank you." I close my eyes. "I love your voice."

He chuckles.

Oh God. I'm doing it. I'm doing it. "Okay," I say.

"Okay?"

"But this isn't... It's just a dance, okay? I'm not promising anything after that. We can just see how the dance goes."

He scrunches up his face. "That's what *okay* means? All this buildup, and that's how you're asking me? This is the longed-for moment? No no no."

I breathe out through my teeth and say, as quickly as I can, "Sasha, will you go to the Snow Ball with me?"

"Oh, sure, I guess," he says, and then he pulls me up in his arms and spins me around.

WHAT WOULD YOU DO IF IT WAS YOUR LAST NIGHT IN NEW YORK?

I would take my wonderful daughter, get on the subway—no, it's our last day, we're taking a cab—and go to Yankee Stadium. We'd get hot dogs and nachos and watch the Yankees. Maybe she'd actually watch instead of playing on her phone like when she was little! Since it's our last night and everything.

—*John Garfinkel, 49, Physician in Chief at Linefield and West Memorial Hospital*

I mean, am I dying, or am I leaving the city? Or is the city about to be ravaged by some Godzilla-type monster? It's kind of an important distinction… No? I have to pick on my own? I need more guidance than this. I am lost in the West Village with no guide. Save me, Isabel.

—*Ashley Baker, 17, found a date*

That's a pretty morbid question. Plus, I think I've told you before. My mom held me while I died, we watched TV, blah blah. What are you wearing to the dance?

—*Claire Lennon, 16, dead*

So in SoHo, there's this apartment building, and if you ring the buzzer, someone lets you up to the second floor. You go up, and it's this entire apartment—like, a big apartment, like a three-thousand-square-foot apartment—and it's completely filled with dirt. Up to your knees in all directions, just dirt. They water it down so it stays in place. So you can go up there, and you can just…look at the dirt. I went there when I was a kid—my mom took me there. She loves it. And I pretended to get it because I love my mother and I love getting things, but…I'm going to be honest with you, Isabel, what I saw was a wasted three-thousand-square-foot apartment in SoHo, even as a seven-year-old. So if it was my last night in New York, I would go back to The New York Earth Room—that's what it's called. I want to see if I've learned anything, if it's really this meditative place like people say it is, or if seven-year-old Sasha was just good at seeing through the bullshit of dressing up a room full of dirt and calling it the earth. And hopefully you would come with me. Though I hope it's not your last night in New York. You should stay.

—*Sasha Sverdlov-Deckler, 16, owns a suit*

have a bunch of people I need to tell to fuck off, I'll tell you that.

—*Louise Kern, 82, works at my bagelry*

CHAPTER THIRTEEN

I was going to get ready with the girls, but my dad's actually home the night of the dance and wants to meet Sasha first, and honestly our "getting ready" parties usually leave me too tired for whatever we were getting ready for, so it's probably for the best.

Dad knocks on my door as I'm finishing up my makeup. "Need help with anything?" he says. He has a dishtowel between his hands and is trying very hard to look casual.

"Yeah, could you look at my earring rack and find the silver ones that are like…spiral-y?"

He picks the rack up and scans it with his eyes narrowed, like he's studying an X-ray. I turn back to my mirror and make sure my highlight sparkles the way I want it to. This is a winter dance. I'm going to look like I'm covered in glittery snow, or I'm not going to bother to show up.

"I like your dress," he says.

It's light-blue cotton with spaghetti straps, a full skirt, and a low back. It ends just above my knees. "Thanks," I say. "It's the one I got for Dr. Leonard's daughter's bat mitzvah."

"Oh, right, right. You're going to be cold, though."

"The dance is actually inside."

He snorts. "Smart-ass. Here they are."

I slip the earrings on, which I hope to God is the last

thing I'm going to have to do tonight that requires fine motor skills, because putting my hair in a French twist and packing on all this eye shadow has done a number on my hands. I hope Sasha isn't expecting me to wear heels. I have sparkly silver flats and that's as far away from my Birkenstocks as my feet are gonna let me go.

My dad sighs. "You know it's going to happen someday, but still…"

"Dad."

"I suppose I should be thankful it took this long."

"It's a dance," I say. "It's not like I'm getting married."

"Well, I should hope not. Would have thought I'd have met the boy before now if you were getting married."

"I've been hanging out with him for like two months. Maybe you should be around more often."

He doesn't say anything. Honestly, I can't believe I said anything.

"Sorry," I say.

"You know I try, Isabel."

"I know. It's fine."

Dad sits on the foot of my bed. "So tell me about him! Is he nice?"

"He's very nice," I say.

"He's responsible?"

"He's, uh…yeah, he's responsible." The doorbell rings. "And he's here."

"All right, get your coat. I'll let him in."

I put my shoes on and take my coat off my desk chair and shove my gloves and a scarf in the pockets, but I didn't put this dress on for Sasha to see me in the same coat he's seen a dozen times. I drape it over my arm and head down the stairs. I can hear them talking in the kitchen. Sasha's answering basic questions about himself and sounds nervous.

"Hi," I say when I'm halfway down the stairs.

He's wearing a suit. I can't believe it. I've never seen him in anything but either five layers of sweaters or a ridiculously oversized T-shirt to try to hide the way his stomach sticks out. But this is a nice suit, tailored, with a jacket lapel that shines in my crappy kitchen lighting. He has a black overcoat on top of it that might be my favorite item of clothing I've ever seen, and he's probably going to lose it to me like he lost his scarf. He's not wearing a tie, and the neck of his shirt is open enough to show a bit of his throat, and he has a white silk scarf draped around his neck. He can keep that one. That little touch is all him.

His cast is sticking out of the left sleeve and his hair is still a goddamn mess. I'm so happy.

"Wow," he breathes.

"Hi," I say again.

I come the rest of the way down the stairs. The kitchen's chillier than my room, and Sasha immediately takes my coat off my arm and helps me into it. His hands brush my bare shoulders.

"I should be home by midnight," I tell my dad.

"All right," he says, though we both know that's like two hours past his bedtime, on the rare occasion he's not working that late. I don't have any sort of defined curfew. I've never done anything worth having one.

Sasha and Dad shake hands and have some sort of male telepathic conversation, then we pull on gloves and get out of there. "I can't believe you have bare legs,"

Sasha says.

"Well what should I have worn, leggings?"

"Yeah."

"You're ridiculous."

"Do you want to take a cab? We should take a cab."

"The train's right there," I say. "I'll be fine."

There's one seat left on the train when we get on. I raise my eyebrows at him, and he shakes his head, so I sit down. He immediately takes his coat off and lays it over my legs. I'm one step closer to making it mine.

"You worry too much," I say, but I pull it over me anyway.

"Yeah, well, you get cold." I can't get over how he looks. Just this study in contrast, all pale and disheveled inside that careful suit. It's perfect. Someone's going to copy this for the Oscars. "Why are you looking at me?" he says with a smile.

I look down quickly. "You're looking at me, too."

"I really like that dress," he says.

I don't know how one sentence can make me feel so awkward and so happy all at the same time. I squirm around a little in my seat, and he chuckles.

The dance is at my school, in our gym. There are a lot of people lurking outside, including at least two girls who are crying to three other girls, and I really want to barge in and ask them what they would do if it was their last night in New York, because I have no shame, but Sasha would probably die of secondhand embarrassment if I did. Mr. Mattrapolis and Ms. Binger, the freshman English teacher, are sitting at a folding table in front of the gym to mark our names off a list and check our coats. Pounding music leaks out of the gym's closed double doors.

"Ready?" Sasha asks me.

"I should be asking you that. My friends are about to swarm us."

He laughs. "I'm ready." We push through the doors.

They swarm us immediately, of course. They must have some sort of tracking device planted in me. Luna, to I assume no one's surprise, has the best dress, this dark-blue sparkly silk thing that looks like she's wearing the whole galaxy. Ashley's stunning in light pink, Maura's wearing red and has a streak in her hair to match because she does not abide by seasonal rules, and Siobhan has a black halter-dress that makes the rest of us look like middle schoolers by comparison.

I twist Maura's face to the side to look at her makeup. "Look at that wing," I say. "You're gonna poke someone's eye out." Ashley and Luna are busy fawning over Sasha in his suit.

"Come dance," Maura says, pulling on my hand.

"Let me put my stuff down," I say.

Ashley points. "We're that table in the corner."

Sasha and I go over, and I put my purse down and consider slipping out of my shoes, but it seems ridiculous, since I didn't wear heels. "It's warm in here," Sasha yells over the music.

"See, that's why I wasn't worried about bare legs. Are you hot? You should take your jacket off."

"No, that's the only thing keeping me from looking like a very tall potbellied pig."

I roll my eyes. "All right, well, drink some water."

"Do we actually have to dance?" he says. "I was

prepared for a night of sitting, and then maybe some gentle swaying at some point."

I look at my girls dancing in a cluster with their arms up in the air. Maura beckons me over. It does look fun. I wish I thought it looked fun.

"I have to do a few with them or they'll never leave me alone," I say.

"Do I come for that, or…"

I try to imagine dancing with Sasha the way the girls who are dancing with boys are dancing—or the way Luna and Siobhan are dancing—and it just feels awkward. It would be the most intimate thing we'd ever done, and it would be in a room full of people who have never seen him before, and we'd be pretending to be open and sexy people instead of neurotic and uncomfortable people and it just… We're already at a dance, wearing fancy clothes. We're already far enough from who we actually are. I don't want this to turn into some night of us being two other people together. It's supposed to be us.

Plus I just try to imagine Sasha dancing, and that's kind of ridiculous all on its own. "Ashley's date isn't with her, either," I say. "The boys usually leave us alone for the fast songs."

He looks relieved. Maybe he was thinking all of that stuff, too. Probably he just doesn't want to dance. "I'll get food," he says.

"Perfect."

I go out with the rest of the girls and screech with them and join our writhing little group. Maura holds my hands and spins me around. I don't remember the last time I danced with all of them like this. I should do it more. So I'm going to feel terrible tomorrow, so what? That's tomorrow-me's problem. It's my body. I get to make it feel terrible for a day, if that's what I want.

The next song is one we all love, and the one after that is one of those bat mitzvah songs with a designated dance, so I end up on the dance floor for a while. I look at Sasha every so often. He's drinking punch with his foot propped up on his knee, watching me like he's amused.

After four songs, my hips are screaming and I'm feeling bad about leaving Sasha for so long. The girls make moaning noises at me as I go, but I extricate myself anyway and limp on over to him.

He pulls out a chair for me. "You good?"

"Yeah," I say. "Are you?"

"I'm fine," he says. "But all they had for food were these dry little cookie things."

"Are these *hamantaschen*?"

"I know. I'm only suffering through that on Purim."

"Wow. That's very culturally broad for this place. Gimme some punch," I say, and he shares his cup. "You didn't get me my own?"

"Of course I did. It's on the table behind you."

"Oh. Sorry."

He laughs. "You're fine."

"That was a terrible idea, by the way," I say.

"Aw, you looked like you were having fun."

"Yeah, but my legs are killing me."

"Put them up on my lap," he says.

"You sure?"

He turns toward me and hauls them up carefully. "There you go."

I fold my arm on the back of my chair and lean my head against it and just… It's blissful, for a minute, just resting. And then a slow song comes on, and we look at each other.

"Next one?" he says.

I sigh with relief, and he laughs. "Next one," I say.

The next one takes a while to come around, which gives him time to duck into the bathroom and deal with a nosebleed and me time to work the room and ask people questions for the column and worry a little about how long he's been in the bathroom with his nosebleed. He comes back eventually, while I'm waiting by the doors of the gym wondering if I should go after him, and he gives me a little squeeze around the waist.

"Do you want to leave?"

"I'm fine," he says. "I promise."

"Drink some punch, though."

"Yes, doctor."

We sit for a little longer to give him time to recover and dissect the cookies to see what's inside them and eventually try eating a few, because if I'm honest, I really thought there was going to be food here, but they're terrible. I spill punch on my dress, and he dabs at it for a while with a napkin, but it's no use.

"It's still a nice dress," he says. "Now it just looks like you murdered someone in it."

They announce the king and queen—it's Ashley, of course, and the senior she got to bring her at the last minute—and they have to dance, which means another slow song. Sasha raises his eyebrows at me, and I nod. He carefully takes my feet off his lap and we go to the dance floor.

He circles his arms around my waist. I reach up and drape mine behind his neck, my wrists crossed. His scarf is cool and smooth under my skin, like water.

Eventually I lean in enough to rest my cheek against his chest.

My legs still hurt, but I don't care. I want to stay here. I want to sleep here, standing up in the middle of a room of people. Me and Sasha.

I'm so scared. I've had crushes before, obviously, but this is something else. I don't know if there's a word for how the world feels survivable when I'm touching him and at no other time.

"You good?" he says in my ear.

"I'm good."

I can hear the smile in his voice. "Not a mistake yet?"

He smells like cinnamon. He always smells like cinnamon. "No. Not a mistake."

I wonder if his lips taste like cinnamon.

And what his hair would feel like through my fingers.

I can't do it. I can't kiss him here, in this room full of people. Pretending like we're the Snow Ball king and queen. That's not me. That's not him.

And anyway, the music stops. Something fast comes on.

We pull away a little and look at each other.

"What do you want to do?" he asks me.

"I'm really hungry," I say.

His eyes widen. "Oh my God, I'm *so* hungry."

"Do you want to get out of here?"

"Yes."

We talk about going to the twenty-four-hour diner in Sunnyside, but honestly, I'm tired, and I can tell he's fading fast, too, so we just stop at McDonald's on the way to the subway. The train's pretty empty, so we spread the food out on our laps and get grease spots on our clothes and share fries.

"Can I ask you a question?" he says. "This has been bothering me all night, but I haven't known how to ask it."

"Of course."

"What's the bra situation with that dress? Is this creepy? I'm sorry. I can't figure it out, and it's driving me crazy."

"Oh, it's a stick-on!" I hold my arms up.

"A stick-on bra?"

"Yeah, it, like… It's two cups, and you stick them on, and then you hook it together in the front."

"Does it hurt?"

"No, no."

"Amazing."

I laugh and lean back against my seat. He bites into a fry.

"Did you have a good time?" he asks me on the walk back to my house.

"Yeah, did you?"

"I did," he says. He pauses. "You're not acting like you had a good time."

"I don't know," I say. "Do you think this is the best time I'm capable of having? Because…I mean, that would be okay. My friends are still there cheering like, I mean, they're at like a level-ten happy right now."

"What are you?"

"I don't know, maybe a seven? And that's good! You can't complain about a seven."

"A seven's pretty good," he says.

"What are you?" I ask.

"Maybe an eight."

I say, "I think I was expecting, I don't know, we'd put on nice clothes and all of a sudden morph into these romance people. But that's not... I mean, I don't even want that. That's how we turn into Frida and Diego, and that's no good."

"So the choice is no romance or Frida and Diego?" He doesn't sound disappointed. Just thoughtful.

And I realize what I've been saying here. I'm telling him that I'm simultaneously glad that nothing happened between us and I'm disappointed that I didn't have a better time with him.

Wow, I am just the world's worst date.

I'm cold, all of a sudden. I haven't been cold all night.

"Maybe," I say. I don't know what else to say. I've ruined everything.

We're at my house now. The lights are off inside. I stand on my bottom step. We're almost the same height like this.

"Thank you," he says. "For inviting me."

I nod. We hug.

I feel my heart pounding against him.

I'm sorry.

I'm sorry I'm not a romance person.

I'm sorry I think too much.

I'm sorry I ruined everything.

Don't let go.

"I'll call you tomorrow?" he says.

"Yes."

He lets go. He's looking down at the ground. He starts to walk away, and I take a shaky breath and go up my front steps.

I've just put my key in the lock when he says, "Ibby?"

I turn around. "Yeah?"

"For what it's worth," he says. "I'm in love with you."

He's a few feet back from my house, standing on the sidewalk. His scarf shines in the streetlights.

His hands are in his pockets. He's not looking down anymore.

I catch my breath. "What?"

"I'm in love with you," he says with this small smile. "I...I love your voice when you call me even though you're falling asleep. I love that you're not afraid of people. I love how much you care about everything you do. I love how you can't eat anything without getting it all over yourself, and how you are with my siblings, and...I like that you're Jewish, I like that, and that you're sick, and that you...you have never been afraid of me. I love that you ask questions, so many goddamn questions, and you..." He shrugs. "I love that you exist in this world. I mean, I love the world even more because people like you exist in it. And I don't even know how people live as long as they do without having someone like you in their life, or how I've done it for this long. I love your dad and your crappy mom because they made you. I want to go hug everyone at your school who made you happen. I love your friends. I...I am all in, here, that's what I'm saying. There's not a caveat. There's not an exception.

There's…I love everything about you."

"Sasha," I whisper.

There are drunk people roaring on the next block. There's a car horn blaring on Queens Boulevard.

There's nothing else but him.

He says, "And I'm not saying this because I want to date you—which I do, just to be clear—or because you look incredible in that dress—which, you know, again, you do, you look like Cinderella—I'm just… I don't think you know that you're destined for a life full of love that is…that is big, and that is sweeping, and that is without penalties or expectations, it's just *there*, and…and I think you should know that you are, and I know that because it's already started. You are going to be loved purely and happily your entire life by people who are just fucking delighted to do it. And if you don't think you're the kind of person that happens for, then you're my best friend and I need you to know this about yourself, because this is a lot bigger than you and me, because you are bigger than you and me, and you are loved, Isabel. You will always be loved. And it will be so good." He nods. "It's good. It's really good to love you."

Every feeling I've ever had in my entire life is right here, right on the surface. And that boy is just standing on my sidewalk, grinning casually up at me like there's nothing I could do that would possibly be wrong.

How is he breathing right now? I can't breathe.

I say, "Y-you can't just say these things and then expect me to know what to—"

"I don't," he says.

He's too far away. "Come here?" I say. "Please come

here right now."

He comes to the bottom of the stairs.

"I need a hand, I can't—"

"Yeah, of course," he says, and he takes my hand and helps me down the stairs.

And goddamn it all, I feel like Cinderella.

And I am going to die if I go one more second without kissing him.

I don't even know which of us moves toward the other one first. It's one of those moments that seems predetermined, like that clock that's been inside me and maybe inside both of us since Thanksgiving at the very latest, tick-tick-ticking away, is finally sounding the alarm. It has to happen. It *has* to happen, and right now.

I stop on the last step, where we're eye to eye, and he holds me by the waist with one hand and cups the back of my head with the other, and my arms are around his neck and scrambling in his hair, trying to pull him closer, closer, and I didn't know kissing could feel like breathing.

Yes—his lips taste like cinnamon.

I wake up the next morning still wearing a dress that looks bloodstained, feeling frozen and sore, like I was caught in an avalanche.

My phone is ringing.

"Are you so sore you feel like you're going to die?" Sasha says. "Because I'm so sore I feel like I'm going to die."

"Yes," I say. I've never been this happy.

WHAT WAS THE BEST THING THAT HAPPENED THIS YEAR?

I don't know. It was kind of a downer year, but I got to watch my best friend be super, super happy, so that's pretty great...*and* we still have Luna's party to come. So the year is not over yet!

> —*Maura Cho, 16, optimist*

The world didn't end, which, considering the current state of, you know, everything, is enough for me to call it a win. Also I got into NYU, and my mom and my sister didn't kill each other, so I'll take it.

> —*Siobhan O'Brian, 17, mediator*

The hospital's doing better than it was this time last year, my baby girl is doing well, and...well, that's enough, I think. I'm not sure I can think of any one best thing, but I think just getting through this year is going to be enough. Oh, a few weeks ago you got those great test results! Maybe that was the best thing.

> —*John Garfinkel, 49, Physician in Chief at Linefield and West Memorial Hospital*

Hmmm, I don't knoooooooow...

> —*Claire Lennon, 16, dead*

So Georgia—the country, not the state—has been participating in the Olympics since 1994. They've won a fair number of medals in the Summer Olympics, but nothing ever in the winter. It's not really a Winter Olympics kind of country. So when Rusudani Mudziri was born in 1990 in Georgia, and she wanted to be an Olympic figure skater from just about the moment she could walk… I mean, first of all, they weren't even an independent country then, let alone one in the Olympics. And on top of that, Rusudani has kind of the classic tragic backstory—raised in poverty, born to a teen mom, war-torn country. But she works her whole life, practicing constantly, training, all sorts of skating things I don't know the ins and outs of. But tons of work. Her mom makes all her outfits because they don't have the money to buy them; her whole family throws every kind of support behind her they can. And, all right, it's Olympic qualifiers, and she wouldn't be the first skater from Georgia to go to the Olympics, but she'd be, I believe, the seventh, so it's a small number. And she gets hurt. Messes up her knee, and she thinks, you know, that's it. All of this training, all of these people rooting for me, nothing. And on top of all that, she gets pregnant. So now she's messed up her knee, she has a little baby, she's getting old—in Olympic terms—everyone has counted her out. But she shows up, and she gets in. And this year, Rusudani Mudziri won the gold medal in figure skating at the Winter Olympics, and I feel like just in terms of…of small, sweet, lovely things, that might be the best thing that happened this year. Also I got a girlfriend.

—*Sasha Sverdlov-Deckler, 16, boyfriend*

CHAPTER FOURTEEN

Sasha and I spend just about all of winter break together.

He takes me to the castle in Central Park. We bring his brothers to Cedar Hill for sledding. We watch horror movies on his couch with Nutella hot chocolate spiked with cayenne pepper when his dad's there, and RumChata when he's not. We take naps every single day. He even comes to the hospital with me for dinner with my dad once or twice. But mostly it's his family, and they fold me in easily and gently, like his dad folds blueberries into muffin batter on Sunday mornings.

What's amazing is how much *hasn't* changed. We haven't turned into romance people. We have the same conversations we've always had. We can be in the same room together and act like friends. And most of the time we do. But when we don't…oh God.

We're both new to relationships, so we're taking it slow, but sometimes when he kisses me goodnight he runs his fingers lightly up my sides and I want to melt into a puddle on my snowy front steps.

He still makes me laugh.

While we're in the throes of domestic bliss or whatever, there's an issue on the other side of my life. Luna's parents have shut down the New Year's Eve party. I can't really blame them. We *really* fucked up that apartment last year. But she's the only one of us with parents who go out on New Year's, so we don't really have another option.

Even I love Luna's New Year's Eve parties. She's been throwing them every year since she moved here. Luna has her hands in a lot of different crowds, so a huge number of people always show up, though it's mostly the drama kids and they know how to have a good time. I don't know why movies about teenagers are always on about the parties the jocks throw. Drama kids are *trouble*.

We have lunch, the five of us plus Sasha plus Tyson, the new guy Ashley's seeing, at the diner in Sunnyside before New Year's. Luna just got home from seeing her family in Jamaica for Christmas, and she still has sunglasses on her head, like she can't quite accept being back in New York.

"We could try doing it at my place," Ashley says. "My parents would probably leave us alone if we asked them really nicely and I promised I'd clean everything up."

"So would my dad," I say, though I can't imagine all those people in our tiny, pristine little house.

Sasha wipes his mouth with a napkin. "We could do it at my place. My dad's going to a party with his new girlfriend."

"What about your siblings?" I ask.

"My brothers are going to be with their mom, and my sister will probably just stay in her room, but she's in high school, she'll fit in if she wants to."

Luna says, "Sasha, seriously? You're my hero."

He looks down at his waffle and does this sheepish

grin that makes me want to die right on the checkered floor. "It's no problem," he says. "My dad will probably be happy I'm doing things like a normal teenager."

"And you can invite all your friends, too," Luna says. "Totally, it can be like an…interschool mixer. We can marry people off."

"Cool," Sasha says.

I say, "You don't have a fake ID, do you?"

"No…"

I give him a look that's like *see, you're welcome* and say to the girls, "So someone else needs to get stuff."

"I can do it," Luna says. "I'm not going to foist the whole party off on you just because it's your house. Oh, see if you can get decorations, though? Something, like… twinkly."

"Do you need an ID for those?" Sasha says, and I kick his leg—carefully, since he's got those bird bones—under the table. He looks up at me, grins, and stuffs way too much waffle into his mouth.

"I'm not sure you know what you've signed on for, here," I tell him later, when we're riding the subway back to Manhattan. The train's pretty empty right now, but once we get to the Times Square station it'll be packed full of tourists and shopping bags. People who come between Christmas and New Year's always think they're going to be the only people who thought of coming then.

"I'm a hundred percent sure that I definitely have no idea what I've signed on for," Sasha says. "Do I look like I throw a lot of parties?"

"Host," I say. "You host, Luna throws."

"See, I don't even know the lingo."

"I'll help you," I say. "It was really sweet of you to step in like that."

He shrugs. "I like your friends. I want them to like me." He blows on his hands. "Can you help me find something twinkly?"

"Yes."

He kisses me.

"I don't know about this," my dad says. It's New Year's Eve morning and I'm about to head over to Sasha's to help him set up. It's also the first I'm telling my dad about the party.

"Dad," I say.

"I don't think I'm supposed to just let you sleep over at a boy's house."

"It's not like an intimate sleepover. Fifty people are going to be there. And it's a lot safer than me coming home at one a.m. on the subway with a host of drunk tourists." I pull on my boots and put my Snow Ball flats in a tote bag, along with my meds and a skirt to change into.

"Yes, I'm not suggesting you go and come back at one a.m."

I straighten out, holding on to the edge of my bed for balance. "You let me go every other year when it's at Luna's house," I say. "You know there were boys there, too, right?"

"And none of them were your boyfriend."

"I thought you liked Sasha." I know I'm being manipulative. But I can't miss this party.

"I do!"

"And don't you trust me?" I'm awful. I'm the worst.

He tilts his head to the side. "You know I do."

"It's a big crowded party," I say. "We're gonna sleep on the floor like kids. I'm going to have two drinks and that's it, and I'll text you before I go to bed."

He sighs. "It's times like this I wish your mother was here."

I don't know what to say to that, so I say nothing and shift from foot to foot and wish he would just make the call so I could get as far away from this conversation as possible.

"All right," he says. "Go. Don't make me regret it."

"Where are you setting up food?" Nadia asks.

Sasha and I are on opposite sides of his living room, putting up a snowflake garland. "Uh, I don't know," he says. "What's wrong with just having it in the kitchen?"

"Well, the drinks are gonna be in the kitchen," Nadia says. "So it's going to be pretty crowded."

I say, "Plus you don't want it to be one of those parties where everyone hangs out in the kitchen because that's where everything is and no one even comes out and sees our awesome snowflake garland."

Nadia hands me some tape. "Exactly."

"Um…" Sasha looks around. He has a piece of tape hanging off his lip. "In here, I guess, then? We could put up like…one of those folding tables."

"That works," I say.

Nadia says, "Not unless someone is bringing a folding table with them."

"We don't have a folding table?" Sasha says.

"Why would we just *have* a folding table?"

"They're very convenient!" Sasha says. "Folding tables are a vital piece of household equipment!"

"You guys have got to stop saying 'folding table,'" I say. "My side's done."

"Yeah, mine too," Sasha says.

"It looks good," Nadia says. "Very festive."

The buzzer goes off, and Sasha's face loses any color it had in the first place. "Why is someone here? They're not supposed to be here for an hour."

"It's just Luna," I say. "She brought cupcakes."

"Oh, okay."

Nadia buzzes Luna in, and she comes up the stairs instead of using the elevator. We can hear her heels clicking from a floor away. She comes in with her hair piled on top of her head and sparkles on her cheeks. "Hiiii!" she says. She hands me the cupcakes and puts her coat in the closet. She's wearing this yellow dress that makes her skin glow.

"Hi, Luna," Sasha says. "You look beautiful. Quick question: is everyone gonna be looking that beautiful?"

Luna looks at me.

"The girls usually dress up," I tell him. "The guys, they wear whatever. They're animals."

He says, "Yeah, but I still want to blend in with the humans."

"I was gonna tell you to change."

He groans and heads to his room. I laugh a little.

"What are you wearing?" Luna says.

"Uh, this top. I brought a skirt."

"A *skirt*? Isabel." She looks around. "It's not exactly sparkly in here. We'll have to dim the lights."

"It's the best we could find. And I wore the only nice dress I have to the Snow Ball. I didn't have tits last time I went shopping."

"You can borrow something of mine," Nadia says. "I have tits."

I hold up my finger. "I didn't say that word in front of you."

"I'm fourteen, not seven."

"I like her," Luna says, and Nadia blushes.

"Come on," she says. "I had to go to, like, twenty-five bat mitzvahs last year. I have plenty of dresses."

"Where are we putting the food?" Luna calls as we go to Nadia's room.

"Did you bring a folding table?" Nadia yells back, and I smack her shoulder and say, "Just put it on the coffee table."

Nadia flops on her bed while I go through her closet. "Did you throw parties when you were my age?" she asks me.

"I don't even throw parties now," I say. "This is all Luna. And Sasha, I guess."

"He's really nervous," she says.

"I know. It's funny. I've never seen him like this before. It's just some dumb party. As long as there's alcohol, people are gonna be happy. And there's plenty of alcohol." Luna dropped it all off yesterday.

"He doesn't want to let you down," Nadia says.

I say, "Hey, do you know if any of his friends are coming tonight?"

"Uh, no, I don't think so."

"Hmm." I pull out a dress. "What about this one?" It's black and made of some kind of stiff fabric.

"Yeah, that's a good one."

I step out of my joggers and pull my shirt off. "Did you invite any of yours? Sasha was supposed to tell you that you could."

"Yeah, he did." She shrugs.

"Well," I say. "It was kind of last minute. They probably had plans already."

She looks grateful. "Yeah. Do you want help with the zipper?"

"Yeah, thanks." I pull my hair to the side while she zips me up. "Y'know…" I say slowly. "Sasha's my first boyfriend."

She pauses on the zipper. "He is?"

"Yep. I didn't want to rush anything. Dating made me uncomfortable, and I didn't… I realized I didn't have to do things that made me uncomfortable just because other people were telling me that being uncomfortable was normal." I don't know if I've actually learned this, but it still sounds like something I wish someone had told me when I was fourteen.

She finishes the zipper and looks over my shoulder at my reflection. "That looks really good on you."

"I bet it looks good on you, too." I step back into my shoes. "Are you gonna hang out in here?" I ask her.

"Yeah, I think so."

"Cool," I say. "I'll bring you a cupcake."

She smiles.

I really don't know why we bother dressing up. It's still an hour until midnight and we already have our shoes off, and our hair is a mess, and four of us are half naked on the couch. Plus there's just something so useless about putting on a strapless bra to drink cheap vodka out of red cups.

I'm two drinks in, in that perfect spot where I'm too drunk to be aware of my joints but not so drunk that I'm doing stupid shit that's going to make me wake up tomorrow and really, really wish I had been feeling my joints. Luna is trashed, which always makes her accent come out, so everyone's having her say weird shit and then squealing at how cute she sounds, and she's living off the applause like Tinker Bell. Siobhan's next to her, drinking and blushing, and Maura and Ashley are dancing on the coffee table next to the suitcase. Ashley still has her heels on.

Sasha rushes by me with two empty bowls and hands me one of them. "Can you help me with this?"

"Yep." I follow him to the kitchen and find the bag of cheese curls. "Have these people not eaten this whole break?"

"Maybe I should order pizza," he says.

"At eleven on New Year's Eve?"

"Oh yeah." He pushes his hair back.

"You gotta relax," I say. "It's a party! It's supposed to be fun."

"What happened to us being boring people who don't do anything?" he says. "That was fun."

"We're on vacation for the night," I say. "We're party humans tonight."

"Party humans must drink more caffeine than I do,"

he says.

I look into the living room. "Yeah, it's not caffeine."

He chuckles. "I'm getting another drink."

"Good call."

"You want anything?"

"I'm fine," I say. He trails his fingers across my back on his way to the drink table. I shiver a little and say, "Hang on."

He stops. "Yeah?"

I wrap my arms around his neck and kiss him, slow and deep.

He laughs a little with his forehead against mine. "You're drunk."

"No I'm not." I pull on his sweater. "Let's go sit down. You've been running around all night."

"I have to make sure no one pukes in my brothers' room or pees on the credenza," he says.

"These people don't even know what a credenza is. Neither do I."

"You can pee on something without knowing what it is," he says.

"Hmm."

He kisses my nose and heads back to the living room.

Ashley's still on the coffee table when I go back in, but she's replaced Maura with Tyson, and they're doing some sort of dancing-making-out hybrid that I would really like to try, but my boyfriend's too busy getting people drink refills.

Maura grabs my arm. "I need to talk to you."

"Yeah, hey, what's wrong?"

"Not here."

"Okay, let's go out to the hallway?"

She nods and follows me out, stumbling a little. She's definitely had more than two drinks.

I don't even have the apartment door closed before she says, "Am I going to be alone forever?"

"What?"

"Ashley has a boyfriend, you have a boyfriend, Luna and Siobhan have Luna and Siobhan, and I'm alone. I'm always alone."

I'm an insensitive jerk, I know, but she does this every single time she drinks, and I really didn't want to deal with this tonight. I take a deep breath. "Hey." I hold her by the shoulders. "You are not alone. You have me."

"Is there something wrong with me?"

"Besides being really drunk?"

"Your boyfriend is so *nice*," she says. "Why are all the boys I meet *horrible*?"

"Because most of them are horrible," I say. "Come on, let's go back inside and get you some water."

"Maybe I should become a *lesbian*," Maura says.

"Good idea," I say, because there's no point arguing with her when she's like this. She's not gonna remember it tomorrow anyway.

"I'll ask Luna how," she says. "Or Siobhan. Siobhan gives better advice."

I drag her inside and back to the kitchen and fill a cup with water.

"Who's gonna kiss me at midnight?" she says.

"Literally anyone here will," I say.

"Will you ask them for me?" She giggles. She's still crying a little. "It can be a question for your column."

Some guy jostles past me on the way to get his drink. I stumble and Maura catches me. "Oh, are you okay?" she says.

"I'm fine."

She looks at my legs. "Poor knee."

"It's fine. Drink your water."

"Okay."

Sasha comes in and leans against the doorway to the kitchen. "Hey, Maura," he says. "Isabel, can I talk to you?"

"Yeah." I squeeze Maura's arm and follow Sasha down the hall. We stop halfway between the living room and his bedroom, a couple feet from some couple I don't know *really* going at it.

"Is Maura okay?" he asks.

"Yeah, she's…drunk and single. She'll be fine. What's up?"

He leans his head against the wall. "I think I need to go lie down for a while."

"I told you to sit down!"

"I know."

I squeeze his hand. "Need me to come with?"

"No, no, I'm fine. Can you just…" He gestures to the living room.

"Of course."

"Don't let me sleep through midnight, okay?"

"You got it."

He hugs me, both arms around my head. "You're amazing."

"Yeah, yeah."

He shuts himself in his room and I go check on Maura in the kitchen. "Where's *Sasha*?" she says. "He was gonna help me be a lesbian."

I'm not even going to touch that one. "Have you been drinking your water?"

She shows me the empty cup.

"Good. Sasha went to rest for a little while."

"Is he okay?"

"He's fine, he's just tired."

She frowns. "That's so *sad*. It's his party and he has to go lie down."

"It's not sad. More people should go lie down in the middle of parties. Come on, let's get you some more water and then back to civilization." I have a whole party to look after now. I can't be stuck in the kitchen with Maura.

"You know," she says while I refill her cup. "You are such a good person."

"Thanks, Maura."

"I don't think I could do it," she says. "He's so lucky to have you."

The cup is full. I turn the water off and just stand at the sink for a minute, because seriously, what the hell? Literally five minutes ago she was crying about how she was jealous of me for having a boyfriend, and now because he's horizontal for a minute, all of a sudden I'm, what, a noble hospice worker? No, thank you, you should still be very jealous of me. Maura wants to know why she's not in a relationship? This is why. Sasha and I have only been together for two weeks, and I'm still pretty sure that part of being in a relationship is putting up with bigger obstacles than whatever annoyances our chronic illnesses decide to throw at us. And this is *nothing*; even if you narrow it down to the category of chronic illness problems, this is barely a complication, and Maura's still making it out to be some great sadness because she has no frame of reference for sick shit, and also because… she's drunk, and there's really no point in me getting pissed at her.

It's that she thinks she's saying something nice. That's what really bothers me. How much shit have I put up with from my friends in the past few years because I know they think they're being nice when they're really being offensive and shitty and boring?

It just took me a really long time to recognize that. I hadn't met an alternative.

I hand her the cup and pat her on the shoulder. "Come on. Let's go sit with Siobhan."

"Oh, I *love* Siobhan."

"See, there you go."

I drop her off on the couch with Siobhan, who's half asleep herself, like she always gets when she drinks, and then I refill the chip bowls—again, these people need to check their blood pressure—and direct some stumbling girl to the bathroom. I wipe up scattered crumbs and spilled drinks in the kitchen and feel strangely triumphant when a girl asks me the address of the building and I know the answer.

I've never really liked hosting duties before, but I like that Sasha trusted me. He's lying down, and I'm taking over. I feel like I'm part of a team.

A power couple. I smile to myself as I wipe down the sink.

We're closing in on midnight now. The TV's on, and people are copying the moves of whatever singer is performing in Times Square, just a handful of blocks from here. There's a countdown clock on the bottom of the screen. Four minutes to midnight. I make sure everyone's settled with drinks and no one's peeing on any furniture, credenza or otherwise, and then slip into Sasha's room.

He stirs and smiles at me when I lie down next to him on the bed. "Hi," he says.

"Hi." I rest my head on his pillow.

"Is it midnight?" he says.

"Almost."

"Is everything okay?"

I push his hair back. "Everything's great."

He rolls over enough to settle his head in the space between my neck and my shoulder. He's sleep-warm and a little sweaty, and I can't even imagine getting up.

"Do you want to go back out there?" he says. "I can get up."

"I'm fine right here," I say.

They start the countdown in the living room. Sasha and I shift around until we're lying there facing each other.

"Three! Two! One!" they chant. Sasha mouths it along with them.

They cheer in the next room, and Sasha and I kiss, very softly.

"Happy New Year," he whispers.

"Happy New Year."

We're up early in the morning to clean the place up before his dad gets home. I'm out of Nadia's dress and in sweatpants and a T-shirt Sasha lent me to sleep in.

A lot of people have left, but a lot more are passed out in various spots—on the couch, on the living room floor, in the hallway, in that claw-foot bathtub.

Sasha and I tiptoe around everyone, picking up all the empty cups. I drag a trash bag behind me like a train.

It's gonna be a good year.

WHAT'S THE BEST THING ANYONE'S EVER GIVEN YOU?

This probably sounds dumb, but when I was seven my dad gave me one dollar and took me to the library on Greenpoint to get a library card. And it turns out library cards are free—there's a one-dollar replacement fee if you lose it, so he got confused—so I had to give the dollar back to him. But I didn't care, because I had a library card, and that was… I mean, that was the beginning of everything for me. I couldn't believe that I could just pick out any of those books that I wanted. I loved the plastic around them. I loved the sound of the scanner the librarians used. Everything. It was life changing.

—Siobhan O'Brian, 17, future NYU student

You asked Siobhan? Ugh, I bet hers was really deep. Mine's gonna sound stupid. But it was my aunt's hand-me-down makeup, about a year after we moved here. I never wore makeup in Jamaica, but after I got here all my friends were wearing it, so I started messing around with it. And my aunt, she came to visit one time, and I had done my face up all nice, y'know. And then the next time she saw me, she came with this whole load of makeup. And it wasn't the same stuff my friends had. Because my friends were white girls. And here comes my aunt, showing me stuff that's actually made for me, and I put it on, and all of a sudden…I don't look like I'm trying to be something else. My eyes are shining, my lips are deep, I don't look like a white little princess. I'm a queen. I know it's just makeup, but it also wasn't, y'know?

—Luna Williams, 16, dancer

The best thing anyone ever gave me was a piece of advice from my mother. I was fifteen, and we were trying to get into a restaurant in Manhattan on a busy night of the year. This other woman—not someone who worked there, just another woman who wanted our table—was trying to argue with us that we didn't have the reservation that we knew we had. She wouldn't stop yelling at us about it and yelling at the hostess about it, and finally my mom told her to cut it out, right before the hostess found our reservation and took us away to our table. As we were walking away, the woman whispered "Bitch" at my mom. I told my mom, "Mom, that woman just called you a bitch." And she looked at me and she said, "You know what happens when a bitch calls you a bitch?" She licked her finger and swiped it in the air like she was making a tally mark. "You get a point."

—Claire Lennon, 16, dead and usually not the type to go to fancy restaurants but needed to hold a memory for someone

Can I say enzyme replacement therapy? It's not a funny answer, I know. But...okay, so the way my disease works is basically, my body doesn't make this specific enzyme called glucocerebrosidase—which you do learn how to pronounce eventually—which really has one function, helping the cells of your body break down cells that are past their prime. So in most people, your cells gobble up the old cells and everything keeps trucking on. But since I don't make the enzyme, my old cells just stick around, clogging everything up, taking up space, rattling around in my lungs or making my spleen the size of nine spleens or sitting around my bone marrow, keeping me from making red blood cells. There's no cure, but I can get infusions of the enzyme that I'm missing, and that helps things stay at a certain balance. It's still worse some times than others—right now, my spleen is just hanging out all enormous like it *wants* to get ruptured—and certain things still get to me. If I get sick or hurt, it's like everything just gives up, but the ERT still keeps it more in check than I'd have any hope of it being otherwise. And I still remember the first time I got it when I was four, and I was *so* sick and had been so sick for my whole life, and that was just…even though I was crying at doctors all the time, I still kind of figured that was just what my life was going to feel like. And I remember them hooking up that IV and watching the liquid drip into me that everyone said was going to make me feel so much better. And it's not as if it happened instantaneously. But I kept going, and I kept getting it, and eventually…yeah. I still remember the first morning I woke up and felt like I wasn't drowning. You don't forget that. And that's the best thing anyone could ever give me.

—*Sasha Sverdlov-Deckler, 16, Sick Boy*

Six hundred dollars.

—*Gwen Partridge, 91, lifelong Queens resident*

CHAPTER FIFTEEN

Sasha gives me a very small ceramic cat the week after New Year's. He comes to meet me after school and drops it into my gloved hand as we're walking to the subway. It's white with bright blue eyes.

"That means it's deaf, probably," Sasha says. "According to Nadia."

It's stretched out with its tail all the way up in the air. It looks happy.

"Nick found it in the snow," he says. "Made me think of you."

I'm not really sure why it made him think of me, since I don't own a lot of things I can't use—or a cat—but it's cute, and he thought of me. And it's not like it will take up a lot of space. I kiss him on the cheek and slip it into my pocket.

I give him all the green Skittles every time I buy a pack. I get them a lot at the bodega on my block, and we'll eat them on the subway or while we're waiting in line at the movie theater or while we're walking. Once I get to the end of the pack, I'll hold out my hand, he holds out his, and I drop all the green Skittles into it, and he eats them one by one.

He gives me a hat halfway through January. It's pink and blue and a little misshapen, like lumpy cotton candy. It's incredibly soft.

"Did you make this?" I say.

He ducks his head. "Is it that obvious?"

I bat it lightly from hand to hand. "I didn't know you knit."

"Yeah, I've been doing it forever, but I kind of go in phases. I won't touch it for a year, then all I want to do is knit for two weeks… The cycle continues. I made this one at school between classes so you wouldn't see. Try it on?"

I pull it over my head and go to his mirror to look. It's baggy and warm and so adorable.

"Do you like it?" he asks.

"I love it." I wear it every day for the rest of winter.

I get him gelato the last week of January when he's had a rough week at school. He doesn't want to talk about it, but he's been calling me every day after school to hang out and then he's just sad and clingy once I get there. I drag him out of his apartment and a few blocks over to the Gelateria on 9th.

"It's January," he says.

"So? British people drink tea when it's hot. We can't eat ice cream when it's cold?"

"Technically this is gelato," he says.

"We're Americans! We call it what we want and we eat

it when we want!" I stick my arm up in the air.

"You tell 'em," he says to me.

I hug him around the waist. "So do you."

He gives me a smallish but very heavy present for my birthday. We're at this hole-in-the-wall pasta restaurant on 7th Avenue in Manhattan that's the only place I'll willingly climb stairs for. It's me, Sasha, the girls, and my dad, who actually got the night off. Dad gives me sterling-silver earrings that glitter in the restaurant's overbright lighting. The girls and I always exchange lots of little things, so I get nail polish and lip gloss, which I'll get a ton of use out of, and cookie cutters and stickers, which I won't, but I give them the same stuff on their birthdays, so I can't exactly complain. Plus, as I learned from Sasha and the ceramic cat, it's the thought that counts, and I'm ready to appreciate whatever little thing Sasha gets me, too, and I'm secretly hoping it's a scarf to go with my hat.

But then he hands me this, and I unwrap a medical textbook from 1923. With illustrations.

"What is it?" Maura asks.

"It's a creepy old book," Sasha says.

Ashley looks over my shoulder at the illustrations. "Oh, gross."

"I'll take it if you don't want it," my dad says.

I close it long enough to hug it to my chest. "No way." I trap Sasha's foot under the table, and he gives me the biggest smile.

I read half of it that same night.

"How did you know?" I ask him on the phone.

"You have a dead-girl imaginary friend," he says.

"That's a good point."

"You're just as much of a freak as I am," he says. "You just hide it better."

I stop reading and close my eyes and just listen to him. "Yeah."

"What does she think of it?" he says.

"Claire?"

"Uh-huh."

"She loves it," I say.

"Does she want a lecture about 1920s medicine as a bedtime story?" he says.

"Yes," I say, and I put my phone on speaker and listen to the quiet rasp of his voice as I fall asleep.

I give Nadia more books after she finishes all the ones I gave her. She and Sasha come over, and I have her go through my shelf and pick out what looks good.

"I recommend the 1920s medical textbook," Sasha says. He's lying on my bed, flipping through my old yearbooks. He just got his cast off, and it's still kind of jarring. I got so used to it.

I point at him. "Shut your mouth."

"Ashley really shouldn't have gotten bangs," he says, squinting at an old picture.

"I know. We told her."

"What about this one?" Nadia says.

"That one's really good and you have to read it because none of my friends will read it and I need to talk about it with someone."

"Why haven't you made me read it?" Sasha says.

I look at the book, then him, and tilt my head. "I don't know. I didn't think you'd like it."

"Why wouldn't I like something you like?" he says nonchalantly, turning a page in the yearbook. "We like all the same things."

I like that he thinks that, even though I'm not sure why he does. "Okay," I say. "You read it, too."

Honestly, I don't expect to hear about it from him again, but three nights later I open my email and there's a whole book report written up. I curl up with a mug of hot chocolate and read what he thought of my favorite book.

He loved it, but he hated all the characters I love and loved all the ones I hate. His favorite parts are the parts I thought were boring, and my favorite parts are the ones he thought were forced.

I reply back, refuting every single one of his points, and he responds almost instantly, defending his just as hard. We stay up until four a.m. arguing about it, and I never stop smiling. Even when I'm typing furiously and whispering, "Fuck you, Sasha Sverdlov-Deckler." Smiling.

He gives the nurses shit when he comes to pick me up after my February infusion and it turns out I haven't even started it yet, and I'm sitting in one of the chairs in the drip room, holding an ice pack to the inside of my elbow.

He zeroes in on it immediately. "What happened?"

"I'm fine," I say.

"You don't look fine."

"They blew the vein," I say. "It's no big deal. They're gonna try the other arm, they're just getting a new tray."

"Why did they blow the vein?"

"I don't know. It just happens sometimes, right?"

"It doesn't just happen," he says. "It never needs to happen. It's always because they did something wrong. Who did it?"

"They're busy. They do a million of these a day, it's going to happen."

"Who did it?" he says. I've never seen him this serious.

"Sasha…"

"Tell me? Please?"

"Lindsey," I say.

He shakes his head. "She isn't careful. I've *always* thought she isn't careful. I'll be right back."

"Please don't be mean."

"I'm not going to be mean."

Lindsey comes in with a new tray before he has a chance to leave. "Hi there, Sasha," she says. "All right, Isabel, let's try this again."

Sasha says, "Is there another nurse on duty who can do this?"

"It's fine," I say to Lindsey.

Sasha says, "You know she's the chief physician's daughter, right?"

"Sasha," I say.

He scrubs his mouth with the palm of his hand while he watches her put the IV in. Once she's gone, he crouches down in front of me and holds the ice pack on my other arm.

"I'm okay," I say.

"These can actually be really serious." He isn't looking at me.

I never get mad, he told me. And it's true that he doesn't wear it like someone who's used to it.

I lay my hand on top of his on the ice pack, and he breathes out slowly through his mouth and bounces a little on his heels. He shakes himself like he's trying to get the feelings off of him. "Shouldn't have happened," he mumbles.

I give him a cold three days after that. We both have terrible immune systems, him from his anemia and me from the drugs I take to keep my arthritis in control. I call him with a croaky voice when he's still feeling fine and tell him he's probably screwed.

"Are you okay?" he asks. "Do you want me to come over?"

"No, if there's any chance you won't get this, we should keep the hope alive."

There's no chance, and the hope is good and dead. I end up with the same sinus and ear infection I get every time I get a cold, and I take a day off from school before I stumble back and fake my way through the day, like I usually do. Sasha, on the other hand, gets a fever of a hundred and three and lungs so congested they almost stop working. Which, I learn, is what happens every time *he* gets a cold.

I try to visit him, but he says he doesn't feel up to company, which is a pretty irritating thing to say, because it sounds like he thinks I expect him to entertain me or something. I think he just doesn't want me to see him like this, and that's frustrating because I didn't think we were like that. If I were in his shoes, I would want him there.

He calls me every night, anyway, when the fever gets high. He wheezes his way through conversations that weave and tangle, and I sit in bed and twist my quilt in my hands. "He's bad at fevers," Nadia says on the phone to me one night. "He always has been." She sounds tired and a little sad but not scared.

The night the fever breaks, he just cries and sounds like he's choking, but I can hear his dad in the background.

"Everything's okay," I tell him, trying to keep my voice as normal as possible, trying to be calm for him. "Everything's okay, you're doing great."

He gives me a plastic shopping bag the week after. He knocks on my front door and I think my dad's home early and forgot his key, but it's Sasha, with a bag and a big smile.

"Hey," I say. "I told you I have to study tonight, right?"

He kisses me. "I know, but I was at the game store and this was on sale. Look look look."

I open the bag. It's a copy of a game called *Situation: Revenant* that I've definitely seen on his desk, and, judging from the art on the back, seen him playing when I wake up from napping at his place. "Don't you have this already?" I say.

"Yeah, it's for you!"

I raise an eyebrow.

"I know," he says. "You don't love video games, but

this is my favorite one, and I thought we could play it together and it would be really fun. And it was on sale, so if you don't like it, no big deal."

"I don't have, like, a thing to play it on. A video game thing."

"No, it's just on your computer," he says.

"I'm using my computer to study."

"Well, you take breaks, right?" He bounces a little. God, he's cute. "I can wait till you're taking a break and we can play a little. I won't rush you or anything."

I say "Okay," because what else can I say? He's so excited. We go up to my room, and he lies on my bed and plays on his phone while I work at my desk. He's true to his word and doesn't say anything to rush me, but I'm still so aware that he's behind me, that he's wondering how much longer it's going to be, that he's wondering if I really need to study this much, because *he* doesn't study and *he* does just fine, and why do I need to take everything so *seriously*? Plus, he's still coughing more than usual, which isn't his fault, but it does mean that even though he's behind me I can't forget he's there for a second.

After half an hour and two-thirds of one of the five chapters I need to review, I say, "Okay, I can take a short break now."

He hops up and pulls up my clothes hamper for an extra chair and sits down next to me at the desk. "Okay, so there's kind of a practice round first, after you get past the opening exposition part."

"Okay."

The exposition part takes fifteen minutes. I don't say anything, but I can tell he's feeling it, too. "Sorry," he says eventually. "I didn't remember it being this long."

"It's fine," I say.

We finally get to the part where I start killing ghosts or zombies or…revenants, I guess, whatever these things are, and I'm terrible at it because I'm terrible at video games. The game keeps telling me what keys I need to hit in what order, but I can't remember them fast enough and I keep hitting the wrong thing and doing some kind of fancy swing move that really doesn't seem to intimidate the revenants.

Sasha coaches me patiently, but I'm just getting more and more frustrated the more times I die on this stupid practice round. "Do you want me to just take care of this round for you?" Sasha says.

"Yeah." I shove the keyboard over to him.

So he plays the round, and then he tells me the next round is kind of tricky, so maybe he should do that one, too, and I should just watch, and I say okay. Eventually he stops talking and I stop watching and take my textbook onto my bed and try making the study guide by hand instead.

He turns the game off after a while. "Sorry," he says.

I shrug.

"I just thought it would be fun to do together."

"I told you I needed to study," I say.

"I know, I just thought, since I read that book…"

"You wanted to read that book," I say. "You asked me to. And you like books. I told you I don't like video games."

He runs his hand through his hair. "I'll just go."

"Okay," I say.

He takes the game with him. A week later, I try playing a round of it at his house. I still hate it. We don't try it again.

I give him my mother's recipe for pumpkin pie three months after Thanksgiving. "Do you think we could make it?" I ask him. "I'd ruin it if I tried it on my own."

"Of course," he says.

There's no canned pumpkin at his bodega, so we have to go to Whole Foods. I stand on the lip of the shopping cart, and he pushes me around until he gets tired. He's wearing this red sweater that makes his skin look yellow and delicate and beautiful, and he chews on his thumbnail while he searches for the right brand of shortening. He pays for the ingredients and winds one arm around my waist while he swipes the card, this casual little gesture like he doesn't even know he's doing it, and in this moment I feel so sure about him. It's the first time I've felt sure in a while. Maybe since New Year's Day.

But God, look at him. Look at the way he smiles at me. The way he checks the eggs before he pays for them, making sure each one is perfect, like it's the most important thing in the world. The way he takes my arm if I'm going to step on a slippery part of the sidewalk. How we're baking and he has this long stripe of flour down his cheek and I don't think he has any idea.

So what if he annoys me sometimes? So what if there's that throbbing feeling in my stomach, *but but but*—aren't I used to feeling disjointed at this point of my life?

When was the last time I felt sure about anything *besides* him? Ever?

There's no one else at home, and his apartment feels big and warm, almost like a third person. He stands behind me to crack eggs into the bowl, with my arms reached around his back and his under my shoulders like they're mine. "You're amazing," he says as he cracks the eggs with one hand. "Incredible chef." We turn music on while it's baking and dance a little in the messy kitchen.

I'm so happy, and I'm honestly not thinking about my mom at all, until the pie is cooled and I put that first bite in my mouth and Sasha asks if we got it right, and all of a sudden I'm seven years old at Thanksgiving and I still believe in love and staying together forever and people who don't end up hating each other, and then it's over, and I'm sobbing in the middle of his kitchen.

He asks me what's wrong about twenty times, going from worried to frantic to resigned, before he gives up and just holds me silently. I pound my fists against his red sweater, very, very gently, and cling on.

He gets me a flower on the first day of March.

"I think the snow's finally starting to melt," he says.

I bury my nose in the flower.

His eyes are hopeful. And sad. "I think it's going to get easier now," he says. "I really do."

WHO DO YOU TRUST?

That's kind of a dark question, isn't it? I mean, who *don't* I trust would be a lot easier to answer, because…I guess I trust everyone until they give me a reason not to. I mean…okay, maybe not. If I'm alone in a subway car at night and a man gets on with me, I don't trust him. I take my earbuds out, I put my keys between my fingers…so I guess I trust women?

— *Maura Cho, 16, lacrosse player*

Nobody. Or at least, I don't trust them as much as I trust myself. Why should I? Teachers tell us what they're supposed to. Our parents tell us what their parents told them. Boyfriends tell you whatever they think will make you happy or will make some, like, image of a girl they have happy. Your friends tell you what they'd want to hear if they were you. You can't trust anyone.

— *Ashley Baker, 17, single again*

So there's this comics magazine called *Heavy Metal* run by a man named Kevin Eastman. It's been in print for a while, since the late seventies, I think. I'd never read it before… I'm not really much of a comics person, which might be surprising. Sure, I like colorful ones with cute monsters and things like that, but this is described as a mix between erotica and dark fantasy, so…I don't know. It takes all types to make a world, as my mother would say. Anyway, there's a specific issue from 1990 that I read about, and then read. It's about Donald Trump rising to power. Yeah, the very same. And what does he do? Builds a wall. And what happens? Rallies. With lots of…well. Arm-in-the-air salutes, let's call it. And no, I don't know what this has to do with dark fantasy, either, except in terms of being very depressing, and I *certainly* don't get the erotica, but what I do know is that Kevin Eastman seems to be a soothsayer, so I guess now I have to go back and read every issue of *Heavy Metal*, so I suppose I trust him. Oh, whatever. I can't keep this up. I'm tired. I trust my dad. I trust my sister. I don't trust my brothers because they're little shits who know nothing about the world, but that's their job. I trust my doctors. I trust my moms. And I trust you, Ibby Garfinkel. To the end of the world, if Kevin Eastman tells us that's coming. If it hasn't already. I mean, Donald fucking Trump.

— *Sasha Sverdlov-Deckler, 16, insomniac*

Nobody, really, but not in that edgy *look-at-me* Ashley way. But…look at Sasha's list, for example. Who on that list are you supposed to trust? Let's go through it point by point. Your dad: yeah, he'll definitely try to do his best, but he doesn't know who you are or what you need. He's doing what's best for some hypothetical child that even he probably doesn't believe he has at this point. Your sister: she's in prison, and you haven't talked to her in two and a half years. You don't have any brothers. Your doctors told you nothing was wrong with you, and when you try to tell them you're still not feeling well, they talk over you about reducing your meds because they're very strong for *such a young woman*. You don't even have one decent mother, let alone two. And…Ibby Garfinkel? You're supposed to trust yourself? That's maybe the most ridiculous one of all, isn't it? Has he met you?

—*Claire Lennon, 17, dead*

*Y*ou should come to schul more often.

—*Tamara Shapiro, 58, surgical nurse at Linefield and West Memorial Hospital*

CHAPTER SIXTEEN

Once a month, our school cafeteria has breakfast for lunch. We all get unreasonably excited. You'd think it was our only chance to eat breakfast food. We load up our plates with pancakes and scrambled eggs and bacon—for them—and hash browns and French toast sticks.

"My uncle sent me some article about how I have arthritis because I eat too many carbs," I say as we're sitting down.

Luna squints at me. "What?"

"Do you?" Maura says.

"No, it's just pseudoscience bullshit."

"Speaking of bullshit," Ashley says, so I guess we're done talking about that. "Lucas canceled on me for this weekend. I'm completely done with boys at this school."

"What a tool," Maura says, her mouth full of bacon.

"Let's make the most of it," Siobhan says. "Let's do something."

"Do you guys want to go to Coney Island?" I say. "Sasha and I are gonna go, he's never been before."

"He's never been to Coney Island?" Ashley says.

I say, "I know, finally a New York attraction I've been to that he hasn't. I'm reveling. He said I should invite you guys."

"I'm in," Siobhan says, and Luna is of course in because there's a part of Coney Island called Luna Park and she never misses an excuse to remind us and to go there and take selfies with all the signs. Maura loves roller coasters, so she's an obvious yes.

We look at Ashley.

"Yeah, I'm in," she says. "Do you ever wonder, though, like… What about Sasha's friends?"

"What?" I say.

"He's always doing stuff with us," Ashley says. "And don't get me wrong, I like Sasha a lot. But do you ever hang out with his friends?"

I shrug and cut into my waffle. "He always suggests doing stuff with you guys."

"And you're not…concerned about that?" Ashley says.

I say, "What would I be concerned about? Isn't it a good thing that my boyfriend likes my friends?"

"I think it's a good thing," Maura says.

"Me, too," Luna says, feeding Siobhan a minipancake.

"You always had to force Justin to do stuff with our group instead of his," I say. "Isn't this an improvement?"

I can tell by the way Ashley looks at me over her orange juice that I've crossed some kind of line. I thought the rule that we had to act like Ashley and Justin were God's gift to high school couples had evaporated when they broke up, but apparently not. The power couple aura torch stays on even if the couple doesn't, and Ashley is not passing it.

No one else says a word.

"Justin wanted me to spend time with his friends," Ashley says. "He wanted his friends to like me, too."

"Of course," I say.

"Doesn't Sasha care if his friends like you?" she asks.

I don't say anything.

Ashley shrugs. "I mean, I guess not, if you haven't even met them."

Luna says, "It is… I mean, it is a little…concerning. That he hasn't even introduced you."

"Concerning of what?" I say.

"Like maybe he knows they're not good guys," Luna says. "You know what they always say about guys like, letting stuff go with their friends even if they know it's bad, because they don't want to call their friends out. Maybe he's ashamed of them and doesn't want you to see them."

"Or maybe," Ashley says, "they don't know you exist."

Siobhan says, "Why wouldn't they know she exists?"

"Maybe he has some other girlfriend at his school," Ashley says. She sips her juice. "Or maybe his friends aren't the one he's ashamed of."

Okay, so 90 percent of Ashley's points are bullshit pettiness. It takes me a few hours to get over myself enough to recognize how painfully obvious that is, but I get there eventually. Sasha is not ashamed of me. He thinks I hang the damn moon, as my father would say. He does not have some second girlfriend, because he spends literally all of his free time with me, and this is not an eighties movie where I'm supposed to leave my cheating high school boyfriend for the mysterious boy who's going to pull up on a motorcycle. No one even has motorcycles in New York City. And as for Luna's points, I mean, I guess it's possible, but it's hard to imagine Sasha letting people get away with shit like that. He might drive me crazy not taking my studying seriously, but just because he doesn't get angry doesn't mean he doesn't stay up until two a.m. arguing with people online about sexism; it just means he somehow schools men's rights activists without getting emotionally involved.

So none of that is a concern. What *is* a concern is that…I haven't met Sasha's friends, and there has to be *some* reason, even if it's a lot less dramatic than what my friends came up with. And even if there isn't really a reason, the effect's still going to be the same: his friends probably now think I'm the girl who took their friend away and who doesn't have any interest in meeting them, and maybe Sasha thinks he's not allowed to have his own friends or something, so…it needs to be addressed, just without my friends' paranoia.

We meet for some kind of lunch/dinner hybrid—breakfast for lunch has me very meal-confused—at a diner near his apartment and then walk back to his place to catch up on TV. It might be March, but it's still freezing. He's in the overcoat that I never successfully managed to steal long-term, and I have the hat he made me pulled down over my ears.

"Are we still doing Coney Island this weekend?" I say.

"Yeah! If you want to. I want to."

"I do." I pause. "I was thinking maybe we'd invite some of your friends to come with us."

"The girls don't want to?"

"No, it's not that."

"We could go just the two of us," he says. "Some sort of romantic midday Saturday date. With cotton candy."

I kind of want to drop all pretenses and just do that,

but I'm on a mission here. "I just want to meet your friends," I say. "Like that one you told me about from school, your best friend."

"Jackson," he says.

"See, I didn't even know his name."

"So?" he says. He's not looking at me.

"So don't you think that's kind of weird?" I say. "You know my friends really well and I don't even know your best friend's name."

"It's just different," he says.

"Why is it different?" We stop the block before his apartment and wait for the walk signal.

"I don't think he'd really be into Coney Island," Sasha says. "He has CP, so he can't do a lot of the roller coasters and shit."

"Which is why we can do it without my friends. The three of us could do, like, a low-key trip."

"You can't even do three-person trips to amusement parks," he says. "Someone always ends up sitting alone. It has to be an even number."

"Sitting alone on what? You *just* said—"

"I know, but…"

"And there would be six of us," I say. "With the girls."

"I thought you were gonna see if Ashley could bring that guy she's seeing. Lucas." The walk signal lights up.

"They're not seeing each other anymore," I say as we cross.

"Really? What happened?"

"Stop trying to change the subject!" I say. "See? This is weird. You know the name of the guy Ashley barely dated for two weeks and I didn't even know the name of your—"

We're half a block away from his apartment, and my hip all of a sudden just *snaps*, like a rubber band, and I completely cave in on that side. Sasha catches me, or I would have just fallen over in the middle of the sidewalk. A couple who was walking behind us brushes past me with this noise in their throats like this is the biggest inconvenience imaginable.

"Whoa, whoa, whoa," Sasha says.

My whole leg is shaking. It doesn't *hurt*, exactly, it just feels like it's no longer interested in being a leg. I try to put weight on it, then the pain hits, shooting all the way down to my foot and up my waist.

"Stop," Sasha says.

"Fuck."

He says, "I'm gonna pick you up, okay?"

"You sure?"

"Yep." He reaches one arm under my knees and sweeps me up, and I put my arms around his neck. In a different scenario, I'm sure this would be very romantic instead of embarrassing and painful, but it's still touch, and it's still comfort, and I still want to bury myself inside of his coat forever.

He kisses the top of my head. "Can you get the keys out of my pocket?"

"Um..." I grope around. "Yeah."

"Good. Let's get inside. Don't rupture my spleen."

"Okay."

"What about this one?" he says.

"Sasha, I'm trying to watch TV." We're lying

next to each other on his bed, me with an ice pack on my hip, him with his laptop balanced on his legs. I can't concentrate.

"Just look, okay?" he says. He turns those big green eyes on me, and I don't stand a chance. I rest my cheek on his shoulder while he turns the laptop toward me. I feel safe here with him and just about nowhere else right at this moment.

He shows me the screen. "See? This one comes with lots of designs."

"It's still a cane," I say.

"So?"

"So I'm seventeen. I can't use a cane."

"Does that argument work when people say you can't have arthritis because you're seventeen?"

I groan and hide in his shoulder. I know he's right, but I still just…can't picture myself with a cane. Going down the hallways at school. Walking to the subway. Everybody annoyed with me that I'm walking so slowly, then seeing the cane and getting filled with that sympathy they feel like they have to have, and then getting mad at me for making them have it. I know the game well enough already, walking around on two feet. "No canes," I say.

He drums on my back while he scrolls down the page. "All right, what about, like… Here, these look, like, sportier or something." He shows me a page of forearm crutches. "And they're more stable than a cane, anyway. And look, this one comes in pink."

"Why, because I'm a girl?"

He gives me a look. "Because you love pink."

Can't really argue with that one.

"So what am I supposed to do, just buy one of these?" I say. "And then I walk out of the house with it in front of my dad? I can't even imagine how that would go."

"You tell him it's helpful," Sasha says.

"He'd think I was ridiculous. He sees me walk around all the time. He knows I can do it."

"Well, maybe he should see your hip freak out and stop working. I should have taken some video for him."

"It's better now," I say. "It hardly ever happens."

He strokes my hair.

"This is all so you don't have to talk about your friends," I say.

He snorts. "Yeah, I threw out your hip to change the subject."

"You would. You're very sneaky." I press my nose into his shirt and just...smell him. "I don't think I could use one of those anyway. It'd hurt my wrist."

"You could get a wheelchair," he says.

"I don't need a *wheelchair*. This is ridiculous. I can walk."

"Lots of people who use wheelchairs *can* walk," he says. "I've used one a couple times when I was really sick. I didn't lose the ability to walk. I was just tired."

"And who gave you the idea to use a wheelchair, Sasha? Was it your boyfriend?"

He doesn't say anything.

I give up and pause the show. "It was your doctor, right?" I say. "You had a medical professional telling you that you needed it. He probably wrote you a prescription for it."

"Is it always going to come down to this?" Sasha says.

"We're always going to come back to this fight that doctors think I'm sicker than you are?"

"You say that like they're wrong," I say.

"No, I say it like it's irrelevant. It's not a competition."

"I'm not saying it's… I'm just saying there are things about each other's experience that we're not going to get. We can talk about how we're both sick like it's some magical thread tying us together, and I'm not saying it's not huge and big and important, I'm just saying…we're not the same. We're not."

He pulls his sleeve down over his hand, slowly, precisely. "Well. I want to be the same."

"I know," I say.

"And anyway, that's not even what this is about."

"Yeah it is," I say. "Because I can't get some mobility aid and then be afraid to use it at a doctor's appointment because they're gonna scoff at me and tell me I don't need it. Because that's what they'll do. If you look this shit up, if you google *do I need a cane*, because yeah, I've looked into this, all you find is people desperately trying to avoid it. People who can barely keep their balance without it who are still doing everything they can to *not* get one. They're not… They're worse off than me. They don't want to use one. You're not supposed to want to use one."

"So you do want one," he says. "You think it would make things easier." He doesn't say it like he's trying to trap me. Just like he's trying to understand.

"I mean, it would be easier in terms of the physical act of walking," I say. "But when you used a wheelchair, wasn't it weird? Everyone could just…see that something was wrong with you?"

"I don't know," he says. "I kind of felt too shitty to care."

"Yeah." I wouldn't, but that seems insensitive to point out. Plus, he knows. He knows me. "I feel like once you start using something, then you're disabled, not sick. And it's not that I have a problem with being disabled, it's that… I don't know. I'm Sick Girl. I'm used to it. To all those, you know, the pluses and minuses of people looking at you and not being able to tell."

He sits up some. "Honestly, I've been thinking about that lately. And I'm not sure there actually *are* advantages to people not being able to tell? I think that's just something that people tell themselves, like when they say it's fine not to peak in high school. I think it's categorically better if people can look at you and know that you're sick."

"That's ridiculous," I say.

"No no, hear me out. Okay, maybe not if you're, like, interviewing for a job or trying to get a girlfriend or boyfriend or nonbinary friend or whatever. But we're not in those situations, so I don't care about them. What do we, like you and I, get out of people looking at us and thinking we're fine? I mean, I know I get threatening letters on our dashboard when we're upstate and we park in a handicapped space. You get teachers who don't believe you when you need a break, and people not giving up seats on the subway, and your dad thinking you're fine. How would your life actually be harder if you looked sick?"

"Life is harder for people who aren't conventionally attractive," I say. "Even if they're not looking for a girlfriend or a boyfriend or a nonbinary friend."

"Sure, if you're trying to be a model."

"No," I say. "For everyone. Just for…being treated nicely at stores. And who knows if you would have even looked at me that day in the drip room if I hadn't been pretty, or I would have looked at you. We're not saints."

"But," he says. "Having a cane wouldn't make you less pretty."

"It would to a lot of people," I say.

He shrugs. "I still think it's just easier if people know."

"But they *wouldn't* really know, would they? That's the thing. I already have a hard time getting people to understand. I mean, remember what you knew about RA before you looked it up?"

He says, "Honestly, not really. Feels like forever ago."

"People think it's just pain, and if I have a cane, that's gonna reinforce that, when really what I have the biggest problem with is how goddamn *tired* I am. So it's just going to be another reason people don't get it." I flop back on the bed. "I tried to talk to my friends about it today, and they just changed the subject. If I showed up next week with a cane, they'd think I was method acting or something."

"So what are you gonna do?" he says. "Just hope you don't fall down when no one's there to catch you?"

I sigh. "I'll talk to my doctor about it. I'll try to make him listen. You can…help me make a list of talking points before I go in. But I can't just take this step without someone I trust telling me it's the right call."

"You trust me, don't you?" he says.

I look up at him. "Of course I trust you."

He smiles a little.

"But," I say. "You can't pretend like *my doctor told me I should try using this* doesn't sound a lot better than *my boyfriend told me I should try using this.*"

"Okay, true," he says, and fuck if I don't love the way he gives in when he knows he's wrong. I feel like everyone I've ever met just holds onto their points and fights like a dog with a bone. But Sasha...God. He listens to me.

And it's not lost to me in all of this that he would be perfectly fine dating a girl using a cane or a crutch or a wheelchair. And I realize that shouldn't be something noteworthy, that any decent guy should be fine with that, especially one with a chronic illness, but...the world is not exactly teeming with decent guys, and here is one right here who has beautiful eyes and good-smelling clothes and the most precious heart, and he loves me. And if his hip stopped working in the middle of the street, I would carry him, somehow. I'd find a way.

And then I'd probably get on him to get a mobility aid, because he would deserve one. I trust him.

"Your wrist," he says quietly.

"What?"

"Nothing. Hang on." He gets up and goes to his dresser and starts digging through. "I thought I found one when I was cleaning...aha!" He finds something and holds it up in triumph.

"What is it?"

"Wrist brace," he says. "From when I broke my *other* arm a few years ago. I found it a couple weeks ago and saved it for you."

I make a face.

"Come on," he says. "It's a wrist brace. People wear wrist braces."

I sigh and hold out my wrist. He smiles, sits down on the bed next to me, and puts it on me.

It's strangely romantic.

"Jackson graduated last year," he says while he adjusts the straps.

"What?"

"Jackson. He's gone. He's in Massachusetts, and we don't talk anymore. We weren't that close. I…" He tugs on a strap. "Fudged the truth at the hospital because I didn't know you yet, and I didn't want you to know I was the loser with no friends who misses too much school and eats alone in the hallway outside the theater and has to beg someone to be his lab partner." He lets go of my wrist. "There. How is it?"

He's looking at me with those big eyes. He's nervous.

"It's perfect," I say. "You're perfect."

"What's that on your wrist?" my dad asks me that evening.

"Oh, I…"

He sounds so confused. Like he's literally never considered that I could possibly, ever, need anything.

"I hurt my wrist in gym," I say. "The nurse gave it to me."

"You all right?"

"I'm fine," I say.

He nods. "Good."

HOW DO YOU FIGURE OUT YOUR PRIORITIES?

I guess I don't do things and then see if I miss them or if something bad happens. It's like ghosting, but with activities instead of people. If I don't do my chemistry homework, then my chemistry grade gets shitty, so I know I have to do my chemistry homework. Okay, so I don't actually have to try that to figure out that my chemistry grade will get shitty. But isn't it *worth* a try? What if the balance of the universe has changed, and now I don't have to do my chemistry homework, and no one told me? I think I'll try it again this week and see. I'll report back.

— *Luna Williams, 16, Roxy in "Chicago"*

It's all about cost-benefit analysis. How much work does something take versus what do you get out of it? You have to do what's going to benefit you the most.

— *Rick Shelton, 18, Republican*

I'm not sure it's really something you figure out. I think… you just know. For example, me and my kids. They're gonna be my first priority. And before they were born, I wasn't really sure I was the mothering type. I thought maybe I was too selfish! And then they're born and… you just know, nothing's gonna be the same anymore. Everything's different now. So I think you just…you can't figure that out, y'know? You can't plan for that. You just have to be ready to adjust.

— *Leighann Thomas, 32, radiology technician at Linefield and West Memorial Hospital* inally, an easy one. It's about promises you've made. What you told people you were going to get done. You stick to your word, you show you're responsible, you take care of your obligations, and you do what you're supposed to do. If you said you'd do something, you do it. That's it.

— *Claire Lennon, 17, dead*

esh. Didn't you used to ask, like, fun, sexy questions? Isn't that why you had to be single? This is…gah. Figuring out priorities? I'm not old enough for this.

— *Sasha Sverdlov-Deckler, 16, Peter Pan in "life"*

CHAPTER SEVENTEEN

Coney Island was fun, Sasha lighting up at every little thing and the girls putting his excitement all over their Snapchat stories and all of us screaming our way through rickety roller coasters, but now I'm having one of those weeks that's just a slog, and it's only Wednesday. People have been warning me about second semester of junior year since I was a freshman, and I guess I convinced myself it couldn't be as bad as they said, because it was the only way I could allow myself to age without existing in a constant state of panic. But…it's bad. We have representatives from colleges coming to meet with us and requirements for how many per month we have to meet with and teachers who are very salty about us missing class to go to these meetings, so basically every junior at my school is walking around feeling like we're doing too much and not enough all at the same time.

"It'll be worth it, right?" Luna says. We're sitting on the banister outside the school after the day's over, soaking up the end of one of the first days of nice weather. She looks like she hasn't slept since before Coney Island. "When we're in college. Or just when we're seniors." She looks at Siobhan. "How did you get through this?"

"Pot, mostly," she says.

"Yes. Okay. Let's go smoke, I need it. You in?" Luna asks me.

"I can't. It's Wednesday. I'm at the hospital today."

"You're at the hospital every day," Luna says. "No wonder you're stressed. Hospitals are stressful! It's like a universal fact."

"You were just saying how stressed you are," I say.

"Yes, and imagine if I went to hospitals. I'd just...pop." She digs her phone out and checks the time. "Okay, I have two hours until rehearsal starts."

"That's enough," Siobhan says.

"Yeah, let's get out of here."

They head off toward their secret smoking spot behind the school, hand in hand. I'm irrationally annoyed at them, because I'm annoyed at everything today, but I shake it off and head toward the subway. My volunteer shift doesn't start for another hour and a half, but most weeks I just head straight to the hospital and kill time until then. Today, of course, I forgot my uniform, because why wouldn't I, so I have to stop off at home first. Maybe I'll take a quick nap or something. I hate short naps, though. Three hours or nothing.

My phone rings, the little jingle I have just for Sasha, as I'm hauling myself up the stairs. He calls pretty often on my way home from school, on days we're not meeting up. I don't love having conversations on the subway, since I feel like I must be bothering everyone, but I'm only on it for a few stops. And also I'm trying to care less about mildly bothering people with my existence, but...it's a process.

Today I don't really give a fuck what any of these people think because I'm so cranky that these strangers are all somehow part of the problem, so whatever.

"Hey," I say.

"Hey," he says. "How'd it go? Today any better?"

"Not really." The train's late, too.

"I'm sorry," he says. "I had a shitty day, too, if that helps."

"What happened?"

"I got a nosebleed in the middle of a Calc test, so I couldn't leave. It was an event. The girl next to me looked personally offended."

"Eesh."

"Are you almost home?" he says.

"I'm on my way. The train's… Hang on, it's coming in now." I step back from the yellow line as it rushes past. In the summer, it's free air-conditioning, that moment when the train flashes past. Right now it's just March. "I forgot my uniform, so I have to go home and get it before my shift, because today wasn't irritating enough."

"Oh," he says. "I forgot you were at the hospital today."

"Every Wednesday," I say, and maybe I don't say it super nicely, but seriously, he *always* forgets, and it's not like it's his enzyme replacement therapy, where it's always a different day of the week. It's every Wednesday. It's not hard. He just doesn't pay attention. Not to anything but weird facts about murder, anyway.

"Well, maybe you should take this week off," he says. "You've had a rough week."

I snort out a laugh.

"Tell me about your day," he says, and I rant about college counselors and teachers who think they're your only teacher the rest of the way home, and we're still on the phone when I get off the train and cross Queens Boulevard and walk up my block, and there's Sasha, sitting on my doorstep with a couple of plastic shopping bags.

"Hi," he says. Into the phone.

I hang up like a rational person, and he lopes over and hugs me. I breathe out and relax into him.

"I brought supplies for caramel marshmallow popcorn," he says. My favorite. "And I've been sitting here looking for the worst horror movies streaming on Netflix, and I found two that might actually kill us."

"The dream," I say.

"Come flop down on the couch and I'll rub your feet."

"My feet are okay." I unlock my front door.

"Okay, so I'll French braid your hair." He does fantastic French braids. I can't do them because my fingers get too stiff. His are so tight he can do them in the evening and I can sleep in them and wear them to school the next day.

That does sound nice. I don't have time for any of the rest of it, but I can have French braids at work and think about him instead of thinking about my hair in my face. "Okay," I say. "Thanks."

My uniform polo is about as close to the door as it could be without falling off the kitchen counter, like it's mocking me for forgetting it. I shove it into my tote bag, because Sasha and I are not at any sort of clothes-removing stage and it seems weird to dart upstairs and change. I'll just do it at the hospital. We sit down on the couch, and he combs my hair out with his fingers.

"Do you want to pick one of the movies while I do this?" he says.

"I can't watch a movie," I say. "I have to be at the

hospital in an hour."

"Call in sick."

"I'm not sick."

"Sure you are."

"I feel fine today," I say.

"That doesn't mean you don't deserve a night off," he says.

"Literally every other night besides Wednesday is a night off. It's a once-a-week commitment. A ton of people have jobs they have to go to after school. Every day." Just because I don't know these people—it's not really the expensive-private-school demographic—doesn't mean they don't exist.

He finishes one of the braids and ties it off with a hair band from the junk mug on the table beside the couch. "I just thought it would cheer you up to spend some time together," he says, and I don't like the way he says it. Like he's bravely trying not to pout about the fact that I'm not throwing away my commitments just because he can't remember them.

"Yeah," I say. "It probably would. But that's not the point."

"You've said before that they barely use you," he says. "That when you step away they just have a nurse take your place like you weren't even there." He starts on the other braid.

"Wow, thank you," I say. "Always good to hear my boyfriend thinks what I do doesn't matter."

"That's not what I meant," he says.

"The *point* is that I'm doing menial shit," I say. "When I'm doing a job, the nurse doesn't have to do it, so she can go do something more complicated instead of sitting there answering the call buttons. Which, by the way, I'm awesome at, and as someone who's sometimes hospitalized, you should be grateful for volunteers because we pay more attention to the call buttons than the nurses do."

"So maybe if you're not there they'll be forced to do it and learn to appreciate them," he says.

"Yes, you're right. They're slow to answer calls because they've never done it before because they have volunteers to do their bidding, not because they're overworked and sleep-deprived."

"You don't have to be mean," he says.

"I'm not being mean. You're the one who's trying to argue me into missing work, like you're going to find some kind of loophole and all of a sudden I'll agree with you that, you're right, I don't actually have to keep up my commitments, I'm so stupid, if only I'd had a boy here this whole time to show me how I was actually…what, hurting the medical process by being around to pick up slack? Is that what we're going with?"

"You know, I had a rough day, too," he says.

"I know, and I'm sorry, but I can't just drop everything."

He's not braiding anymore, so I turn around and face him.

"I was just trying to do something nice for you," he says.

"I know, and it would have been really nice if it was yesterday, or tomorrow, or literally any other day besides Wednesday, and honestly, you should know that by now. It's *just* Wednesdays, and it's every Wednesday."

"Okay, well…" He runs his hands through his hair, like he always does when he's stalling for time. "I'm not good at stuff like that. I don't remember dates and stuff."

"Because you don't pay attention," I say. I can't help it.

"What?"

"You don't pay attention to things you don't want to hear. You don't listen when I say what days I work or that I can't hang out because I have to study or…"

"Okay, I'm sorry I want to spend time with you?"

"That's not it," I say. "It's that you don't take me seriously. Like…I ask you questions for my column, and you turn them into a joke."

He looks hurt. "I thought you liked when I did that."

I do. This is all getting too big, and there's still so much more shit I've been holding on to. "Or when I tell you that I don't like video games and then you still come over when I *told* you I have work to do and make me play one."

"I wanted to show you something I love," he says. "I read that book for you."

"I didn't ask you to read it! You wanted to!"

"So we just do the stuff you like and not the stuff I like?"

"How about we just do the stuff that we want to do?" I say. "You like books. I don't like video games. It's not some contest."

"So what you want to do right now is go to the hospital and work for no money when you could be hanging out with me," he says. "That's what you're saying."

"That's a completely different thing. This isn't about what I want to do. It's about the fact that I made a commitment and I have a responsibility, and if I don't show up everyone's going to think I'm a flake."

"I just don't get why you—"

"You don't have to get it!" I'm standing up. I don't know when I stood up. "You just have to listen to me when I tell you it's important to me. I'm sorry we can't all bounce through life not giving a shit about anything, but that's not me, okay?"

He crosses his arms.

"I have to go," I say. I walk to the door too fast, and my hip aches. He tries to stop me, and it's not until I'm halfway down the block that I realize it's probably because I just left him in my house like this is some kind of TV show where people don't have to worry about leaving their doors unlocked, and I'm two stops deep on the subway before I notice half of my hair is braided and the other half isn't.

What a fucking day.

Maybe I should just…be easier. Be the kind of girlfriend who loves to watch her boyfriend play video games and who is happy to toss her life aside anytime he wants to hang out with her. Because if the situation were reversed, Sasha would do those things for me. Which would be a great revelation, I guess, if that's at all what I wanted from him.

It's not my fault that he stood on my sidewalk and told me he loves everything about me and then apparently expected me to turn into some other person. He knew what he was getting into. I'm not going to change, not for anyone.

I repeat the argument to myself all the way to the hospital and through my shift, and I get peak mad about half an hour in and then deteriorate into just exhausted from there. By the time my shift is over at eight, I'm just sleepwalking. I have to get home and finish my lab reports for Bio, and I can't stop thinking about how close I was to having caramel marshmallow popcorn to eat while I did them, and now I'm going to just go home hungry because I'm too tired to socialize with the cafeteria people and we don't have any food in the house. I don't even stop by my dad's office to say hi to him. I just leave.

Except there's Sasha, sitting on a bench by the reception desk.

He doesn't look great today. I noticed it at my house, but I didn't really process it. I mean, it's Sasha, so he always manages to look irritatingly handsome no matter how sick he is, in that sort of dying-from-consumption way, but he's paler than usual and kind of shaky, and honestly my first thought when I see him here is maybe that he's here because it's a hospital and not because it's me. But that's stupid. This isn't the ER. This is where you wait if you're visiting someone.

He stands up when he sees me. "Hi," he says.

"What are you doing here?"

"I have your key."

Oh. "Thanks."

He looks for it in his pocket. "I used to," he says softly.

"You used to have my key?"

"No, I…" He finds it and drops it into my hand. "I used to bounce through life not giving a shit about anything," he says. "Like you said."

I put my key in my jacket pocket and don't say anything.

"I think it was charming for a while," he says. "You know, the sick boy who doesn't worry. Playing against the type."

"Sure," I say quietly.

"But…see, the thing is…I do," he says. "Care about things." He's watching me.

It's hard to look at him. It's too much. It's not enough, standing here and not touching him, with the receptionist at the desk, with people walking past us. "I know," I say.

"I'm sorry," he says. "You were right. And I'm gonna do better. I'll listen more. I'll stop trying to make you blow stuff off. I'll stop, you know. Acting like I'm heartless. I'm not heartless."

"Sasha, I know you're not."

He shrugs a little, this sad smile on his face. "It's not charming anymore," he says.

It's too much power. I'm scared. "Just not to me," I say.

"Well, who else do I need to be charming for?"

I fold into his arms, in front of anyone who's looking. He wraps himself all the way around me.

I didn't ask him to change. I didn't ask him to apologize. He just shows up and says he'll be different because I don't like something about the way he is. It's sweet, and it's thoughtful, and…I wouldn't do it for him.

But he didn't ask me to. He said I was right, so I don't have to.

I let him hold me for a while, and I feel comforted and safe and guilty.

"Can you please keep coming up with funny answers for my column, though?" I say. "People really like them."

"I don't care about people," he says. "It's your column. Do you like them?"

"Yes."

"Then I will."

ARE YOU WHERE YOU'RE SUPPOSED TO BE?

Interesting question! Well, it's ten p.m., and I'm at home, for once, so I would say yes, I'm exactly where I'm supposed to be. But I won't lie to you. I do have some nagging worry about a patient I left with a rather new doctor overnight and some financial paperwork that I still need to go over, and there's always a part of me that feels guilty for relaxing in my beautiful home with my beautiful daughter when there are so many people still working at the hospital and so many patients who can't go home. So I suppose where I'm "supposed" to be is really a relative term, huh? But I bet you did that on purpose, to make us think about what "supposed to" really means. You're very clever with these questions.

—*John Garfinkel, 49, Physician in Chief at Linefield and West Memorial Hospital*

No, not in any sense of the word. First, I'm going to AP Psych, which I shouldn't even be in, because I wanted to take AP Art, but the college counselor told me that AP Psych would look better on my applications, and yeah, okay, it worked, I got in to NYU, but they even *told* me in my interview that they wished I was taking AP Art because it would have shown them that I'm passionate about what I do and I'm not just trying to win points by taking something like Psych. Also, I'm late for Psych.

—*Siobhan O'Brian, 17, artist*

No! At my age? I deserve to be somewhere warmer than this. You know, I have a girlfriend, and she and her husband just moved to Aruba. Aruba! Imagine moving to Aruba. That's not something they tell you is possible, you know? They say no, that's a vacation, then you have to come home. And we just believe it! But people do it. Probably someone new moves to Aruba every day. Why not me!

—Judy Bluth, 79, retired chef

Right at this moment? Looking at that boy, sitting on this train? Yes. Look at him. Yes, we are.

—Claire Lennon, 17, dead

No. We should be in Disney World. We're very sick! Why aren't people constantly taking us to Disney World?

—Sasha Sverdlov-Deckler, 16, gravely ill

CHAPTER EIGHTEEN

Sasha and I are in sync.

I'm judging myself for being so worried, for the neurotic way that I can never calm the fuck down and enjoy anything, except...I am, right now. I'm doing it. I am enjoying something.

I'm enjoying him.

And he's trying. I can tell. He pauses, sometimes, when he's talking, and then he'll say something more patient or thoughtful than he would have said before we fought at my house. He doesn't push when I tell him I have a paper to write and I can't hang out. He listens to me rant about how stressed out I am about this college stuff and doesn't tell me I'm overreacting or suggest some dumb solution. He just listens.

And I was right; this was what we needed. We're a finely tuned machine now, performing some choreographed relationship dance. We circle around each other. He comes up behind me and wraps his arms around my waist, and I forget how to breathe and don't mind.

One thing no one ever told me about relationships—and it's honestly a good thing they didn't, because it sounds so stupid and overdramatic that I never would have believed it—is that desperate, deep sense of *loss* you get every time a kiss stops or he lets go of your hand. He'll still be *right there*, but the fact that I was just touching him and now I'm not makes me feel this gnawing at the bottom of my throat, every time. He pulls back from me, and it's like I'm watching it in slow motion, trying to will it not to happen, and I feel a bit of me pull away with him, like it's attached.

But then he touches me again, and I think, *home*.

I am allowing myself to think, *home*.

I'm doing this.

March is almost over, it's finally starting to get warm, and Sasha and I are having a rare day where we're both not feeling all that bad. This will probably never happen again. I go over to his house for our usual Saturday night horror movie ritual, but the movie's over and it's not even nine and we're both antsy. I'm on his laptop on his bed, checking out what's playing nearby or if there's some restaurant we haven't been to or some bar that won't card two teenagers who really do not look twenty-one. Sasha's pacing the floor and brainstorming.

"There's nothing good in theaters," I say. "It's all sequels to shit."

"We're too poor for theaters anyway," he says.

"True. So why am I looking at restaurants?" I close a bunch of tabs.

He claps his hands together suddenly and points at me.

"Idea?" I say.

"Yes. Let's go to Times Square."

I laugh. "What?"

"Come on, when was the last time you went?"

"I…transfer at the subway station a lot?"

"It'll be fun," he says. "We'll look at the lights. Watch the people. I'll get you a pretzel."

"We're New Yorkers," I say. "New Yorkers don't go to Times Square."

"They also don't call themselves New Yorkers! You've backed yourself into a corner." He's being patient, though. A week ago, he would have already been putting my jacket on me. Now, if I really didn't want to go, we wouldn't.

And honestly, it has been a long time since I've even walked through Times Square. I usually do everything I can to avoid it. We all do. Hating Times Square is a New York point of pride. We're supposed to hate everything that tourists like.

But I have no idea how I actually feel about it. I'm just repeating the things other people say.

I do know I like pretzels.

"Okay, what the hell," I say. "Let's go to Times Square."

We're the only people at Sasha's apartment for the first time since we baked my mom's pie recipe. Nadia's at dance class, the boys are at their mom's, and Sasha's dad is out with the woman he's been seeing for a little while now. Sasha hasn't complained as much about him dating as he used to, so she must not be that bad.

We go down in the elevator and out of the building and toward the subway. He's all hyped up like he's never left the apartment before, bouncing a little as he walks, shooting me these completely disarming smiles that make me want to kiss him and never stop. This is what's in the air on the first warm evening in New York every year. We still have to wear jackets and hats, but it's finally reasonable to be outside as a destination and not just as a way to somewhere else. Preteens are lurking outside Sasha's bodega, talking shit about people who pass by and kicking around a hacky sack. There's an old man sitting in a plastic chair in the doorway of the dry cleaner's. When we get down to the subway station, there are devastatingly dressed, extremely drunk women laughing so loudly you'd think the subway station was the place they wanted to get to tonight.

We stand up together on the train, because there's only one seat and I want to be with him, and he gradually leans in closer and closer to me, our eyes on each other's, until our noses touch. We don't say anything. We don't have to. The train stops suddenly, and we slide into each other and giggle.

We get off the train at Times Square and weave through the crowd transferring onto other lines and get to the escalator to go above ground. "You ready?" he says.

I laugh. "You know I have been here before."

You can see the Times Square lights through the big glass windows before you even step out of the station, even though the Times Square from the movies, with the red steps and the sidewalk-to-sky lit-up billboards, is still a few blocks away. Sasha takes my hand as we leave the station.

"I took my cousin here, once," Sasha says. "His very first time in the city. We walked out of the subway station, and he goes...*is this outside?*"

I squeeze his hand. It's just cold enough out here for his cheeks to flush a little pink. His lips are chapped in the center, and his hands are soft, except for little calluses right at the base of his fingers from his bike.

"I used to beg my mom to take me here when I was little," I say.

"Oh yeah?" He has a voice he uses for me when I talk about my mom, like I'm a frightened little animal he's worried about scaring away if he's too eager, but I don't mind.

"Yeah." We keep walking toward Times Square. There are a lot of tourists here, of course, but it's not as bad as I would have guessed. People are on the street corners, handing out coupons for comedy clubs and pamphlets about Hell, and there are a couple of guys dressed like Spider-Man wandering around the street. "She always wanted to do stuff as a family, but my dad had to work, and…I guess this was easy. She'd bring me here and I was so dazzled by the lights she didn't actually have to do anything to entertain me, just watch me and make sure I didn't run off. She wasn't really much for playing and stuff. We got along better when I was older and we could just exist."

"What about your dad?" he says. "Better when you were younger or now?"

"I don't know," I say. "I thought when he took the promotion to Chief it was so he could spend more time with us. That's what he said it was going to be. But I guess it didn't work out that way. She was really upset about that."

"He's been busy lately, yeah?" Sasha says. "Like, even by his standards, I haven't seen him much."

"Yeah, there's something going on with the hospital. They're gonna have to stop accepting an insurance they were accepting. Which they already had to do last year."

"Wow, that sucks."

"Mmmhmm. And otherwise they can't keep the doors open."

"Lose-lose."

"Yeah."

He takes a deep breath, or as deep as he goes, as we finally reach the square. "On the bright side," he says, his face tilted up to the lights.

I smile without meaning to. "Yeah."

I know we must look like tourists, standing here holding hands and marveling at the ads around us, and usually that's something I take great pains to avoid, but right now, I don't mind so much. The buildings around us are lit up with billboards playing videos of girls putting on lipstick and M&Ms spinning and pictures and tweets from people who use a special hashtag. Up above those ads, the Broadway billboards peek over like the flashy signs' more serious parents. Tourists are posing for pictures in front of the steps, but there's always a ton of room to sit on them. I think maybe they don't know they're allowed to sit there.

But we do, of course. Sasha says, "Go ahead, I'll get you your pretzel."

"With—"

"—tons of mustard, I know."

I sit on the steps and watch him walk to one of the hot dog and pretzel carts in that loping, long way of his, his hair blowing back off his face. He jokes with the vendor a little, those dimples showing up so deep on his cheeks I can see them even from here. He reaches into the wrong pocket for his wallet first and gets embarrassed and flustered and adorable. He covers it with another joke.

And honestly, all these people in Times Square…are they aware of what they're in the presence of right now? This boy who's terrified of ordering food, who's getting me a pretzel so I can sit down? Who's so self-conscious that he doesn't know what else to do besides brush everything off but who's trying something different for me?

Bow down, New York City. Look at my person.

And all I have to do is sit and watch and clamp down on that feeling in my stomach that never lets me enjoy anything, to put my fear that another shoe is going to drop, that I am not allowed to be this happy, into a tiny little box and store it away and open it sometime when I'm alone and it can't ruin our night. When it can't ruin him. Because maybe it's baseless. Maybe this time, something is actually as good as it seems. We've had the arguments. We hashed it out. We figured out solutions. Maybe we actually really do get to the good part. Maybe if my parents had done that, they'd still be together. This could be all it takes.

It's possible I deserve something. Or that he messed up karmically in some past life and somehow I'm really the best *he* deserves.

I'll take it, is what I'm saying.

As long as it's real.

And it could be.

It's possible.

It's…okay. He's heading back toward me. Try acting like a normal human who knows how to enjoy things.

And then he sits next to me and hands me the pretzel and kisses me on the cheek, and all of a sudden, I am.

We don't say much. We don't need to. We just sit on the red steps for a while, sharing a pretzel with tons of mustard, watching the billboards change, watching tourists gape at the buildings, and I fall in love with this stupid little tourist trap and with this amazing city and with this boy who has me under his arm.

I remember that first day in his apartment, how it felt when I first sank into that bath, and for a minute nothing hurt.

That's what it's like.

"So it was fun, right?" Sasha asks. We're back in Chelsea, walking to his place from the subway so I can grab my backpack and we can make out for a while before I head home.

"It was definitely fun."

"And I didn't… I know it was my idea, but I didn't…"

I grab his hand. "You didn't make me do it. I had fun. Everything's good."

He smiles at me. "Okay."

We stop outside his building and kiss for a while, even though we're about to go upstairs together. I drape my arms around his neck and feel like I'm falling and caught.

Sasha starts chuckling in the middle of the kiss.

I pull back a little. "What?"

"Sorry, it's, uh." He covers his eyes. "My dad is at the end of the block, doing the same thing we're doing."

I turn around and look. Dmitri has his arms around some blond woman in a short black skirt, and they are really just going to town. They make Sasha and me look like prudes.

They pull away a little to gaze at each other, and this crawling feeling starts at the back of my neck and itches its way up to my scalp before I even understand what's going on, and then it's my whole body, and I'm suddenly very aware of my heart and my lungs, and this can't be happening—

"He's shameless," Sasha says.

"That's my mom." My voice doesn't sound like mine.

"What?"

"That woman that your dad is... That's my *mom.*"

This is why we don't trust good feelings.

WHY ARE YOU THE WAY YOU ARE?

I think we're all just copying what we see. Scenes from movies. Feelings that songs say we're supposed to have. Fights that our parents have. We just reenact them. And of course they're all reenacting stuff, too. I don't know. There should be Oscars for real life, and we give them to all the people who are still married.

> — *Maura Cho, 16, lapsed optimist*

It's kind of the nature versus nurture argument, right? It's not like that only applies to gay stuff, though of course that's where you hear it the most often. Was I born 100 percent, you-are-definitely-gonna-be gay, was I born neutral—which I guess to them means *straight*, uh, okay—and then I had gayness thrust upon me by, I don't know, I guess the argument is my parents or the media, or was it somewhere in the middle and I had, like, a predilection toward gayness that had to be nudged, but not all that hard, by something outside of me? I don't know. I'm not a scientist. But if you know any, tell them they can study me if they pay me a lot.

> — *Luna Williams, 16, certified gay*

Because of the government and capitalism and all that shit. And the baby boomers destroying the economy and then blaming us for it. Did you hear we're killing the napkin industry? How about you fucking pay us, and then we'll buy some napkins, sound good?

> — *Anna Spumoni, 21, activist*

It's genetic.

—Sasha Sverdlov-Deckler, 16, Gaucher disease

I don't know. Why *did* you make me? Why'd I have to die? Wouldn't I have been more affecting for you as someone just wasting away beautifully and getting all that motherly love and attention? But no. You killed me off. There's got to be more to this, don't you think? Because it's not that you want to be dead. Do you, Isabel? Or do you just think you deserve to be?

—Claire Lennon, 17, dead

CHAPTER NINETEEN

I make Sasha go up to his apartment and get my backpack because I need to go back to the subway station and not up to an apartment where Dmitri could potentially be bringing my mother, or coming up to tell us about his date with my mother, or smelling like my mother's perfume, or with her lipstick on his cheek, or...*my mother my mother my mother my mother.*

I wait underground by the subway card machines and stare at cracks in the tile until he gets back. He has my backpack over his shoulder. "Are you sure it was her?" he asks.

"Yes, I'm sure."

"This is pretty weird," Sasha says.

"I should have known this would happen."

"You should have known my dad would date your mom?"

"Not this specifically, just...something. God, this is awful. I take back everything I ever said about you being a baby about your dad dating. He clearly has terrible taste in women and should not be allowed to date."

"Well, I don't think you ever said the word *baby*, but...I appreciate it?"

"God." I hold my head. "God, God, God."

"He told me her name," Sasha says. "Ann...not Garfinkel."

"Levine. She didn't change it when she got married."

He says, "Oh, that reminds me. Would we be Sverdlov-Deckler-Garfinkel or Garfinkel-Sverdlov-Deckler? I'm fine with either."

"Can you *please* be serious right now?"

He takes my hand. "Sorry."

"I feel like I'm gonna throw up," I say.

"Listen, I'll talk to my dad about it, okay? I'm sure he has no idea. He'll end things with her if I explain it to him."

"Why would he do that?" I say. "They've been dating as long as we have. I don't have priority."

"Yeah you do, because you're also my best friend," he says. "My dad's best friend is this guy Steve on the Upper East Side. I'm not asking him to dump Steve."

"I should have known this would happen," I say again.

"I'm gonna make sure you don't have to see her again, okay? I promise."

"It doesn't matter. She's just... This is just proof of everything I was telling you. I tried to pretend I was bigger than this, or we were bigger than this, or something."

"Ibby," he says gently. "What are you talking about?"

"I'm cursed," I say. Someone pushes past me to get to the subway card machine. "Either my family is cursed or we are just horrible fucking people, but either way, we are a fucking curse."

"Okay, I love you, but you know you sound kind of ridiculous right now, right? You don't believe in curses."

"There is something *wrong* with me," I say. "I keep telling you and you keep not listening." This gets a very helpful *ooooh shit* from a group of girls walking past us, who ironically probably think I'm talking about a disease or something.

"I am listening," Sasha says.

"No, you're not. I can't… This was a mistake," I say. "Thinking I could have this. Thinking this was even a *thing*."

"If you want me to listen, you're going to have to explain to me—"

"*The women in my family are terrible*," I say. "I'm terrible. I don't need to explain it to you because I *told* you and you didn't listen. That woman, who left her family and changed her phone number and who, *by the way*, is still married, is up there making out with your dad, and you don't get why it's a problem that that woman is half of me?"

"Okay," Sasha says. "I don't know if this is the wrong time for this, but…I mean, just going from what you've told me, I know your mom isn't a saint or anything, and I'm not saying she is, but…didn't your dad kind of jerk her around?"

"What?"

"He kept telling her he was going to be around more and then leaving her alone," he says.

"He had to work."

"I mean, so did she, right? And she still took care of you."

"He—" I can't believe I have to explain this to him. "What he does is really important."

"I'm sure it is, but it's also kind of… I mean, he's turning away people because of insurance stuff. He's making those decisions."

"It's not like it's *just* him. There's a whole board and shit."

Sasha says, "You have an imaginary friend who died because she didn't have the right health insurance. Are you sure you don't have some kind of resentment toward him that you're just...channeling all onto your mom?"

"I mean..." This is so incredibly not the point, and does he really think he's going to introduce some new idea about my father to me? He really thinks I haven't considered this? "Okay, so what if I am?" I say. "So I'm the spawn of two terrible people instead of one? That's supposed to make me feel better?"

Sasha sighs. "I didn't say—"

"I shouldn't have even asked you to the Snow Ball," I say. "I shouldn't have started any of this."

He settles back on his heels. "Wow."

This is all happening too fast. "I just... I think this might have been a mistake."

"That was the point, remember?" he says. "Making a mistake."

"Garfinkels don't make mistakes! They make decisions."

He laughs and takes a few steps away from me, his hands in his hair. For a second, I lose him in a flood of people leaving the station.

"Why...why are you laughing at me?"

He turns around. "I'm not," he starts, and then he runs his hand over his mouth and comes back toward me. "Honey, I'm sorry, but you don't...you don't make shit!"

"What?"

"You don't decide anything without asking everyone you can find. I still don't know if we'd be together right now if most of the people you asked hadn't said yes.

Would we?"

I don't say anything.

"I never know how you actually *feel* about anything because you're too busy overthinking everything to death," he says. "How do you feel? What do you actually want?"

I swallow and try to keep my voice measured. "This isn't about you—"

"I know very well this isn't about me, Isabel! Or about you. It's about your mom and your friends and literally *everyone else* who isn't in this relationship. You have been looking around waiting for us to fail since we got together."

"That's not true."

"I see it all the time," he says. "Every time I do something you don't like, you're calculating. Trying to figure out if the positives still outweigh the negatives."

"Everybody does that," I say.

"No. They don't. People *commit*. So I am asking you. Do you want to be in this relationship? Not do you think you *should*. Not do you think we're going to last forever. Not...not do you think anything, do you *want* to be in this relationship? That's it. That's all that matters."

I say, "Just because you think it sounds nice doesn't mean that's all that matters."

He puts his hand on his chest. "Do you want me to go first? I'll go first. Yes, I want to be in this relationship." He holds his hands out to me, waiting.

I say, "I just don't know if—"

"Yes or no, Isabel."

"It's not that simple, I just think—"

"Yes or no!"

I say, "If you would just let me explain—"

"There is no explanation that is more important than just telling your boyfriend whether or not you want to be with him! Explain *after,* I don't..." He's breathing hard. "If the next word out of your mouth isn't either yes or no I swear to God I'm walking out of here."

"Yes or no," I whisper.

"Exactly. If you want to be with me, Ibby, we will figure it out. We can get through all the bullshit, but you have to want it. And it's...fuck, it is not right that we've been together for three months without me feeling like you actually want to be with me. So...please. Just stop crowdsourcing your life and tell me. Yes or no, or I'm walking out of here."

So many thoughts are competing for attention in my head.

Remember when he told me this wouldn't mess up our friendship?

If he walked away, I could just go home and not have to worry about anyone but me ever again.

If he walked away, it would feel like ripping out my stomach and I might curl up and die right here in the subway station.

I can't believe we're doing this in front of people.

Why won't he just let me explain how complicated this is for me?

Maybe I'm just not doing it right.

Maybe I'm not doing anything right.

He's really not breathing well.

But he just needs to listen, and then he'll understand.

Except I don't even know what I'm going to say.

I don't know isn't yes or no.

Can you give me some time to think about it isn't yes or no.

Can I call someone and ask isn't yes or no.

I don't even know who I'd call anymore.

"Isabel, come on," he whispers.

I take a deep breath. He watches me.

I say, "There are a lot of things about you that—"

He drops my backpack at my feet and disappears up the stairs.

WHAT'S THE WORST THING YOU'VE EVER SAID?

—column postponed—

CHAPTER TWENTY

I don't sleep. I don't write my column. I don't go to school. I wait in my bed until my dad's left for work, and then I go downstairs and eat peanut butter cups, standing over the sink and staring out our tiny window.

So I'm just supposed to believe that people fall in love and stay in love and don't hurt each other? That's some trajectory that supposedly happens?

I'm going to be the first woman in my family not to slaughter the person she loves?

I'm going to be the first person on this planet to be happy?

Sure.

This is exactly where I was standing two years ago, washing plates after dinner, when my dad stood behind me and screamed at my mother that she could disappear from this family and no one would even notice.

She stuck around for two years after that.

Let's not act like everything Sasha said was wrong just because he hasn't called.

Oh look, the couch.

This is where I was sitting when my mom told me she thought all the time about how she didn't have a life since she'd had me, and no offense, but she just wondered every day what her life would have been like if she'd run away to Europe when she was twenty-six instead of settling down and marrying my father.

Cool, cool, no problems here.

Now let's sit on the stairs, where I was standing when I screamed at my mom that if she was that unhappy, she should just leave instead of constantly beating us over the head with how unhappy we made her.

That was years ago, so it's not why she left, and I've been kicking myself over it for months, and I'm done now.

This is where my father announced his promotion and told us he'd be home more.

This is where she made Passover dinner alone.

This is where she stroked my hair until three a.m. when I had a fever, even though she had work in the morning.

This is where she left the note for my dad and not for me.

This is where this is where this is where this is where Sasha hasn't called.

My dad comes home at six, which feels like some kind of personal attack. The one day I want to be alone, all of a sudden he's coming home at a reasonable hour?

He frowns at me sitting on the stairs, still in my pajamas. "Did you stay home today?" he says.

I wish I had a cigarette, which is a weird thing to wish for because I've never smoked one, but I think it would make me look bored and nonchalant instead of pouty and unshowered. "Yes."

He's so uncomfortable. This might turn into talking about *feelings*, so he's unprepared. "Are you sick?" he says.

Am I sick.

"I'll be at school tomorrow," I say.

"All right…"

I get up and go upstairs.

"Isabel," he says.

"I have homework."

I eat an old bag of chips I find under my bed for dinner and stare at my phone.

My boyfriend, who I love, asked if I wanted to be with him and left before I could give my answer.

Which was: *there are a lot of things about you I really like.*

That's it. That's what I was going to say.

To my boyfriend. Who I love.

There are a lot of things about you I really like.

Thank God he walked out, honestly.

I go to school the next day like I'm supposed to, but on the subway I dream about confronting my father. I play the imaginary conversation over and over in my head and perfect what I would say to him.

"I've been thinking about it," I would say. "And I've decided it's your fault. You lied to her. You belittled her. You chased her away. The only thing you did better than her is stick with me, and you don't even know me. And that's your fault, too. I'm a mess because of you. I have to be perfect because I have to prove to you that I'm not like her, and it will never work because I'm always going to be half her. But that's not even my actual problem, which is that I'm half you."

I don't know what he would say. I've never confronted my dad about anything before.

It's not as if I'm going to do it now.

But it's nice to think about.

I barely listen in class. I write Sasha's name in my notebook like an eight-year-old with a crush.

"*Would we be Sverdlov-Deckler-Garfinkel or Garfinkel-Sverdlov-Deckler? I'm fine with either,*" he said.

"*Can you* please *be serious right now.*"

I slam my notebook closed.

"Please remember the elevators are for maintenance staff and wheelchair users only," says a prerecorded voice over the PA system. I've heard it a hundred times. "There will be no exceptions."

"*I'm sorry. I'm going to do better. It's not charming anymore,*" he said.

And I stood there while he promised to change and owned up to everything he'd done wrong, and I said, "*Just not to me.*"

My friends try to get my attention all through lunch, and I try to remember to smile and look like I'm listening. I guess it doesn't work, because while we're changing after gym—just me and Ashley and Maura; Luna and Siobhan have a different gym period—they start talking about how great Sasha is, which is a reasonable thing to expect would cheer me up, except nothing about me is reasonable right now.

The locker room's just about empty, except for the three of us. They always take forever. I usually don't mind. I sit on one of the benches and watch Ashley spin her combination lock. She locks it in between taking out her real clothes and putting her gym uniform back in. Why does she do that?

Maura puts on lip balm in her locker mirror. "He just has such a great attitude. He's always, like…bouncy."

That first day after he broke his arm, when he saw me in the hospital: Hitting the call button. Asking for something.

He must have been so nervous to do that.

"And he's cute," Maura says. "That's very important."

She laughs a little at herself.

Ashley's brushing her hair. "Do you think he ever thought he'd date someone like you?"

I look up at her.

"Um, yeah," I say. "Of course. Why wouldn't he?"

"Oh, you know." She tugs at a tangle. "You're a catch. It's a compliment."

If it's a compliment, then why won't she look at me?

"So's Sasha," I say.

She doesn't say anything.

"Sasha's *great*," Maura says, but even she sounds like she feels the tension.

"You flirt with him all the time," I say to Ashley. "Outside the school that time. At the skating party."

"That was before you guys were together," she says.

"That's not my point. I'm not jealous. I'm just... You were flirting with him as what, a sport?"

She puts her brush back in her locker. "Would you rather hear that I was seriously hitting on the guy you liked?"

"Yeah, I would."

She sighs and closes her locker. "I don't know, I just didn't see him as like...a serious dating contender. I guess I thought he might like being flirted with. I thought maybe it didn't happen to him very often. Sue me for trying to do something nice."

I stare at her. Maura's behind her, chewing on her nail.

"What?" she says.

"That's a fucking horrible thing to say." And the worst part isn't even that she said it, it's that she said it like it was *nothing*.

She shrugs. "I was trying to give you a compliment. Won't try that again."

I grab my bag and stand up. "I wouldn't worry about that," I say on my way out of the locker room.

It's the first thing I've done that I've felt good about in a long time.

I lie on my back on my bed, eating the crumbs out of the bottom of that bag of potato chips.

He still hasn't called. Then again, neither have I. Everything he said in that subway station plays over and over in my head and I can't make it stop.

I think he needs me to be someone that I'm not.

And that's the kiss of death for a relationship, right? Imagine, changing for a boy. I always told myself if I ever got in a relationship, this would be me, take it or leave it. And now a guy wants me to...think less? That's horrible. If a girl was asking me this question for my column, I would tell her to dump him, no questions asked.

Not that I ever answer questions for my column. I'm not going to do that. What if I'm wrong?

Goddamn it, I am so fucked up.

When Sasha agreed to change for me, I stood there in the hospital lobby and thought less of him for it. He was doing something nice for me, and I *judged* him for it.

If I make an exception for Sasha, where does it stop? I start changing every time someone wants me to?

And why? Because he loves me?

Because he wants me to be able to say what I want?

Because he sees me curling up inside myself instead

of saying something that might not be the right thing to say?

Because he wants me to be able to enjoy something?

Because I'm literally going to ruin my life before it's even started if I keep pretending that everything is fine and that nothing will ever be great?

I bite down on the sleeve of my sweatshirt.

His smile when we played Monopoly in his hospital room. The soft rasp of his voice telling me I didn't have to go skiing. His soft hands when he fastened the brace around my wrist or when he led me away from the roller rink or when he took me to Times Square and I looked up and just for a second...

Imagine. Changing for a boy.

Imagine. Someone who wants me to be happy.

Imagine being happy.

I can't keep this up. The most perfect people I know are a workaholic who drove his wife away and an ableist jerk in a locker room. That's what happens when you're trying to be perfect. You end up not accepting anyone who doesn't fit the plan. Like a floppy-haired, green-eyed, emotionally stunted goofball with a debilitating chronic illness.

Or like me.

Goddamn.

I think I need me to be someone that I'm not.

Maura plunks her cafeteria tray down across from mine. I don't look up.

I'm sitting alone at one of the tiny tables. Luna,

Siobhan, and Maura sent me a bunch of texts last night, but I didn't even look at them, and today I just came and found my own table without pausing at our regular one.

It's fine. I need to think, anyway. I have a pen and a blank piece of paper in front of me, so clearly I'm making a lot of progress.

"I told Ashley I'm not sitting with her until she apologizes to you," Maura says.

"I don't care if she apologizes," I say. "That's not the point."

"I know," Maura says quietly.

I stab my mashed potatoes with my fork.

"She's got some shitty ideas," Maura says. "You know Ashley, she…she takes something and runs with it and doesn't know when to…stop running with it."

"It's not just Ashley," I say.

"What?"

I look up. "You say shitty stuff, too. And Luna and Siobhan, and fucking *everybody*. How about what you said at the New Year's Eve party, about how I was dating Sasha like it was some kind of act of charity?"

"Okay, I was, like, blackout drunk. I don't remember, but—"

"Were you blackout drunk when you said I shouldn't date him because I shouldn't settle for someone sick just because I think I can't do better?"

"I just don't want you to feel like you're not worthy of anyone you want, whether or not they're sick, just because you have, like, a condition."

"Being sick is not a bad thing," I say. "And you guys don't get that. You will never get that."

"Okay," she says. "Maybe we'll never get that. But also…have you really given us a chance to?"

"I've had RA for nine years," I say.

"Yeah, you have, and you've wanted to talk about it for like, what, the last two months? It's a pretty quick adjustment. If I'd asked you a year ago, I'm pretty sure you'd say being sick was a bad thing." Maura stirs her soup, shaking her head. "You used to say you didn't want to talk about it."

"Okay, well, I shouldn't have said that."

"I mean, you can feel however you want to feel about it, who am I to judge? But it seems like Sasha's really, like, opened your eyes to feeling positive about this thing you have, and that's great! I'm super happy for you. But you can't just…you can't make this big shift and not even tell us about it and then dump us because we're not adjusting when you didn't even give us a chance to adjust."

"I don't have time to go back and grab Ashley from—"

Maura waves her hand. "Okay then, fuck Ashley. Ashley's controlling and bossy and…whatever, fuck her, but what about you and me? We've been best friends for years. You can't just not even give me a shot to get on board with this new thing you're doing. I want to be on board. You're the one who changed, and I'm happy about it for you, but you're the one who changed, not me. You can't just drop me for not changing when you didn't even tell me I was supposed to. I deserve better than that, Ibby."

I swallow and look down at my roll. It's sitting half on and half off my plate. I feel bad for it for some reason.

"I changed," I say quietly.

"What?"

"I didn't…" I take a deep breath. "You're right. I changed, and it was good. I didn't know I could change."

She smiles at me a little.

"Okay," I say. "You're right. I'm sorry."

She nods.

"I still don't want to talk to Ashley, though."

"Fuck it. I've been looking for an excuse to spend less time with Ashley. Siobhan and Luna already told me they want to stay neutral."

"That's fine."

She spears a few pieces of pasta and slips them into her mouth. "So what's going on with you?" she says. "You were weird yesterday even before the thing with Ashley."

"Yeah." I open my yogurt. Sasha loves yogurt. "Stuff's not great with Sasha right now."

She puts her fork down and pushes her plate aside. "Okay. Let's talk it out."

And God, everything in me wants to. All my instincts are telling me to put it all on Maura, to get her advice, to do exactly what she says. I look down at the blank sheet of paper where I've been trying all day to write what I'm going to say to him. I could give it to her and have her write it. She'd love that. Let her make the decisions. Let her take the fall.

I changed, and it was good.

I lick my lips. "I think I need to figure this out on my own."

WHAT ARE YOU AFRAID OF?

*D*ogs. Why do people have dogs in the city? Don't they know they live in tiny apartments? Are they living somewhere else? Where are all these dogs coming from?

> —*Abby Lincoln, 29, lawyer*

*D*id you know more people are afraid of public speaking than are afraid of death? I learned that from *Seinfeld*. I don't know if it's actually true. It doesn't seem right to me. I think everyone's so afraid of death that they don't even think to mention it, but people who are afraid of public speaking… I don't know. Maybe they think they're special. Honestly, everyone's afraid of that, too, right? Who wants to get up and talk? After answering this, I'm gonna have to be quiet for two days to make up for it.

> —*Jenna Shields, 31, writer*

*C*ops, mostly. And I don't like needles!

> —*Mason Carter, 22, assistant manager at Pete's Diner*

*D*on't ask me, girl. I'm not taking the fall for this one. You're on your own. Can ghosts slam doors? I'm gonna try.

> —*Claire Lennon, 17, dead*

*F*ailure.

> —*Melanie Drake, 19, actress*

CHAPTER TWENTY-ONE

I spend the rest of the day drafting out what I want to say, and then I go home and keep working. I read it over a few times, then recite it in front of my mirror, then crumple it up and throw it away because I'm doing this wrong and it's supposed to be spontaneous. Sasha didn't write what he was going to tell me after the Snow Ball. That wasn't planned. He's never planned anything in his life.

I think about putting on my Snow Ball dress, but that seems like overkill. At the last minute, I dig through my closet to find a white scarf—not silk, but something—and drape it over my neck. He probably won't notice, but it makes me feel braver.

I get on the subway and head into Manhattan and spend the entire trip typing what I remember of the speech onto my phone. I'm hopeless.

I can't believe I'm about to do this. Sasha hasn't called. He's given no indication he has any interest in ever talking to me again, and here I am taking the train to his apartment at ten on a school night. If not for the fact that I'm obsessively taking notes on my phone right now, I'd think I'd been body-snatched.

But at the same time I have this electric feeling inside of me. I drum my fingers on the empty seat next to me and stare out the train window. I can't remember ever feeling this energized before, not in a very long time.

At least something is going to happen. I remember how I felt when he called me on Thanksgiving and how it felt when he kissed me for the first time, the kind of inescapable inertia of it all. This is a much-higher-stakes version of that. Back then, I knew it meant we'd eventually get together. Now, I just know we're about to...something.

But at least I'm doing *something*.

I transfer at Times Square, take the 1 down to Chelsea, and walk to his building. I take a deep breath and call his phone.

He picks up on the fourth ring. "Hey," he says. No rasping *hi there, Isabel*. Just *hey*, like a normal person.

"Hey," I say. "Can you come out?"

"What?"

"I'm outside your building."

"You're outside my building."

"Come out? Please? It'll just take a minute."

"I...yeah. Let me put some shoes on."

"Okay." I hang up and look up at his apartment and wring my hands.

He comes out of the building a minute later, in sweatpants and a thermal long-sleeved tee and shoes with no socks. He starts to come toward me, but I hold up my hand to stop him.

"Stay there," I say. There aren't any stairs in front of his building, so I back up down the sidewalk a little. This will have to do.

He crosses his arms and watches me. There's nobody else on this block right now. His doorman's off duty for the night. I'm sure someone will turn the corner and walk past us any second, but right at this moment, there's only Sasha and me.

And of course I've forgotten everything I was going to say. But he's standing here, and he's waiting for me, and I cannot let this go, so…bombs away.

"I know I overthink things," I say. "I just…all the time am overthinking everything. I think about things that don't need to be thought about. And I know it drives you crazy, and trust me, I get it, because it drives me crazy, too."

He watches me.

"I get a little rash over my infusion site and I think what if I'm having some major allergic reaction and I'm gonna die? The train stops when it's not supposed to and I think what if someone jumped in front of it? I hear a key in the door before my dad's supposed to be home and I think maybe it's my mom. And…and you do something that annoys me, and I think, maybe this was a mistake. And I know. I know that's frustrating."

He doesn't say anything. I wait for a couple to pass by me but start talking again while they can still hear me.

"I'm going to do better," I say. "I'm going to commit. I—oh fuck, the first thing I was supposed to say when I got here was *yes*. I was going to say that first. I was just gonna say yes, and then I was gonna stand here and… Can I start over?"

He's trying not to smile.

"Okay, fine, yes, this was rehearsed!" I say. "I wrote this all down! I practiced this on the train on the way over! I'm going to do better, but I'm still… I am always going to overthink things. But, like… Oh okay, this part is good, I remember this part."

He rubs his hand over his mouth. It's so casual and so beautiful and I'm messing this up and it's still working and I think I'm crying.

"No wait, okay, this part is good," I say.

"Okay," he says. His voice sounds muffled.

"I'm going to do better. But I think you should know that I'm already, even right now, before I'm doing better, there's…" I shake my head fast. "Okay so I think too much, I think about bad things, but I also think about… what you and I should do this summer. And if, like, if we had kids, would we do genetic testing first. And if"—I catch my breath—"if we should be Sverdlov-Deckler-Garfinkel or Garfinkel-Sverdlov-Deckler."

He clears his throat. "Or Sverdlov-Garfinkel-Deckler," he says. "That'd be weird."

I do some kind of laugh-sob. "Or that. And I know that those are not responsible things to think about, because we've known each other for not even five months, so I'm not saying we actually do anything about the fact that I'm thinking these things, I'm saying… I mean that's my point, that they're irresponsible and ridiculous and sappy and I'm thinking about them. I've been thinking about them for a long time. So while I'm overthinking everything else, I'm overthinking that *too*. I am in this. I am so in this that it's embarrassing. But I'm going to try to stop being embarrassed and just…and just be in this."

He nods.

I say, "Oh, there's an ending, wait. I…okay, and…and for what it's worth, I'm in love with you."

He smiles, slow and big, his face lighting up like a jack-o'-lantern.

"I think…I think Sverdlov-Garfinkel-Deckler?" he says after a moment. "I want to really confuse people."

I sniffle. "Sounds good."

"Okay."

"So…is that good?" I say. "Is that yes enough?"

"Really just yes would have been fine," he says.

"I hate you. I hate you so much."

"Are you going to come here and kiss me now?"

"Yeah," I say, but he catches me halfway and kisses me so hard I see stars.

Or maybe that's just the moonlight.

Sick Girl loves Sick Boy.

We sit on the sidewalk outside his building and talk for a long time. We haven't gone two days without talking in months, and it's weird how much we have to catch up on. I tell him about the thing that happened with Ashley, and he tells me about Nadia's new friend at school. His moms sent him a postcard. And my mom got dumped by his dad. I thought maybe I'd feel a little bad, but I don't.

"That reminds me," he says, taking out his phone. "She gave my dad… Hang on, I have it in my phone."

"This better not be some kind of STD picture."

"Yes, I have a junk shot of my dad on my phone," Sasha says.

I make like I'm gonna get up and walk away, and he laughs and pulls me back down.

Gently.

"It's a phone number," Sasha says. "After my dad

explained everything to her, she wanted you to have it. Here."

"Oh," I say.

"I'll text it to you, okay? Whether you want to use it, that's up to you. But at least you know how to find her now. If you want to."

"Yeah," I say. "Thanks."

I lean my head against his shoulder, and we sit there on the sidewalk a while longer, watching the Empire State Building spear into the sky. It's lit up green tonight.

I'm not even thinking about the number, not right now.

I missed him so much.

SHOULD SICK GIRL CALL HER MOM?

Honestly? Yeah, I think you should. You have so many unanswered questions, and she deserves to have to answer them. She shouldn't just be able to walk away and forget about how much she hurt you. Call her and yell at her. Otherwise you're just going to wonder forever, and maybe she's going to think you're okay.

— Maura Cho, 16, best friend

Yeah. I mean…yes, she messed up, but that was about your dad, not you. Clearly, she wants to reach out to you; she's just trying to be respectful, so she wants it to be on your terms instead of her just calling you. That's kind of the best possible thing she could do at this point, right? I think you should at least hear what she has to say. I mean, someday you're going to run into her again, like some cousin is going to get married or something and you're going to see her so at least this way you're controlling when it happens. Facing your demons and all that. Plus, she's your mom. She gave birth to you. She deserves a phone call. And if she doesn't deserve anything after that, then that's up to you. But you should do one phone call.

— Luna Williams, 16, junior

I don't know, girl. My gut wants to say yes, but I would really understand if you didn't. I'm not sure I could do it. But also, I just… God. I don't even know how you've gotten through the past six months. I can't imagine a mom doing this to her kid. How do you give advice on something like this? It wasn't supposed to happen.

—*Siobhan O'Brian, 17, senior*

*Y*ou're asking people about your mom, now? I'm so confused. You're not supposed to be crowdsourcing your life, but it feels like talking about your mom is progress? You're so confusing.

—*Claire Lennon, 17, dead*

*W*hatever you decide to do, I'll support you.

—*Sasha Sverdlov-Deckler, 16, patient*

CHAPTER TWENTY-TWO

I'm sitting at my desk at eleven thirty in the morning on Saturday, the last weekend in March. There are birds screaming outside and a number entered on my phone, and my thumb hovers over the green button. I'm about to tap it or erase the number or do *something* when a text pops up.

Sasha: **Come over?**

I don't hesitate.

Sasha and I watch a movie in his room, my head resting against his collarbone while he does a nebulizer treatment to open his lungs up. It's a good movie, this coming-of-age thing from Sundance, but I can't concentrate.

"Should we have sex?" I say.

He starts coughing. I wait patiently.

"Are you trying to break my lungs?" he says.

"No. I'm just wondering."

"Like right now?" he says. "We're in the middle of a movie."

"No, just like…in general. We've been together for a few months now. I'm just wondering if it's something that you're thinking about. It's okay if you're not."

"Ibby, I'm a red-blooded bisexual with my hot girlfriend

lying on my chest. Of course I'm thinking about it."

"Oh, you're going with bisexual officially?"

"Yeah, well, I've been staring at the love interest this whole movie instead of the lead girl, so I feel like I should at least try it out."

"Yeah, he's pretty cute."

"He can wait." He reaches for his remote and pauses the movie. "Have you ever done it before?" he says.

I shake my head.

"Me neither," he says. I don't know if I'm supposed to act surprised by that just for his ego or whatever, but I pretty much know his life backward and forward at this point.

"Do you have condoms?" I ask.

"Yeah…"

I sit up. "Well…do you want to? Because I want to."

"I do, I just…"

I wait for him to finish his sentence, but he never does. I say, "Oh my God, you're nervous!"

"Shut up."

"I've never seen you nervous in a situation that doesn't involve ordering food before. Or phones."

"Is this how you seduce guys? You mock them?"

"Yeah."

"I'm just worried about my shitty body," he says.

"No, I planned for that already."

He takes a pull off the nebulizer, one eyebrow up. "You planned for my shitty body?"

"Yeah," I say. He laughs. "What! I don't want to like crush your organs. I figured I'd be on top, so we wouldn't have to worry about putting pressure on your stomach, and I'd kind of…angle myself. Like this." I slide my hips forward.

He puts a hand over his eyes. "Ibby."

"Oh my God, you're not supposed to *cover your eyes.*"

"I'm sorry, it's a little weird to see you fully clothed and, like, miming sex positions with the quilt my bubbe made for me." He peeks through his fingers, nebulizer mouthpiece dangling out of his mouth like a cigar. "Plus that's not even what I was talking about," he says.

"Okay, then what."

He says, "You realize you've never seen me with my shirt off."

"You're worried I won't like your shitty body?"

He scoffs. "What? No, you think I give a shit if you enjoy looking at my shitty body? If I have to live in it you can fucking *look* at it, you'll survive."

"Okay good."

"What I'm worried about," he says, "is how *I will feel* if you don't like my shitty body. It's a very important difference."

"Nuance."

"Yeah, nuance."

"I have *never* seen you openly self-conscious before," I say.

"Well, you've never tried to get me naked before," he says. He cocks his head to the side. "It's a pretty gruesome sight."

"This isn't working. You're not scaring me away."

He groans. "And yet *I'm* still scared, and I've told you I'm solely concerned with my feelings on the issue."

"Right. Your reaction to my reaction."

"Exactly."

"Okay," I say. "Tell you what. I'll make you a deal."

"I'm listening."

"Simple deal. One-to-one trade. You take off your shirt, I take off my shirt."

He points at me, hesitating. "I'm interested. Question, though."

"Go for it."

"How does your bra play into this?"

"Oh, okay, good question. Um, okay, first I take my shirt off, then you take yours off on good faith, then I take my bra off. Fair?"

"Is it a stick-on bra?"

"Sasha, what? Girls don't just walk around in stick-on bras."

"*Look.* I think they're fascinating now. It's your fault."

"I'm taking off my shirt now," I say.

"Hang on!" He shuts off the nebulizer and hurries to his bedroom door and locks it. "Okay, go ahead."

I pull my T-shirt over my head. I feel very confident while I'm doing it, but as soon as I feel the air on my skin, I'm suddenly very aware that this is the first time a boy has seen me without a shirt in any sort of non-bathing suit situation. I try to project confidence.

He gestures toward me. "Oh, come on, that's not fair. You look like that and it's supposed to inspire me to show you my grotesqueness? You look amazing and I want to staple my shirt to my body."

"Sasha," I say.

He groans.

"Look, I have a belly, too." I grab it and shake it.

"That's not the same," he says. "I look like I'm

pregnant with twins. You look like you're…sitting down."

"Fine, I'll just put my shirt back on."

"No…"

"Then take yours off."

"Can't we have sex with my shirt on?" he says.

"Sure, yeah, we could, this time. But at some point, I'm going to see you with your shirt off. It's going to happen."

"That's true," he says.

"It's just me," I say. "Plus, then I'll take my bra off."

"Sure, if you don't run screaming into the night."

"It's day."

"Well, that's how long you'll be screaming." He wheezes out a sigh. "All right," he says, and he pulls his shirt over his head. He looks at the ground.

"It's not that bad," I say, which might not have been the perfect thing to say but feels better than saying *there's nothing weird about it* or *what stomach?* He doesn't want to hear that. I don't like when people pretend I'm normal.

"I look like John Hurt in *Alien*," he says.

I reach behind my back to unfasten my bra and wince a little.

"You okay?" he says.

"Yeah, can you do it?"

He comes back over to me, still avoiding eye contact. He kneels in front of the bed and reaches around behind my back to undo the hooks. I let it fall forward off my shoulders.

"Oh, fuck," he whispers.

"Feel better now?"

He cups the back of my head and kisses me.

My legs are still shaky when I get home that evening. I'm turning on the oven to reheat some of the pizza Sasha and I ordered for lunch when my dad comes in.

Act normal, act normal. "Hi," I say. "Want me to put a piece in for you?"

"Yeah, thanks." He kisses my forehead. "How was your day?"

"It was fine. I hung out with Sasha. And his family."

"How are they?"

"They're good. His mom called while I was there, so I said hi to her for the first time. They're in Tanzania, and they're about to move all the way across the country for some new project." I turn the dial on the oven.

"And how's Sasha?"

"He's good, too. He's doing some project on Machu Picchu where he has to build a model out of clay. His lungs have been giving him trouble lately, but the last round of ERT helped a lot."

"Must be hard," Dad says.

"It is, sometimes." I slide the pan into the oven. "But it helps having someone who understands."

And he laughs. He laughs at me. It's just this soft little chuckle, but for some reason that's the last straw.

I stand up and cross my arms.

"It's not as if you and he are...the same."

I look at the chair at the kitchen table where I used to sit and drink Shirley Temples and pretend it was medicine and someone was taking care of me.

"No," I say. "No, it's the same. It's not... It's not identical, but it's the same experience. And it's not something that healthy people understand."

My dad doesn't say anything.

"I'm sick," I say. "And I don't wish that I wasn't. And I don't really care how uncomfortable that makes you anymore."

"It doesn't make me uncomfortable," he says, and I just shrug my shoulders, and he suddenly has something he needs to check on his phone. I want to run up and hide in my room, but I force myself to stay here, waiting by the oven, not getting out of his way. Not being convenient.

It's been a pretty big day for me.

"So did you end up calling your mom?" Sasha asks me. We're walking back to his place, licking ice-cream cones the next day. It's sunny and bright, and I would skip if I had another person's body.

"Oh, I didn't tell you?"

He shakes his head.

"I decided to call the prison where my sister is instead," I say.

"The credit-card-fraud sister?"

"Yeah. I got a mailing address for her, and I sent her a care package."

"Huh," Sasha says. "I thought she was awful."

"She's not great," I say. "But…I thought I wanted to call my mom, but then I really thought about it, and the urge that I actually had was to reach out to somebody and be the bigger person, but I didn't actually want to talk to or interact with or think about my mother in any way. So I did something else."

He's smiling at me.

"What?" I say, even though I know what.

He licks his ice-cream cone. "I just think you're the most incredible person I've ever met."

Well, I wasn't expecting *that.*

"You're not so bad yourself," I say, and I skip just for a few steps.

WHAT'S THE WORST THING THAT COULD HAPPEN?

That's a good way of looking at it, I think. Just do it! What's the worst that could happen? Probably not as bad as you think. Probably nothing you can't get through.

> —*Linda Janis, 44, surgical nurse at Linefield and West Memorial Hospital*

I would say…death. It seems to me it would be death.

> —*Hwan Cho, 52, father*

Oh God, don't get me started thinking about that; I'll never stop. I'm trying to be more prepared, though. I feel like I'm always… I don't know. I'm sick of being the one who doesn't see what's going on.

> —*Maura Cho, 16, best friend*

So if we're looking at this statistically, the three deadliest natural disasters of all time took place in China. Makes sense, when you think about population density. However, one of those was in the 1550s, and even the most recent one—that'd be the deadliest, the 1931 China floods—was, as you can tell from the name, more than a minute ago. If you look at stuff that's more recent, say, since the 1970s, now you have to start worrying about other areas of Asia, mostly India and Pakistan. And, of course, Indonesia. So that brings us to what I think is, as far as I can see, the biggest threat to us right now as a human race, which is the Lake Toba supervolcano in Indonesia. It's the largest volcanic lake in the world, located on this *really* populated island, like fifty million people. Plus, it's close to the ocean so, yeah, more tsunamis. Last time it exploded it unleashed, like, a metric fuck-ton of shit, give or take a few, and some scientists are doing studies that make it look like it could explode again at any point. So I think that's something we all need to be concerned about, and that's probably the worst thing that could happen. Everything else is doable.

— *Sasha Sverdlov-Deckler, 16, realist*

That sounds like the Ibby I know and love.

— *Claire Lennon, 17, dead*

CHAPTER TWENTY-THREE

"So, like, asking if you wanted to help carry Luna's books when she sprained her ankle…" Maura says.

"Right, that's a good example." We're stretched out on her bed with about twenty bottles of nail polish. She's working on her toes while I do my fingers. It's a little after ten at night on a Thursday, and we've already had dinner with her parents and studied for our Spanish test, so this is our reward. Maura lives in Forest Hills, the same neighborhood as my dad's hospital, in a very cramped and impeccably decorated apartment. "That made me feel like this thing that's wrong with me is old and boring and not important when something new comes up. Like Luna's temporary injury is more valid than this thing I live with every day. Not that her sprained ankle wasn't valid, but… it made me feel like you're sick of my thing. And it's not going anywhere, so what am I supposed to do with that?"

"I think it was like…" She paints on a stripe of nail polish. "We didn't want you to feel like you were less capable."

"And I appreciate that, but I don't actually need to feel more capable. I need to feel like it's okay to *not* be more capable."

Maura flops backward on the bed. "This is so complicated. I'm not complaining, it's just, I don't want to get it wrong."

"I know, but once you get the idea of it, it all kind of

starts to come together. It's not a list of rules to memorize; it's just a mindset."

"Okay, but, like…right now you're sitting here doing your nails, and it's like I'm supposed to expect that you couldn't ever do that."

"Yeah, today's a good day," I say. "But it's better to not expect good days, 'cause then they're a nice surprise instead of everyone getting disappointed when I'm not having a good day. This isn't the usual." My phone rings over on her nightstand, and I blow on my nails.

"Who's calling you?" she says.

"Sasha. I told him I was with you tonight." I look at it and consider not picking up.

"So scold him for bothering you," Maura says.

"Good point." I reach for my phone, trying not to smudge my nails. "Hey."

"Isabel, it's Dmitri."

Sasha's dad, calling me from his phone. And his voice sounds funny.

Everything kind of slows down.

"What's wrong?" I say.

"Everything's all right. Sasha's okay. But we're at the hospital."

He's not supposed to be at the hospital today. "What happened?"

"His spleen ruptured. We were on the train, and it stopped suddenly, and someone elbowed him in the stomach and…that was enough."

Shit, shit, shit. "Do they have to take it out?"

Maura tugs on my pants with worry on her face. I hold up my hand.

"They do," Dmitri says. "They're bringing him into surgery as soon as they can, but if you—Nick, hold on—if you can get here soon, you can see him before he goes in. He's in a lot of pain, but he wants to see you."

"Yeah, I'm in Forest Hills already. I can be there in ten minutes." I start gathering my stuff. "How's he doing, can't they drug him?"

"They are. They're going to sedate him soon, before they bring him in for surgery. That should help." Dmitri sounds pretty calm, all things considered, and I grab onto that like a life raft.

"Okay," I say. "I'm leaving now. I'll be there soon."

"What's wrong?" Maura asks as soon as I hang up.

"Sasha has to have surgery; it's an emergency."

"Holy shit, is he okay?"

"He'll be fine, I just— Do you know where my socks are?"

"Yeah, here," she says. I tug them on and then my shoes and start messing with my phone. "Who are you calling?" she asks.

"No one, I'm getting an Uber. I don't want to wait for a cab."

"In this traffic, either one's gonna take way longer than walking," Maura says. "It's just, like, six blocks."

It's eight blocks. I take a deep breath. "I'm taking an Uber."

"Seriously, it'll be easier to—"

"*Maura*," I say. "I'm taking an Uber."

don't know this girl at the front desk. She's probably a volunteer. Ordinarily I would blow right past, but they're strict about visitor's badges in the pre-op areas. I lean on the desk and try to smile. "Hi. I'm here to see, um, Aleksandr. Sverdlov-Deckler." I spell it for her.

She types on her computer for a really, really long time. I'm holding my keys just to have something to do with my hands, and I dig the teeth of one of them into my thumb. "I'm not seeing him," she says.

"Yeah, he just got here; he might not be in the system yet. Can you try Sasha?"

"Sasha…"

"Sverdlov-Deckler, yeah."

She shakes her head. "I'm not getting anything."

"He's in pre-op, can I go up? I know where it is, my dad's a doctor here, I've been walking around this hospital since I was two. It's my boyfriend, he's scared, I…please? Can I just get a badge? Please."

She sighs and takes out a visitor's badge. "What was the name?"

"Sverdlov-Deckler." I swallow. "Aleksandr."

I grab the badge and head to the elevator and push the button for the floor about a hundred times. "Come on come on come on."

I text Sasha's dad on the way up to get the room number—why didn't I ask for that on the phone?—but he doesn't answer. It's fine. I can poke around pre-op. But the first things I see when I get off the elevator are Sasha's little brothers kneeling and playing with one of those clunky wood-and-wire puzzles in the waiting room. Nick runs over and stops me before the woman watching them, probably a nurse or a social worker, can stop him.

"It's okay," I say to her. I give Nick a hug. "Hey, short stuff."

"Sasha's sick," he says.

"Yeah, do you know which room he's in?"

"Uh-uh."

I take his hand and bring him back to Josh and the woman with them. Her hair's down, so I'm thinking social worker. Nurses never wear their hair down. "Do you know which room their brother's in?" I ask.

She says, "I think it's eleven forty-two."

"Perfect. Thank you."

Eleven forty-two is about as far from the waiting room as you can get. No wonder Dmitri left the kids with a social worker. I head through hallway after hallway. There's a woman wailing in one room, and it carries all the way through the floor.

Eleven forty-two. I pause with my fingers on the handle.

Relax, I tell myself.

You've seen him in the hospital before.

Splenectomies are easy surgeries.

They do a hundred of them a day.

This is part of what you signed up for. This is real life.

I turn the handle.

Sasha's curled up as small as he can get, facing away from me, and something about that seems wrong, like it's not allowed and he's supposed to be stretched out neatly in his bed, filling it like people always do on TV. Dmitri's sitting next to him, Sasha's hand clasped tightly in his, and he looks up when the door opens. The room's divided by a green curtain, and on the other side, a doctor's talking quietly to someone. Dr. Yates. I know her. That doesn't matter right now. I'm not thinking straight.

Dmitri smiles at me and touches Sasha's arm. "Hey, bud. Isabel's here."

He rolls over very slightly as I come to the bed. His eyes are swollen, and his hair's tamped down with sweat. He grabs onto my shirt, and I kiss him lightly. His lips are really chapped. "Hey," I say softly. "You good?"

"I'm Frida," he says.

I push his hair off his forehead. "What?"

"I had a train accident."

I laugh a little. "I guess you did. How are you?"

He closes his eyes. "Hurts." I see him squeeze his dad's hand.

"I know." I can't stop touching him. His cheek, his shoulder, his arm. Right in front of his dad. But he's still hanging on to me, and I just feel like something really bad is going to happen if I take my hands off him. Like he'll just vanish.

"Did you see my brothers?" he says.

"Yeah, they're with the social worker, they're fine."

He nods, eyes still closed.

"They're doing the surgery tonight?" I ask.

He licks his lips. "Yeah. They said it's not gonna take very long."

"That's good."

He winces and pushes his head back into his pillow. His whole lower body is curled up to his stomach, like he's trying to protect it. "Fucking *hurts*!" he says, yelling the last word.

"I know," Dmitri says.

"How much longer is it gonna be?" Sasha asks him. "I just want them to knock me out. This is fucking…" He blows air out of his mouth.

"Hey," I say. "You're doing great. Do you want me to find your nurse?" There's a white board on the wall with the name of his surgeon and his nurse. Betsy. I don't know her.

"Yeah," Sasha says. "Find out why the fuck they won't give me more morphine."

"I'll do my best."

"Thank you. I love you."

I smile. "I love you, too."

I talk to four different nurses who lead me down three different hallways before I finally find Betsy. Even though I try to channel Sasha instead of being my appeasing self, she gives me the answer I was expecting—no more morphine, and they'll get to him soon.

"He's in a lot of pain," I say. "And he's upset, and this is going to be a long recovery for him… He's the one with Gaucher disease."

She pats my arm. "I know Sasha."

I didn't give any indication she could touch me, and I'm really pissed off about it. "Okay, but…he's not used to this, this sudden kind of thing. Emergencies like this, he's not used to it. He's scared, and he just wants to know what's going on."

"I know as much as you do, unfortunately," she says. "The OR schedule depends on how long it takes the surgeons to do the people in front of him. If someone takes longer than usual…"

"Right, but—"

"He'll be in as soon as we can," she says.

"And he can't drink anything? He's really thirsty. Not even like some ice chips?"

"No, I'm sorry." She gets a page and starts to walk away.

I say, "Can you please give me something I can go back in there and tell him?"

"Just tell him it'll be soon," she calls over her shoulder.

"Great, thank you," I mumble. Maybe I should get my dad down here. Have him pull some strings. I hate myself for even considering it, but…it's Sasha.

I head back to his room. Dmitri's outside, just finishing a phone call as I walk up. "Is everything okay?" I say.

"I'm trying to find a sitter who can come get the boys and bring them home, but I can't find anyone last-minute," he says. "Nadia's at a friend's house. Can you stay with Sasha until I can bring them home and…"

"And what," I say gently. "Leave the boys alone all night? I'll bring them home."

"No, I can't ask you to—"

"Yeah you can, because this is what makes sense," I say. "They're gonna bring Sasha in soon and I can't be with him in recovery anyway. You can. It makes no sense for you to be at home when you could be here with him."

"Are you sure?" he says.

"Please? Let me help. I…I need to do something."

He nods. "Yeah, I know that feeling. Okay." He takes his key ring out of his pocket and pulls one out. "And let me get you money for a cab."

"It's fine," I say.

"No," he says firmly, and he hands me a few twenties—a cab from Forest Hill to Chelsea is not cheap—from his wallet. "The boys will be very excited. They never get to ride in cabs." He pushes his hair back and laughs a little. I'd never noticed how much he looks like Sasha.

"You don't have to worry," I say. "I'm good with kids."

"I know," he says. "And you don't, either. Sasha... He's gonna be fine."

"I know. I'll come back in the morning and see him? I can take the kids to school first and everything."

"No, no, I'll come home in the morning and take care of that. He should be okay to be alone for a little by then. And don't you have school?"

I wave my hand.

"Fair enough," he says. "But if your dad asks, I told you to go to school."

"Okay."

He smiles, then says, "Oh, you should know, typically he doesn't do great on anesthesia. It's because he's so anemic, I think. It just takes him a while to get it through his system. So he's probably still going to be pretty out of it when you get here tomorrow."

"Okay."

Dmitri nods.

"I'm just..." I point at the door. "I'm gonna go say goodbye to him real quick?"

"Sure, of course." He steps out of the way.

"Thanks."

Sasha's on his other side now, so he sees me when I come through the door. "Hi," he says. "What'd she say?"

"She says soon."

"Morphine?"

"No more morphine."

He breathes out. "Damn."

"I know." I pull his dad's chair around to the other side of the bed and take both his hands. His cuticles are red and irritated where he's always bothering them. They're the only part of him that isn't ghost pale, besides the pink around his eyes.

"I'm really scared," I say. "I probably shouldn't tell you that. Should just be letting you be scared."

He shrugs a little, winces. "I'm not scared, honestly. Just in pain. But I'm not scared."

"Small favors, I guess."

"Yeah. It's just a thing. We'll take care of it and... God. It just hurts right now."

"I know."

"Don't decide I'm too much work and break up with me."

"Come on. Don't do the thing."

He smiles. "Okay."

"We're not gonna suddenly become those people because you have to have minor surgery. That's gross. Plus, at least right now you're still. It's the least work you've ever been."

He snorts.

"You just look really sick," I say. "It's weird. We're not supposed to look sick."

"How are you?" he says.

"No, shut up."

He chuckles. "Fair enough."

I rest my head next to his on his pillow. It reminds

me of New Year's Eve, when we lay there watching each other.

"You should be on oxygen," I say quietly.

He watches me. "I'm okay."

I tuck his hair behind his ear. "Still."

He leans into my hand, closes his eyes. His cheek is scratchy against my fingers, and for a minute I really, really hate that I said I'd take his brothers home.

But it's what he asked me about as soon as I came in. It's what makes sense.

It's how I'm part of this, instead of just being someone who's hanging around.

So I kiss him slowly and let him pull away to breathe. "You're leaving, aren't you?" he says. "That was a goodbye kiss."

"Yeah."

"Are you…" He looks down. "Is it too much?"

Five days ago, he had that same look on his face when he was taking off his shirt for us to have sex. Five days ago, we were having sex.

I squeeze his hand too hard. "No. What did I just say? Don't do the thing. That's not us and you know it."

"Sometimes I have to check."

"I'm taking your brothers home."

"You are?"

"Yeah."

He breathes out. "You're in this."

He gets it. Thank fucking God.

Why do I ever think there's a risk this boy isn't going to get me?

"I am in this."

He ducks his head into my collarbone. "Fuck, it hurts."

"Just a little longer, then they'll pull that thing out of you, and you're gonna be a loopy mess all night, and then I'll be here in the morning, okay?"

"My dad's staying?"

"Your dad's staying."

"Okay." He nods.

"You're gonna be fine."

He nods again. "I'm gonna be fine."

"It's his stomach?" Josh says in the back seat of the cab.

"It's his spleen, so, close to his stomach." I point to where I'm pretty sure it is on my own belly. "Right here."

"And they have to take it out?" he says.

"Uh-huh."

"Can you live without a spleen?"

"Of course," I say. "Otherwise they wouldn't take it out."

Nick says, "My friend Sam got his heart taken out." This must be a very strange conversation for the cab driver.

I say, "When they do that they have to put a new heart in. Sasha doesn't have to get a new spleen."

"Then why does he even have one if he doesn't need one?" Nick says.

"Good question," I say, though really I know why we have spleens, because I remember some from Bio and read what I could on the Uber ride to the hospital. Some people with Gaucher actually do better without their spleens because cells build up there so quickly, but it's still not like the appendix or anything that literally does nothing. It helps with your immune system, and since Sasha already has a crappy immune system from being so anemic…this is probably going to make things harder, forever.

But I'm not about to tell the kids that.

It's way past their bedtime, and they're both asleep before the cab even gets into Manhattan. I wake them up once we're parked and guide them to the elevator and up to their apartment. Nick's so sleepy that he'd walk into walls if I'd let him. I have them brush their teeth and get into bed, and as soon as they're asleep I realize how tired I am.

I think about sleeping in Sasha's bed, but it just feels so disrespectful, plus it'd be really embarrassing if Dmitri came home in the morning and found me there. So after I text my dad, explaining what's going on, I start setting up a little bed on the couch, just as the sound of a key in the lock makes me jump about a foot.

It's Nadia. "God, you scared the shit out of me," I say.

"Sorry."

"I thought you were at a sleepover," I say.

"I was, but I…" She shrugs. "I felt like I should be home."

Sasha will be disappointed. He's been so happy she's making friends. But any friend who doesn't understand leaving because your brother's having surgery is probably not a friend she needs to have.

"Why are you here?" she says.

"Oh, I'm watching your brothers. Or I was, I guess. I can go now that you're here."

"You don't have to," she says, so clearly my offer to leave sounded as sincere as it felt. I just don't want to go home right now, even if it is closer to the hospital. I don't want to deal with the fifty questions my dad's already texting me. I just want to be here with three people who already understand everything, even if they are kids. And be close to Sasha's stuff, even if he's not here.

"Okay," I say.

"It's good he's at his hospital," she says. She sets her stuff down on the coffee table. "It sucks when he has to go to the ER and they don't know him or anything."

I nod. "Plus my dad's in charge there, so if anything happens…"

"Yeah, that's good." She breathes out heavily. "I talked to my dad and told him I'd get the boys to school tomorrow," she says. "So you don't have to worry about that."

"Okay. Thanks."

She shifts her weight from foot to foot. "You don't have to be worried, okay?" she says. "Sasha always gets through everything."

"Yeah. And a splenectomy's an easy surgery."

"It is?"

"Yeah."

She nods. "That's good."

I smile at her. "Yeah, it is."

She clears her throat. "Are you gonna go see him in the morning?"

"Yeah."

"He has kind of a hard time every time they have to put him under, so you should be prepared for that."

"Your dad told me already," I say.

"Okay. Good. Well, um…I'm gonna go to bed, I think. Thanks. For getting the boys home."

"Of course."

"Night, Ibby." She goes to her room and shuts the door.

I really love that girl.

I turn off the lights in the living room and the kitchen and crawl into my makeshift bed. I hear all those noises you always hear when it's quiet in a place you don't know: a clock ticking, the hum of the refrigerator, traffic outside that's a different frequency from the traffic at home.

I wonder if he's in surgery yet.

I wonder if they've called his mom.

What time is it in Tanzania?

They probably wouldn't want to wake her up for this. For all of them, this is just a thing, like Sasha said. It's just something that happens. They're tired, but they're not scared.

I'm scared, but honestly I'm surprised how much of me is just tired.

He hates being in pain.

I try to sleep for what must be an hour, but every time I close my eyes I see flashes of scalpels and Sasha's miserable red eyes. Finally I give up and go to his room. I pretend like I'm just going to get one of his T-shirts to sleep with, but as soon as I'm in there, I curl up in his bed and bury my face in his pillow.

Cinnamon.

HOW ARE YOU FEELING?

I'm fine. How's Sasha?

    — Luna Williams, 17, dancer

Doing all right, thanks for asking. It was a long night, but it's gonna get easier from here. Always does. Easier and easier until it's not, right? I'm sorry, I'm not making any sense. Is there coffee on this floor?

    — Dmitri Sverdlov-Deckler, 39, father

You know what? It's gonna be a good day. I can tell. So you can go ahead and jot that down. I'm feeling like it's gonna be a good day.

    — Yvette Laurence, 27, surgical nurse

Sore. Next time, you think you could *start* the night in a bed instead of on a lumpy couch? You don't stop having arthritis just because your boyfriend's spleen falls apart, remember?

    — Claire Lennon, 17, dead

CHAPTER TWENTY-FOUR

"Isabel?"

I startle and open my eyes. Nadia's standing over me.

And I'm sleeping in Sasha's bed. That's awkward.

Oh God, right. Sasha.

I sit up as quickly as I can, even though it makes every joint I have scream in protest. "Hey," I say.

"Hi. I don't know if you drink coffee or anything? I don't know how to make it."

"No, it's fine." I can't find my phone. I must have left it out in the living room before I came in here to sleep. "Any news?"

She nods. "He's awake, sort of. Dad said he had a rough night, kept waking up really confused and in a lot of pain, but that's kind of standard for him… He's always really groggy for a long time. He's mostly just sleeping, Dad said."

"He's okay?"

"Yeah, he's good."

I breathe out and sink my head into my hands. She laughs a little.

"You get used to it," she says. "That's probably hard to believe right now."

"It's not, actually," I say. "You guys make it seem possible."

She shrugs. "I'm gonna take the boys to school before

my first class," she says.

"You sure? I can do it."

"No, I know where their school is and everything. It's just easier."

"Okay. I have your dad's key, so I can lock up."

"Are you going to the hospital?"

"Yeah, I just need to take a shower first," I say.

I don't take a shower. I take a bath, and I tell myself I'm going to be quick and I'm only going to stay in for as long as it takes for my joints to relax a little, but I end up closing my eyes and thinking back to the first time I did this. How strange it felt, and how new Sasha was. He was just this boy whose tub I was using. He wasn't…

Everything was so simple. People don't tell you that being patiently miserable can be a lot less work than being happy. Miserable is just a baseline. Happy, there are always steps. There is always so much that can go wrong.

He's just this fragile thing with swollen organs and bird bones, walking around for breaking and being loved.

I just want to stay in the tub, just for a minute.

How can loving someone as much as I love him be this delicate?

My wrist throbs in the water.

We're so delicate.

I can't wait to see him, though.

He's got a room, now. The woman at the front desk — same one as last night; doesn't she sleep? — gives me a tag with 319 and "Alexander Svedler-Deckler" on it. Close enough.

When I get to the third floor, though, Kayla, a nurse I've known for as long as I can remember, holds up her hand to me the second I get off the elevator. She's on the phone, so I have to stand at the desk waiting for her to get off it, and she doesn't seem to be in any sort of hurry. I try to look pleasant and not like I want to strangle her.

Finally she hangs up. "Are you here to see Sasha?" she says.

"Yeah."

She leans over the desk and scrunches up her face. It's that face you give a little kid when you're about to tell them something they don't want to hear and you're hoping they don't throw a temper tantrum. "His dad wanted me to tell you that it might be better if you come back tomorrow."

"Why?"

"He's having some trouble with the anesthesia—"

"I know that," I say.

"—and he's a little agitated right now. I think his dad was worried it might upset you."

"I'm not a child," I say. "I'm not going to get my feelings hurt if Sasha isn't nice to me when he's drugged up the morning after surgery."

"Why don't you just come back tomorrow?" she says. "He'll be in better shape by then."

"That's the point," I say.

She sighs. "Look, I'm just passing on the message."

"Did Dmitri say I *can't* see him?"

"No, but—"

"Then I'm gonna go."

She rolls her eyes and sits down. "Go ahead."

Sasha's blanket on the floor is the first thing I notice. There's a nurse standing at the foot of the bed, and Dmitri's standing up next to him, both hands on Sasha's arm. Sasha was in the middle of saying something, but he stops when I come in. He squints at me like he hasn't seen me in years. "Isabel?"

"Hi," I say. "What's going on?"

"I need to get out of here," he says.

Dmitri says, "He's pretty confused."

"I know," I say.

"I'm *not* confused," Sasha says, and he kicks his feet. I'm guessing that's how the blanket ended up on the floor. The nurse tries to hold his feet down, but Sasha tries to sit up, and not in a nice, gentle, post-surgical way.

"Hey hey hey." I come to the side of the bed Dmitri's not on and put my hand on his shoulder. "You're gonna rip your stitches if you do that."

He pulls his arm away. "Let go of me."

Dmitri says, "He doesn't mean — "

"I know," I say.

Sasha reaches up and tries to rip the oxygen cannula out of his nose, but his hand is slow and clumsy and he can't make it do what he wants, and that just makes him even more pissed off. He tries to sit up again, and Dmitri takes both his shoulders and holds him down.

"Get *off of me!*" Sasha yells.

Dmitri looks at the nurse. "I really think we need those restraints."

"All right," she says, and she leaves.

"He's gonna hate that," I say.

Dmitri sighs. "Last time he went under general, he

was…smaller."

"Stop talking about me like I can't hear you!" Sasha says. "I'm not supposed to be here. This isn't *right*. Something's *wrong*."

"Sasha," I say, and he looks at me, and God, he doesn't look confused. His eyes are so clear and sure.

"Please," he says, and it's the exact same voice he uses when he's asking me for something real. When he knows what's going on.

It's hard.

I tuck his hair behind his ear. "I know this doesn't feel right. You just gotta trust us and get through this part, okay?"

"Fuck you," he says. "I don't want you here."

Dmitri says, "He doesn't mean—"

I feel like I'm about to scream at him, and it's not his fault, but dude, *come on.* "You really can stop saying that," I say. "I understand."

"He's gonna tire himself out soon, anyway," Dmitri says.

"I have to *go*," Sasha says, and then he gags, and Dmitri quickly turns him onto his side and grabs the basin on the counter next to the sink and gets it under his mouth right before he throws up.

"He's been doing a lot of this, too," Dmitri says, rubbing his back.

Sasha's shaking so hard. I put my hand on his hip and whisper "Shh shh shh" as his body jerks.

"I hate this," he whimpers once he's done, and after that he just sobs until he falls asleep.

The rest of the day is just that, basically, fits of confusion broken up by bouts of sleeping. But the sleeping stretches get longer and longer, and he seems a little less angry every time he wakes up. His oxygen levels won't stay steady, so they switch the cannula out for a mask, and he seems a lot less upset after that, and I'm really pissed it took them that long to do it. Not as pissed as Dmitri, who, it turns out, had been fighting for that since the second Sasha was out of surgery. I sit in Sasha's room while he barks orders at his doctor in the hallway.

He was only six years older than me when Sasha was born.

"Your dad loves you so much," I whisper to Sasha. He's asleep, breathing hard through his nose and fussing with the bandage over his IV, no matter how many times I stop him. I run my hand down his arm and feel him stretched skinny and tight like a tree branch.

"You're doing great," I tell him.

I should probably eat something. Sasha's been asleep for over an hour, and I've just been playing on my phone while Dmitri's passed out in the armchair. It's almost three in the afternoon, and I haven't eaten anything besides a packet of pretzels from the vending machine. Nadia will be here soon to visit, and I'm just going to be taking up space. I kiss Sasha's scratchy cheek and go down to the cafeteria, but once I'm on the floor, I end up ducking into the bathroom and sitting in the stall just to be alone for a minute.

I take some deep breaths and fan my face. *Keep it*

together. Keep it together.

I don't know how I'm supposed to balance the contrasting truths that today is probably the worst day and he'll be back to normal tomorrow, and that if I'm really in this for the long haul, then a minorly bad reaction after a routine surgery is nothing compared to what we're going to have to face down the road. That first thought is enough to keep me going, but it feels irresponsible to cling to that. It makes me feel like someone who needs something to cling to, and I don't want to be that person. That's not what he deserves.

He's just *so upset*, and he doesn't even know why.

And I am so tired. I am tired all the way through my bones. I don't know how I'm even supposed to eat, let alone do anything else, when I'm this tired.

I shouldn't have come in here and sat down. I have to keep moving.

I wash my hands and go out into the cafeteria and start filling a tray with food, and right before I check out, I go back and add another serving of everything. Maurice, the checkout guy, asks me how Sasha's doing while I figure out how to balance two plates of pizza on my arms and stuff the sodas into my purse.

"He's doing great," I say.

He says, "You know you two are our little resident couple. We better all be invited to the wedding."

"We'll try to make you proud," I say.

I walk slowly toward the atrium so the plates don't fall and take the elevator up to five. I probably should have texted first to see if my dad was in his office, but there he is, sitting at his desk. I wonder if he misses when he got to actually get up and do things. He probably does. He used to be happier.

I wonder if he really believed he was going to get to spend more time with us.

I think he did.

He looks up and smiles when I come through his door. "Hey, munchkin," he says.

"I brought lunch."

"I can see that." He pushes the paperwork he's filling out aside. "Pull up a chair."

I do. "I hope grape soda's okay."

"It's perfect." He takes the plates away from me and sets them out in front of us. "How's Sasha doing?"

"The surgery went well," I say. "But you probably know that already."

He smiles a little. "I asked around."

"Have you been in to see him?"

"Uh-huh, I checked on him when he was in recovery right after he woke up. I'm sure he doesn't remember."

"I don't think he's going to remember anything for a while," I say. "He's still really out of it."

"That's not uncommon," he says.

"Yeah, his dad says it happens every time he gets put under. Because of his anemia, I guess. It's, like, extra strong on him or something." I wave my hand at him. "I don't need the medical explanation."

Dad laughs a little. "All right." He starts to take a bite of his pizza, then cocks his head and looks at me. "How are you doing?" he says.

I shrug. "I'm fine."

"You look tired."

"You're not supposed to tell a woman she looks tired," I say.

"Is that a fact?"

"Mmhmm." I take a bite of my pizza and chew it slowly. "It's just hard. Every time he wakes up I try to calm him down and it doesn't work. And it's not like… He's not normally the kind of person who needs to be calmed down. So I don't have a lot of practice at it. And I know this isn't him, that it's just the drugs or whatever, but at the same time, like, yeah, it is him. He's feeling all this stuff. You know?" I shrug. "It just feels like there's nothing I can do that's right. I feel bad right now that I'm not with him, but I also feel stupid that I've been sitting there mostly just watching him sleep all day. I don't know what I'm doing. And you'd think since I volunteer here I would have some idea, but…"

"It's different," my dad says. "When it's someone you care about, it's different."

"I know that. I just feel like I should still be better at it than, like…someone who's just walked off the street with no experience at this kind of thing, and I don't think I am."

Dad wipes his mouth. "Y'know, one thing I've noticed is when people get some kind of crisis like this, they tend to think they need to turn into a special crisis version of themselves. Someone who's more capable, more logical, more serious."

"And then they wear themselves out," I say. I've heard this lesson before.

"Well, that," he says. "And also, it's not who the people in the crisis want."

"Hmm."

He says, "When something bad happens, you want the people who love you to be around you, and you want them to be acting like themselves, to be familiar, to be all the beautiful and strange things that are the reason that they're in your life. It doesn't really make sense to not act like yourself when something's wrong with someone who loves you, because probably the only thing they really want is the people who make them happy every day. You have to be the same person to remind them that they're still the same person."

I think about this. "Okay...but sometimes you have to be more logical and businesslike or whatever. Sasha's dad is like the nicest guy ever, but he still had to yell at a doctor today because they were too busy to give Sasha the oxygen mask he needed. I get that we're just supposed to be the loved ones and they're supposed to be the doctors, but it's really frustrating when doctors won't do *their* jobs."

"They're very busy," Dad says.

"I am so tired of that excuse. Were they very busy when they told me for a year that nothing was wrong with me? No, they were lazy, and they were writing me off because of assumptions they made about me based on my age and my gender and probably my religion. And a lot of those things apply to Sasha, too, and they apply to every single person here, and I'm not saying all doctors are bad; I'm just saying...why do you guys keep acting so fucking bad? We're really frustrated, and we get to be, because you treat us like we're lying, all the time, like I'm trying to get high off you running another blood test or some shit. It's ridiculous. They can't stand being wrong, because it threatens their egos, so they just keep insisting they're right even when they *know* they screwed up, because they know that there's nothing you can do about it."

"Well, hang on—"

"No," I say. "You guys are messing up a lot of people, and that's just what it comes down to, and I am sick of having to worship doctors when all they do is tell me I'm okay when I tell them I feel terrible and tell me to lose weight and sign a prescription pad, and they won't give my boyfriend a fucking oxygen mask. You want us to do our jobs as loved ones, or as patients? You have to do your jobs so we don't fucking have to do them for you."

"Everyone's trying," he says.

I slump back in my chair. "I know, I know. Everyone's always *trying*." I take a deep breath. "And it's good advice. What you said." I push my pizza around my plate. "You're a good doctor."

"I didn't learn that from being a doctor," he says. "I learned that from being your father." He looks down at his plate. "She left, and you were you. And that was everything."

I look at him.

"You know I…" He clears his throat. "I wouldn't change anything about you."

That's as much as I'm going to get from him, I think.

And it's kind of everything.

I kill time browsing the gift shop to give Sasha's family some more time alone with him and go back to his room at around five. I literally run into Nadia in the waiting room, who tells me her dad's in the bathroom and she's going to make him go home for a few hours to get some sleep.

"That's a good idea," I say. "How's Sasha?"

"Still pretty out of it," Nadia says. "But he knew who I was and everything. Last time he had surgery he didn't recognize me for, like, two days."

God. "That's good," I say.

"You should get some rest, too," Nadia says.

"Yeah, I'm just gonna go in and sleep in his chair, probably. I'll go home after your dad comes back to take over."

"Okay." She looks up. "I like the balloon."

"Seemed better than flowers, lungs considering."

She nods. "Definitely better than flowers."

Dmitri comes back and they both hug me goodbye, and Dmitri thanks me for last night, which I guess he hadn't really had an opportunity to do until now. He looks about as beat as I feel. After they're gone I go into Sasha's room and shut the door. It's a double room, but there's no one in the other half right now.

"Just you and me for a while," I say.

He blinks his eyes open.

"Sorry," I say. "I didn't mean to wake you."

"Hi," he says softly. His breath fogs up the oxygen mask.

"Hi. I got you a present." I hold the balloon between my hands so he can read it. I watch his eyes slowly trace over the words—*Congratulations, it's a boy.*

"It's true," he says, a little bit of a smile on his mouth.

"Yeah, they didn't have any *it's a spleen*, but I figured

you're, you know. Also a boy. So at least it's still accurate."

"How'd it go?" he says. He's been asking that every time he wakes up.

"Good," I say. "Everything went great. Are you feeling better?"

"Hurts," he says.

"Yeah, I bet. Let's see what we can do… Can you scoot over a little?"

"I think so."

"I'll help… Good." I get him closer to the edge of the bed, then I take off my shoes and climb over the rail on the other side and lie down behind him. I curl my body around the shaky, bony curves of him, and he relaxes back into me with a sigh. "Better now?" I say.

"Mmmhmm."

I kiss the back of his neck. "Y'know, the other day when you took your shirt off, I was thinking, 'I like his stomach like this, but I would like it *more* if it had a huge scar running across it.'"

"Too bad," he says. His voice is so small and tired. "Laparoscopic. Just a little scar."

"I can fix that."

He actually laughs a little. "You shouldn't threaten me right now," he says. "I'm very frail."

"Good. That's how I like my men."

He turns his head enough to nestle into my collarbone. "Lucky me."

He's mostly asleep, and I am, too, when he suddenly starts snickering a little. "*It's a boy,*" he mumbles. "You fucking weirdo." We both laugh for a long time.

I knew it would work.

It's eight thirty, and I'm on the train going home. It's a Friday night, and we're headed toward Manhattan, so most of the train is people dressed to go out for the night. Girls in sparkly tops, a few guys in suits. Plenty of people my age or younger, some of them swinging from the poles as I sit and look out the window at the industrial scenery.

And then all of a sudden everything hits me, like a car hitting a wall, and I start crying. And not, like, pretty, private crying, like everyone does on the train from time to time, but gross, sobbing, body-racking crying, like I'm trying to get every feeling I've ever had out of my body, and honestly, maybe I am. I'm just so relieved, and so worried, and I'm so, so, so fucking tired.

Nobody gives me more than a glance, and God, I am so in love with this city that lets me just be a full person outside of my house, surrounded by strangers, lit up with an outer-borough skyline.

And I am even more in love with that boy.

WHAT HAPPENS NEXT?

I mean, you tell me, right? Are you and Ashley just never going to talk to each other again? I mean, what she said was terrible, don't get me wrong, but, I don't know, you're just going to drop someone from your life because they said something terrible? Can you...do that?

— *Luna Williams, 16, actress*

We're collecting donations for a nuclear medicine department, if that's what you mean. How's Sasha doing today?

— *John Garfinkel, 49, Physician in Chief at Linefield and West Memorial Hospital*

It's a series of steps. Like from the bed to the door, and then from the door to the nurses' station, and then a loop. And then after that, who knows how far I'm going to be able to walk. I'm going to be amazing. I'll go to the Olympics in walking. You want to go to Canada? Give me four days, I'll be walking to Canada. Or do you mean what's next in a global sense? I'm still concerned about that volcano I mentioned.

— *Sasha Sverdlov-Deckler, 16, spleenless*

I don't know. And I'm not the type of person who typically copes well with not knowing, but I'm trying. Before we got together but when I could already feel that it was going to happen, I said it was like watching a movie I'd already seen before, but now…actually being in a relationship is like listening to a song you've never heard, and you really like it so far, but there's that anxiety that it's going to fall apart at the chorus. But when you're with someone like Sasha, it's a drumbeat, really, this steady kind of throbbing keeping everything steady. Like a heartbeat. I remember what Siobhan said a long time ago about how a good relationship isn't something you have to gather up strength to do. It's where you recharge. And I think when you're me and Sasha, and you're so tired all the time…that's just not always going to be reality. Sometimes even things you love are going to be too draining. But you've got to be with someone who understands you. That's really all it comes down to. All the complicated rules and compatibility tests… Really, it's so simple it sounds stupid. And the truth is, even when the song is too loud for me, I always love the drumbeat. I don't think people our age get what we have very often. I guess we'd be those people who peak in high school now, except I'm not planning to grow out of this. I'm already old, and Sasha's never going to grow up, so I think we'll be fine. I don't know what happens next, but I know how I'm going to get through it. Close my eyes and feel it all the way through me. You know what happiness is? It's a boy in a hospital bed. Who would have guessed.

—*Isabel Garfinkel, 17, columnist*

CHAPTER TWENTY-FIVE

A lot of splenectomy patients are up and walking around a couple hours after they wake up from surgery. Sasha is not most patients, but we do get him up on his feet when I visit him on Saturday. He makes it from his bed to the armchair, where he promptly falls asleep for three hours, the balloon I got him bopping gently against the ceiling above his head.

"Was I awful yesterday?" he asks me later. His dad's downstairs getting us something to eat, and I'm helping Sasha sponge himself off. "I don't remember anything."

"You were fine," I say.

"So I was awful, but you're not mad about it?"

"Pretty much."

He sighs happily. "I'll take it."

His brothers come to visit that night. They bring board games and run laps around the bed and gently hug Sasha, who manages to stay awake for a full ten minutes at once. Afterwards, I play Monopoly with them on Sasha's tray table while Dmitri stands in the hallway and calls their extended family and fills everyone in. Sasha sleeps through the whole thing.

"You're supposed to walk to the nurses' station today," I say to him on Sunday.

He has his pillow pulled over his head. "I've decided to become a bed person."

"I think you already *are* a bed person," I say.

"Good. Then there's nothing left I have to do today."

I sit down in the chair by his bed. "I'm making you get up later."

"Well, I like the later part." He turns his head and looks at me with those sad eyes. "I feel like crap today."

"I'm sorry. To be fair, you did just have surgery. I don't think you're supposed to be feeling spectacular."

"True. Sorry I'm so boring." He shifts around. "All I do is sleep."

"That's what you're supposed to do in the hospital, right? Relax and be taken care of. Plus, that's why I brought a book." I kick my shoes up and rest my feet on the bed next to his leg and take out the book I finally thought to bring. He rubs my feet until he falls asleep.

I get a text in the middle of the night between Sunday and Monday and I freak out and wake up my dad and he comes to the hospital with me.

Given his lungs they think it's probably pneumonia. He spiked a fever, and they're hoping they don't have to intubate. Nobody can see him except for Dmitri, who doesn't come back to the waiting room. My dad rushes around, getting all the information, and I sit there next to Nadia, and we squeeze hands.

This was supposed to be boring and routine and stressful and exhausting.

This was not supposed to happen.

This can't be happening.

His voice is rough on Tuesday. He blinks his eyes open and gives me a small smile under the oxygen mask.

"You should probably go back to school at some point," he tells me.

"Shut up."

I stop by on Wednesday during my volunteer shift. He's eating green Jell-O, and he has a stack of empty cups already on his tray.

"You know I can hear you coughing from down the hall," I say. "You're disturbing my other patients."

"This isn't even your floor."

"You caught me."

"You look sexy in your polo."

"Thank you."

"You look like you're going to tell me the schedule of events on my senior citizens' cruise."

"Shut up."

"You look like you're about to rattle off a list of what plants were traditionally used as herbal remedies on our nature hike."

"Sasha."

"You look like you're about to buzz in at the mathletes finals to tell me the limit does not exist."

"I'm leaving now."

"No, I have more! Stop! I'm in love with you!"

"*Y*ou feel up for Monopoly yet?" I ask him on Thursday. We're squished into his bed together, eating popcorn I got from the vending machine.

He coughs for a while. He's back to just the cannula now, and he says it's okay, but he sure has been coughing a lot. "Mm," he says. "Maybe tomorrow?"

"We've got all the time in the world," I say.

"How was school today?"

"I don't know." I throw a piece of popcorn into the air and catch it in my mouth. "Do you think it's wrong of me just to cut Ashley out completely? I think the girls think it makes me soulless."

"Well…do you miss her?"

"No. But she's sad."

"You don't have to be friends with someone out of charity," he says.

"I know I don't have to…"

"Do you want to be friends with Ashley?" he asks me. "Yes or no?"

"Yes or no."

I eat a few pieces of popcorn. "No."

"Then there you go. Plus, she's graduating in two months anyway. You'll both move on."

"You're right."

"How's stuff going with your dad?"

"He's…trying." I give Sasha a look. "You know doctors. They're always trying."

"Poor doctors," he says. "We should be more understanding."

"It's very hard for them, having to look at all these sick people."

He nuzzles my shoulder. "Do you want to go to Africa this summer? See my moms?"

I toss a piece of popcorn into his mouth. "Sure."

I draw a Community Chest card. "Gimme ten dollars," I say. "Second prize in a beauty contest."

He hands me a ten. "I got first prize."

"Yeah, they don't give you any money for that."

It's Friday, April twelfth. I realized this morning that this past Monday was the day we would have been in the drip room together again, five months after we first met. It would have been the first time we'd seen each other again, if everything had gone as planned. Except we wouldn't have, because he would have been in the ICU with post-operative pneumonia, and we would have had to have waited another five months.

None of this was supposed to have happened.

He lands on Tennessee and my hotel. "Ah, fuck."

"Can you do it?"

"Yeah, let me mortgage everything I've ever owned."

I look out the window into the hallway and watch the people while he works. It's amazing how many stories are going on all at once in this one hospital. How small Sasha and I and our little coincidences really are, even just in this one building.

What if he hadn't broken his arm?

What if I hadn't been assigned to his floor that day? What if I hadn't gotten up to deliver water? What if he hadn't recognized me? What if he'd been too shy?

What if I'd dated some nice boy at school instead? It's a Friday night. I'd probably be out somewhere, wearing something cute instead of these ratty sweatpants, with my hair in something other than the sloppy bun I slept in last night. Doing something sexier than playing Monopoly.

"All right," he says. He hands me a pile of unorganized money. "Nine-fifty."

"You know what?" I say.

"What?"

I sort the money and slip it underneath the board. "I still haven't made that mistake I was supposed to make."

"Dating me was supposed to be the mistake," he says.

I shrug a little. "Yeah, well."

"Oh, that one ended up working out okay?" He nods at the board. "All right, come land on my hotel instead. That'll be a good mistake." He looks up at me, green eyes, pale lips, dimpled smile.

I hold my breath and roll the dice.

ACKNOWLEDGMENTS

The amount of support I've received since the second I first mentioned this book is truly like nothing I've ever experienced. So many people encouraged me to write this book as happy and as true as I could make it, and I so hope I've made you proud.

There's no way to name everyone who supported me, but there are a few who need special recognition. Jen and Kate fell in love with this book before I even knew it was ready to be seen, and we wouldn't be here without them. John and Rebecca put their all into my career time and time again while still going along with the incredibly strange decisions I tell them I already enacted at three a.m. Lydia and the whole team at Entangled adopted this book and gave it a beautiful cover, a dedicated marketing plan, and a lovely home.

My incredible family, from my parents who never stopped seeing me as myself and my sister who always promised me that no, not everyone feels this way, on whose futon I came up with the idea for this book two years ago, remain so patient with my pathological secrecy about my books and give me plenty of space and even more food. The burden of emotionally supporting me is, thank God, staffed by a large team, and I'm eternally grateful to, just to name a handful, Seth, Emma, Kat, Jessi, Parker, and Amanda.

Thank you to Roz and Jed, who I hadn't even realized I needed to know until, thankfully, I already did.

And thank you, always, forever thank you, to anyone who has ever had to ask how to spell their disease, who has ever smiled and nodded when they were asked if they'd tried yoga, or who has cried on the phone with their insurance company, who has sat in a doctor's office and wondered if they were losing themselves, who has lost themselves, who has found a community. We are here, we are here, we are here.

READERS' GROUP GUIDE

Sick Kids in Love, by Hannah Moskowitz
Prepared by Nancy Cantor, media specialist,
NSU University School

1. The author wants us to understand how people live with what she calls "invisible" illnesses. Readers learn about Gaucher disease and rheumatoid arthritis. What others can you identify? Do you know anyone with a chronic illness? If so, how do they handle their issues?

2. On page 40, Isabel and Sasha discuss that they define themselves as sick, and that society does not want them to. Sasha says, "You either have to be overcoming it or you have to be completely disconnected from it. God forbid it be an important part of your identity that you're just living with. Why is that?" After reading this book, do you agree with society or with Isabel and Sasha? Why or why not?

3. Isabel is glad that her father doesn't think of her as sick, and yet she can't discuss being sick with him, even though he is a doctor. Is her father being overprotective? Unrealistic? A good dad?

4. Isabel is surprised when Sasha and his father speak candidly about Sasha's illness. What are your experiences with an ill person? Would it be different for a young person than say, a senior citizen who is closer to death?

5. On page 21, Isabel describes her first crush, a boy she and Maura fought over in seventh grade, until they decided they hated him more than each other. What was your first romance like?

6. Isabel's friends make plans to go skiing and don't include her. Isabel doesn't feel bad about it, however. Should the girls have made plans that would have been difficult for her to enjoy? Is this typical of friend dynamics in your circle?

7. On page 74, the girls discuss their experiences with breaking up. What are your experiences with ending a romance?

8. Isabel and her dad do not "do" holidays. Why do you think this is? Do mothers have a greater capacity for creating memories and traditions? What traditions from your childhood will you carry on into adulthood?

9. Do you think people from the same religious or cultural background have better relationships? What are the advantages or disadvantages of dating someone much like yourself?

10. Isabel thinks her illness has made her "a mean, angry, worse person." Do you agree? Why or why not?

11. Isabel is worried that she is faking her illness because she was always fascinated with illness as a child. Sasha says she must have always felt it deep inside, like one feels their religion deep inside. Whom do you agree with? Why?

12. At the beginning of their romance, Isabel is worried that dating Sasha could mess up their friendship. What are your experiences with dating a friend?

13. The New Year's Eve party at Sasha's is a sleepover. Does your crowd do coed sleepovers? Is everyone appropriate? How would your parents react?

14. When Sasha and Isabel have an argument and Sasha says he will change for her, Isabel is frightened

because she senses she has too much power in their relationship. Has that happened to you? Is equality in a relationship possible?

15. Isabel fears that she can't be happy without a tragedy happening. Is this because of her illness or is it just her personality? Do you know people who are afraid to be happy?

16. The girls discuss being gay and whether it is nature vs. nurture. What are your thoughts?

17. Were you satisfied with the way Isabel left things with her mother? Did you think she should have called her mom? How could the author have changed this part?

18. Each of Isabel's questions for her column would be interesting to go through with your group. Here's one that seems especially relevant: Why are you the way you are?

Easy A *meets* The Carrie Diaries *in this edgy, contemporary new release*

ASK
ME
ANYTHING

by Molly E. Lee

I should've kept my mouth shut.

But Wilmot Academy's been living in the Dark Ages when it comes to sex ed, and someone had to take matters into their own hands. So *maybe* I told Dean, the smartest person in my coding class—and the hottest guy I've ever seen—that I was starting an innocent fashion blog. And *maybe* instead, I had him help me create a totally anonymous, totally untraceable blog where teens can come to get real, honest, nothing-is-off-limits sex advice.

The only problem? I totally don't know what I'm talking about.

Now not only is the school administration trying to shut me down, they've forced Dean to try to uncover who I am. If he discovers my secret, I'll lose him forever. And thousands of teens who need real advice won't have anyone to turn to.

Ask me anything…except how to make things right.

One spark and everything can disappear.

P*A*PER G*I*RL

by Cindy R. Wilson

I haven't left my house in over a year. My doctor says it's social anxiety, but I know the only things that are safe are made of paper. My room is paper. My world is paper. Everything outside is fire. All it would take is one spark for me to burst into flames. So I stay inside. Where nothing can touch me.

Then my mom hires a tutor. Jackson. This boy I had a crush on before the world became too terrifying to live in. Jackson's life is the complete opposite of mine, and I can tell he's got secrets of his own. But he makes me feel things. Makes me want to try again. Makes me want to be brave. I can almost taste the outside world. But so many things could go wrong, and all it takes is one spark for everything I love to disappear…

*A driven teen must accept the present can hold
more value than the future.*

LOVE AND OTHER UNKNOWπ √ARIABLES

by Shannon Lee Alexander

Charlie Hanson has a clear vision of his future. A senior at Brighton School of Mathematics and Science, he knows he'll graduate, go to MIT, and inevitably discover solutions to the universe's greatest unanswered questions. He's that smart. But Charlie's future blurs the moment he reaches out to touch the tattoo on a beautiful girl's neck.

The future has never seemed very kind to Charlotte Finch, so she's counting on the present. She's not impressed by the strange boy at the donut shop—until she learns he's a student at Brighton where her sister has just taken a job as the English teacher. With her encouragement, Charlie orchestrates the most effective prank campaign in Brighton history. But, in doing so, he puts his own future in jeopardy.

By the time he learns she's ill—and that the pranks were a way to distract Ms. Finch from Charlotte's illness—Charlotte's gravitational pull is too great to overcome. Soon he must choose between the familiar formulas he's always relied on or the girl he's falling for (at far more than 32 feet per second squared).

A sexy, witty novel that will remind you
Life loves a good curveball...

whatever
LIFE
throws
AT YOU

by Julie Cross

Seventeen-year-old Annie Lucas's life is completely upended the moment her dad returns to the major leagues as the new pitching coach for the Kansas City Royals. Now she's living in Missouri (too cold), attending an all-girls school (no boys), and navigating the strange world of professional sports. But Annie has dreams of her own—most of which involve placing first at every track meet...and one starring the Royals' super-hot rookie pitcher.

But nineteen-year-old Jason Brody is completely, utterly, and totally off-limits. Besides, her dad would kill them both several times over. Not to mention Brody has something of a past, and his fan club is filled with C-cupped models, not smart-mouthed high school "brats" who can run the pants off every player on the team. Annie has enough on her plate without taking their friendship to the next level. The last thing she should be doing is falling in love.

But baseball isn't just a game. It's life. And sometimes, it can break your heart...

A chilling, intricate mystery perfect for fans of We Were Liars.

we ~~told~~ six lies

by Victoria Scott

Remember how many lies we told, Molly? It's enough to make my head spin. You were wild when I met you, and I was mad for you. But then something happened. And now you're gone.

But don't worry. I'll find you. I just need to sift through the story of us to get to where you might be. I've got places to look, and a list of names.

The police have a list of names, too. See now? There's another lie. There is only one person they're really looking at, Molly.

And that's yours truly.

Let's be friends!

🐦 @EntangledTeen

📷 @EntangledTeen

📘 @EntangledTeen

📰 bit.ly/TeenNewsletter